A NEEDLE IN THE EYE

A Retired Detectives Club Novel

SHAWN SCUEFIELD

For Mom and Dad
And for Horace Jones, miss you Grandad

Prologue
SUNDAY, BLOODY SUNDAY

3:45 a.m.

IN THE FORTY-PLUS years I had worked for the Chicago Police Department, twenty-two of which were spent in homicide, I'd been called to many crime scenes. I had lost count of the number of times I'd received an early morning phone call before the sun had come up. None of them had been to deliver good news. And the call I'd received some twenty minutes ago had been no exception.

Like many times before, I walked into a room that was in a state of complete disarray. My eyes took in the scene with its telltale signs of violence: blood spatter on the doorjamb, along the living room walls and overturned furniture. A dead body lying face down on the floor in the corner completed the picture.

In each of those past cases, it was my job to determine what made person X stab, shoot, or poison person Y. What were the reasons that the prone bodies laid out before me had their existence extinguished that day? At the start of any such investigation it was important not to miss any clues, and to sift through everything, because in the absence of a live witness to the events that had taken place, I had to put the story together from scratch.

Even with all of that experience, I wasn't prepared for what lay before me this Sunday morning. The neighbors had called police roughly two plus hours ago reporting gunshots and sounds of a violent struggle. That my former commanding officer, Lt. Andrews, called and urged me to get here quickly was stunning. I recognized the address immediately when he recited it to me.

"Robert, come on in," Andrews said, and led me past the other officers and the forensics team that were already on the scene. "Look, this is just a courtesy call. It's not even my case, but with his former ties to the department, the investigating officer called me, and I called you. I know what he meant to you."

"Meant?"

"Means. I know what he *means* to you," Andrews said.

I glimpsed the body lying prone on the floor. "Who's that?"

"We don't know. No ID. The only thing he had in his pockets were three, crisp, hundred-dollar bills and some change."

"Well, where is he? Where's Ashe?"

"We don't know that either," Andrews said. "He's missing."

Ashe, one of my closest friends and one of my partners in RDC Investigations, is missing. *How the hell is that possible?* As I struggled with the concept, my eyes continued scanning the room to see what else it would tell me. I picked up on the bullet holes in the doorway immediately. There were no shell casings, so I wasn't sure how many rounds had been fired, but at least one shot had left a canoe like groove in the head of the mystery man on the floor. There were two more entry wounds in his back. A blood trail started at the door and tracked into the living room. I'd only taken a cursory glance around, but the shooting seemed to had begun from the hallway and then the struggle continued inside. *Who'd be crazy enough to show up at Ashe's door?*

I walked through the apartment, and the sign Ashe had on his wall, "There's no easy day, but yesterday," caught my eye. That was one of the marine sayings he was most fond of. His Navy SEAL trident was also on prominent display on his bookshelf. I had always marveled at his dedication to our country, and to service, that after he finished his tour with the marines, he enlisted with the navy, and became a SEAL. It was actually on a dare, he'd told me once. But one that he was more than willing to take on. He was proud of serving in both branches of our military.

I eyeballed the body on the floor again. He was a decent sized man, but Ashe goes six-three, two-forty. No way this guy could've taken Ashe one on one.

Two assailants, then?

Maybe that explained why there was so much blood. But if they somehow got the drop on him, that just as well could be Ashe's blood smeared around the apartment.

"It just doesn't seem possible," I said.

"His car is outside, but there's no sign of him in the area. Early forensics indicates the blood could be from the deceased over there, and a second subject. But that won't be known for sure until all the tests are run."

"So, he could be hurt," I said.

"We'll know when we find him and ask him." A face I didn't recognize interjected.

Andrews made the introduction. "Robert Raines, this is Detective Mark Royce."

Royce was the detective in charge of the investigation. He worked out of the sixth precinct and looked to be in his early to mid-thirties, and wore a sour expression on his face as he limply shook my extended hand. Royce twirled a toothpick around in his mouth as he eyed me up and down. His tone and body language seemed to suggest that my presence upset him.

"I know who *he* is," Royce said.

Apparently, my reputation preceded me.

That scowl never left his face as he continued, "Ex-cop. I watch the news so I know about the thing in Louisiana, and that you were involved with Senator Dietrich. Guess that makes you hot shit, huh?"

It appeared that reputation of mine would not do me any good this time around. "That's one way to put it," I said. "Look, I'm not here to step on any toes. I'm just concerned about my friend. Can you tell me what you know so far?"

Royce pointed toward the corpse. "One dead guy over there, and your friend in the wind. That's what I know. Unless you have anything of substance to offer, we're gonna put out an APB on Ashe. He's got some questions to answer."

"What? Like he's a suspect?" I asked.

"Well, he has a dead body in his apartment. And with his, uh, history, until we know more, yes, I guess he is."

"That's a mistake."

Royce laughed and pulled the toothpick from his mouth.

"Did I say something funny?"

"You old guys, man. You really do love the smell of your own farts, don't you? Always think you know everything. The great private investigator is going to figure this all out for me. Let me guess, you know exactly how I should run this investigation."

"Yeah, punk. Because I was doing this job and doing it well, while you were still popping pimples and hanging out in your momma's basement, jerking off to lingerie models in the Macy's catalogue."

Andrews stepped in between us.

"Easy guys, easy. We're all on the same team here."

Royce popped his toothpick back into his mouth, and said, "You and I are sir, but he's not. Not anymore. I want him out of my crime scene. You were here as a courtesy only, courtesy is over."

He may have been a prick about it, but Royce was right. I'm retired. It's his crime scene, his case, and he was handling it as he saw fit. As he should. And that was just fine, because I'd be handling my own investigation just as I saw fit.

Questions swirled around in my head in rapid fire fashion. It had been only three months since my team's encounter with Walter Rand, and he and Ashe had quite the face to face.

Could Rand have had a hand in this?

I don't think he'd have been crazy enough to confront Ashe personally, but he could've hired someone, or brainwashed someone, wound them up and sent them after Ashe.

I also wondered if whatever had taken place here had anything to do with the investigation Ashe and I had recently taken on. A case that has sent me tumbling down memory lane. Reminiscent of one of the most heated, charged, and gut-wrenching cases I'd worked in all my years on the force.

The corpse in Ashe's living room wouldn't be providing any answers on either front, and the hothead detective in charge had dismissed me, so I made my way out as getting into a pissing contest wasn't going to do me any good. Either way, my hands were full.

As I headed out, I could only hope that my friend was still alive.

Part One

TWO DAYS AGO ...

CHAPTER

1

Friday morning

Iᴀᴀᴀᴀᴀᴀᴀᴀ Kᴇʏᴇꜱ sᴀᴛ ᴘᴀʀᴋᴇᴅ with the engine running at the corner of 56th and Ada. The sun had just barely crawled across the horizon, adding a peach hue to otherwise gray skies. He sipped his coffee and checked the Omega Speedmaster strapped to his wrist. It was eight-thirty. His targets were due to pass by any minute.

The three young girls weren't the reason he'd been paid to be in Chicago. The job he was scheduled to pull at Wynn Pharmaceuticals held that distinction. But even though those three little ladies weren't his primary business, they were still important to him. They were part of a *necessary distraction*. To a man like Ishmael Keyes, those necessary distractions were critical. They helped him keep his edge. As he'd always said, *a man that doesn't challenge himself isn't a man at all.*

Keyes adjusted the temperature in the Ford Transit, driving the heat to seventy-five degrees to combat the winter winds swirling outside. He'd heard about Chicago winters, and the season had more than lived up to the reputation. All the same, he had run his customary six miles earlier in the morning. His heart rate barely crept up over sixty, even when he had to trudge through packed snow. Most of the streets had been cleared, but some remained covered even though the Department of Streets and Sanitation trucks worked through the night cleaning up after the most recent snowstorm dumped its load on the city.

It was important to stay in shape. Keyes had always believed so. In his line of work, and with his *hobbies*, physical fitness was a premium asset. He was a fit and trim two hundred five pounds, which his six-foot frame carried extremely well. His clean-shaven good looks put most people in a mind that he was in his early twenties, though his thirty-fifth birthday wasn't far off.

After his run, he stopped off for breakfast before picking up the supplies needed for today's excursion. His trip to the south side, in the white cargo van he'd *borrowed* days ago, was uneventful. There wasn't much foot traffic that passed by after he parked. And Keyes attracted little attention from the few people that did see him. Dressed in blue Dickie's coveralls, a bright orange safety vest, and yellow safety helmet, he seemed to blend into the cityscape as he setup orange traffic cones in front of his vehicle before returning to the driver's seat.

Keyes's eyes darted toward the intersection. There were no signs of his quarry yet, but after observing them over the past month, he was confident his targets would show. And once he got that ball rolling, there was no stopping it. This was one genie that would not go back into the bottle. The raised stakes also excited him.

Plenty of times as he'd worked around the world as a gun for hire, however difficult his assignment, Keyes would always find an additional challenge. A way to test himself both mentally and physically. It was his compulsive nature that drove him to do so, but rarely had he found an opportunity where he'd be so evenly matched. This go-round, he'd be dealing with men that were as smart and as deadly as himself. The possibilities sent a rush of adrenaline through him. He shuddered and cracked a smile. Keyes sipped more of his coffee and checked his watched again. Eight-thirty-three. *Shouldn't be more than another couple of minutes.*

His cellphone rang. "Keyes," he answered.

"I'm calling for an update," a familiar female voice said in a heavy French accent.

"Tell your boss that everything is on schedule as expected. I've cultivated an asset that will get me access to Wynn Pharmaceuticals. I will acquire the package as discussed and deliver it upon receipt of the balance of my fee." Keyes paused, sipped his coffee and said, "Has my travel out of Chicago been arranged?"

"I'm making the arrangements as we speak. You'll be briefed closer to the date."

"Excellent. Thank you, Sophie."

"On another note, did you receive the dossiers you requested?"

"I did, Sophie. Very detailed. They were exactly what I needed."

"I'm glad you're pleased, Mr. Keyes. Also, as you've done such exceptional work for us in the past, my employer was hoping you'd be available for another assignment after your business in Chicago is completed."

"No. I'll be lying low for a while after this one."

Sophie Bisset let out a heavy sigh. "This job should be rather easy for a man of your talents, Mr. Keyes. I can only assume it's your *other* endeavor that will have you taking a sabbatical."

"You know me so well," Keyes said.

"My employer will be disappointed. What should I tell him?"

"You can say I'm sorry, if you like," Keyes said sarcastically.

"With the money you're paid, I don't understand why you feel the need to—"

"That's right, you don't. And I have neither the time nor inclination to explain myself. The job your employer is paying me for will be completed on schedule. Whatever else I do is my business."

Movement in the intersection caught his eye. "Will that be all?"

"*Oui*. I guess so," Sophie answered.

"Good." Keyes disconnected the call and eyed the three young black girls crossing the street. They were bundled up against the cold; big coats, hats, scarfs, the works. Each had a heavy book bag draped across their shoulders. His targets had arrived. While he had no particular desire to do them harm, that was a necessary evil. It was the only way to lure the prey he sought. The girls were…*collateral damage*. Besides, bad things happen to good people all the time. This wasn't personal, they just so happened to fit the bill.

Keyes picked up a black ski mask from the passenger seat. He removed the plastic safety helmet and slid the mask over his head. Keyes drew his Glock 17, checked that a round was chambered, and then shoved it back inside the dark blue coveralls he was wearing. He picked up the Vipertek stun gun from the dash and clicked the power button. Blue sparks flew, and it cracked with power.

It was show time.

Chapter

2

LAYLA MONTGOMERY MADE CERTAIN that her younger sister, Kayla, and their eight-year-old neighbor, Shameka Barnett, held hands as they all made their way across 56th Street.

Being Kayla's big sister—and the oldest of the trio at eleven—the responsibility was hers. Her mom had always said so. Layla didn't mind it much. Being a big sister, that is. Except, on those days when she had to babysit her kid sister and got in trouble for any mischief Kayla got up to while their mother was out working. And their mom was always working. Holding down two jobs at a time would do that; which left other responsibilities in Layla's lap.

Not only did she have to get her own homework done, she had to help Kayla with hers as well. On the nights where their mom had to work late, Layla also had to "cook" dinner. Most times this consisted of heating frozen Encore Salisbury Steak dinners, Ramen noodles, or Hot Pockets in the microwave and mixing up a pitcher of Kool-Aid. Tropical Punch was Kayla's favorite, or as she liked to call it, "the red kind," while Layla herself was more partial to Grape.

Sometimes the dinners were a little *fancier*, as their mother recently began trusting Layla to use the stove. Those nights she'd cook rice to go along with Aldi's brand chicken nuggets. It was a lot of work, but again, Layla didn't mind. This was what big sisters were supposed to do, especially since their mom needed the help.

Momma's got to work to keep the lights on and food in ya'll stomachs, she'd said on more than one occasion. More times than Layla ever cared to count, but she believed it was true.

While they didn't have fancy things around the house or expensive clothes and shoes (Layla had always hoped for a pair of Jordan's for Christmas—even though she didn't get them this past jingle bell season either), there was no denying, their mom took care of them.

After the girls crossed the street, Layla said, "Ya'll take your time. There's a lot of snow on the ground."

Kayla and Shameka responded in unison, "Okay."

"Are you going to see Brian, today?" Kayla asked. She swiped at the frosty air billowing from her mouth.

Layla's eyes narrowed. "He's in my class, so like, yeah I am."

"Who's Brian?" Shameka asked.

"Her boyfriend!"

"He is not! And you ain't supposed to be talking about that, anyway."

"Well, you like him, right?"

Shameka's nose turned up in a frown. "Wait, she likes boys? Yuck!"

"Both of you shut up!" Layla said with a scowl on her face. "You keep it up, and I won't help you next time LaDarius dumps you in the snow." She was lying. Of course, she'd always help her sister. As their mom had said on multiple occasions, they both had to look out for each other. Besides, LaDarius James was an annoying little jerk. No doubt he picked on her sister because he liked her, but just the same, Layla had no problem popping him in the head any chance she got.

Being bigger than him helped, too.

The threat, though, served its purpose as Kayla blurted out, "Okay, okay, okay! I'm sorry!"

As Kayla apologized profusely, and little Shameka shook her head, muttering, "boys," Layla's attention was drawn to the white van they were passing. There was something odd. She couldn't put her finger on it at first, but a chill ran up her spine and it had nothing to do with the winter winds whipping around them.

Layla's mom had always told her to keep an eye out for any strange movement. To watch after her little sister, their neighbor, and herself as well. And as far as little kids go, Layla had done a fairly good job of that.

But the man in the coveralls was just too fast. In an instant he sprang from the van and was upon them. The black ski mask he wore startled the girls. They froze. All three of them. He closed in on them without saying a word.

Summoning all the nerve she could, Layla jumped in front of her younger charges. But in an instant, there was a burst of heat, a loud crackling sound and staggering pain. Then the world went dark.

3

THE GRAB HAD GONE by the numbers. Literally as easy as one, two, three. Keyes had caught the girls' mid-conversation. They were scared stiff, and the Vipertek did its job. Their little bodies seized up, and went limp, long enough for him to round them up and toss them into the van.

Keyes hopped in the back with them. Moving quickly, he produced a small pouch that contained a syringe. It was already loaded and ready to go. The girls squirmed and moaned—the effects of the Vipertek already wearing off. Within seconds, Keyes had injected each of them with ketamine. Just enough for a nice, long nap. Not enough to stop their little hearts.

"Relax, ladies," he said. "I'm not going to hurt you. We're just going to go for a ride." He secured them by the wrists and ankles with zip ties. Satisfied with his work, Keyes pulled the ski mask off and climbed through the van to the driver's seat.

Everything had gone according to—

"Hey! Hey! I saw you! What the hell do you think you're doing? I'm calling the cops!"

Keyes turned and peered out of the driver's side window. There was a man running down the steps of a home across the street, yelling at the top of his lungs, and headed toward the van. He looked like he could've been in his late forties, maybe early fifties. The man had made his way outside in the blistering cold, dressed in only his robe and slippers with cellphone in hand. *A bit of a slob*, Keyes mused observing the snug fit of that robe.

You should've waited a little later in the day for that morning cup of coffee and staring wistfully out the window, my friend.

Keyes hopped out of the van and in the same motion pulled the Glock 17 from inside his coveralls. He fired two quick shots. Each struck his target center mass, dropping the good citizen in the snow-covered street.

This was almost clean.

Keyes climbed back into the van and peeled off. The tires dug angrily into the snow, sending chunks of white powder and ice flying. The vehicle lurched and skidded, but then found its footing and took off.

With the little beauties secured in the back of the van, and sleeping away, Keyes turned on the Uniden Bearcat mobile scanner.

It wasn't long before he heard calls of his exploits going out across the police airwaves. "….we've got a report of shots fired…a single victim is down…caller states victim is still breathing… ambulance is in route…"

"…Dispatch, any id on the offender?"

"…negative…"

Still breathing? Well, that just won't do. That won't do at all.

Keyes made a hard-right turn. He could hear the unconscious children slide across the back cabin. "Sorry, girls. This ride might get a little bumpy." He raced up the block, making another right, completing what amounted to a U-turn, and proceeded toward the scene. The roar of the ambulance siren could already be heard. He stopped at the top of the block and waited. Within moments, the ambulance arrived. Keyes watched as the paramedics hopped out and began tending to the victim he'd left lying in the street.

The snow around the wounded man had become stained in crimson. Within minutes, the paramedics had him stabilized and loaded into the back of the hospital wagon. Keyes had always preferred the term, "meat wagon," and today, that term would be all too fitting. The siren fired back up signaling they were ready to begin the trek to Stroger hospital. It wasn't the closest, but Stroger has the best trauma unit in the city.

The ambulance screamed toward the top of the block and Keyes floored the gas pedal in the Transit, sending it speeding directly in its path. The paramedic behind the wheel reacted with a mix of horror and anger as he swerved hard to the right, coming to an abrupt stop.

Keyes hopped out of the Transit, his Glock 17 already in hand. He fired two quick shots into the cab, striking the driver in the chest and head. He then raced to the back of the ambulance and snatched open the rear doors.

"What the hell are you—"

Two more shots ended the stunned paramedic's line of questioning. Keyes hoped into the rear and fired one more shot, this time to the head of the good Samaritan strapped to the gurney.

There, now that's tied off nicely.

Keyes could hear the police sirens wailing off in the distance. Only a minute or two out by the sound of them. Keyes exited the rear of the *meat wagon* and raced back to the Transit. He threw the gearshift into reverse and floored the gas causing the tires again to furiously churn up snow and bits of ice before the Transit lurched back onto the cross street. Keyes then shifted into drive and fled the scene.

Chapter

4

THE PAST NOVEMBER SEEMED like a lifetime ago to Dale Gamble. Thanksgiving, Christmas, and New Year's had all passed in a blur, he reflected and sat a bowl of broccoli cheddar bisque, along with sliced roasted chicken breast, in front of his wife, Millie, who was seated in what had become her all too familiar place. On the sofa in the living room in front of the TV.

Her physical scars were healing well. She'd been making a remarkable recovery from the attack she suffered four months ago at the hands of Walter Rand's sadistic errand-boy, Fallon Krieg. But the faraway, dull look in her eyes reminded him that mentally, she still had a long road, with many hurdles, to go.

Any time he caught that far off look from her, his blood boiled. Memories of the helplessness and guilt that he felt for her being kidnapped would flood his mind and nearly drive him into a rage. Luckily, his partners had his back. Ashe had saved

Millie's life, but the cost was letting Walter Rand go free. To this day, Ashe hadn't been able to locate him. But he hadn't given up, and he'd given Dale his word that he would find him. Whatever it took.

"You need anything else, hon?" Dale asked.

Millie said nothing, absorbed by a rerun of *This Is Us*. She'd taken to watching the show on-demand of late. Dale stood up from the couch.

"Wait! Where are you going, Dale?" Millie asked, suddenly in a panic.

"Easy, sweetie. Easy. I'm only going into the kitchen. Clean up the mess I made from lunch, then take out the trash. That's it."

"You promise?"

"I promise."

"Don't be gone long," she pleaded.

"I'll be back before you know it." Dale kissed her forehead and gave her hands a gentle squeeze. It seemed to put her at ease.

Dale entered the kitchen. The aroma of fresh garlic and rosemary from the chicken he prepared still danced in the air. But it wasn't the aromatics on Dale's mind as he filled the kitchen sink with dish water. It was Millie's scars. The mental scars. They were not healing as fast as their physical counterparts, and Dale could see that all too well. She was skittish. Afraid in their own home. And why wouldn't she be? After all, this was the very place that madman broke into, attacked and kidnapped her from before he held her hostage while he barbarously tortured her. It only made sense that she wouldn't feel comfortable here.

But in all truth, Dale knew, Millie wouldn't feel comfortable anywhere.

He had broached the subject of moving away, finding a new home elsewhere. Millie would have none of it. In the bravest voice she could muster, she'd said, "No one's going to run me from my home, Dale. Our whole life is here."

That ended the discussion. They were here to stay.

Since he'd decided to take a break from working with RDC investigations, the detective agency he founded with long-time partner Robert Raines and Ashe, his life had slowed. Taking care of Millie was a full-time job. But he still craved…*something* to keep his mind occupied.

Occasionally ol' Bobby Raines or Ashe would drop by to check on him and the Mrs. In between updates on her condition (and his), he'd ask about any interesting cases they were working. For five, maybe ten minutes, he got to pretend that he was back with the boys. Part of the action.

Not that he had any regrets. He firmly did not. Just months ago, he wondered if he'd ever get to hold Millie's hand again with all that had gone down. This time they had together now would not be taken for granted. Not for a minute. But still…

After he finished the afternoon dishes, Dale tied up the garbage and headed out into the yard. He pulled his collar up to brace against the winter air. The skies had dumped another three inches of snow on the city last night. He needed to get out later and shovel. As he surveyed the mounds of powder in his yard, thinking of the work he had in store, something caught his eye.

He thought it odd, given the downfall that one of the garbage cans in his yard, the closest to the back gate, had no snow on the lid. As a matter of fact, it looked like someone had brushed the snow off of that one lid. And there was something else. Flapping in the wind, there was a envelope or *something* taped to the lid? Dale peered around his yard. It and the neighboring yards on either side were empty. He trudged through the mounds of snow and made his way over to the trash cans, and after tossing the trash into the one closest to him, he snagged the envelope off of the other.

It was unaddressed and sealed. He ripped it open. There was a note inside. Dale slowly pulled it out. There were two words written on plain white paper in an almost child-like scrawl. Written in black crayon were the words:

I know.

Dale's brow furrowed. The note didn't make sense at all. And *if* its mystery author knew, exactly *what* did they know? He decided he wouldn't waste any time on it. Whoever left it undoubtedly had the wrong house.

"Pranks don't work if you don't get them to the right address." Dale crumpled the note and tossed it into the trash. It was time to get back inside; no doubt Millie was looking for him.

Chapter

5

THE THREE SLEEPING BEAUTIES hadn't stirred or even whimpered since Keyes delivered a dose of the trippy stuff into their little bodies. Not that he had expected they would, but they'd been so still that he'd already pulled over twice to check their pulses. It would be a shame if they'd suffered any unintended damage this early. Although, given how he saw this all playing out, it really didn't matter.

All the same, he had more vials of ketamine on hand for the duration of this event as he had no desire to answer questions or hear the inevitable crying and whining, they were sure to do once they'd awaken. Besides, now that he had them, business was about to pick up. Big time. But first thing was first. He had to get the girls stashed away. Then he could focus on the other thing.

The *main* thing. Wynn Pharmaceuticals.

As that thought crossed his mind, Keyes's cell phone rang. "Keyes," he answered.

"It's me," a male voice said.

"Perfect timing. How are we looking?"

"Everything's set. You'll have a fifteen-minute window. Fifteen-minutes flat and I mean not one tick past. Can you handle that?"

"I can. And I will. Thank you," Keyes replied. "When will you be ready?"

"There's one more thing before we get to that," the caller said. His breathing became raspy and heavy.

"Oh?"

"Yeah, sorry, man. I know what we agreed and all, but I have to change the deal."

"Do you now?" Keyes's eyes left the road for a moment, looking up into the mirror. His charges were still slumbering peacefully. Keyes returned his gaze to the road.

"If you want to do this, and you want my help, I need to change my fee. It'll have to be seventy-five instead of fifty."

"Really?"

"'Fraid so, slick. I'm taking a big risk here, man. I just figure, I'm just figuring that's a fair price for what you want me to do. So, that's the way it has to be."

"Very well," Keyes said evenly. His voice registered neither shock nor displeasure. "If that's the way it's got to be. Seventy-five it is, then. Now, again, to my question, when will you be ready?"

"Sunday night. It has to be this coming Sunday night."

"I'll be there," Keyes said, then disconnected the call. *Always a hiccup with any plan*, he thought. He pulled the work van around to the back of an abandoned property, which was located a mere six miles from where he scooped up the little beauties.

Keyes had scoped out the homes on this block over the past two months. There were three abandoned two-flats in a row. With every other window smashed out of the front, the buildings each looked like crudely carved jack-o-lanterns. The only thing they were missing was a candle. Each had been a drug den, drawing traffic, vagrants of all sorts, looking for shelter from the world. A private place to shoot up and keep warm. Posing as a construction worker, Keyes had taken time to board up the building farthest from the corner.

It would be a temporary stop; a sufficient place to stash the girls while he ditched the van. With the heavy police presence in the area, that task would be much easier without lugging the kiddies around. This wasn't a family affair, after all.

He had a busy weekend ahead of him. It was time to get started. After carrying the girls, wrapped in thick painter's tarps, inside one by one, he laid them on the floor of an empty bedroom, in a nice, neat row.

The place had been abandoned for years. A story told by the peeling paint on the walls and ceiling. In areas where there were still walls and ceiling. The floor boards creaked and groaned, threatening to give way with every step. Just the same, the place was going to serve its purpose.

Keyes returned to the van and retrieved a knapsack. Back inside, he took out three lengths of chain. One by one, he clasped a section around the right ankle of each of the three girls, and then secured the other end by padlock to exposed piping in the walls.

Keyes again fumbled around in the knapsack, this time producing three juice boxes and some graham crackers. He sat the provisions within arm's reach of the nearest child. It wasn't the finest last meal, and surely didn't make him the last of the big spenders, but it was better than nothing. Just a little something to help them out should they wake while he was away. Sure, their time was short for this world, but as he saw it, no need to be a prick about it.

Keyes headed back outside. He opened the rear door and pulled out a red, black, and white car magnet. It advertised "Carl's Plumbing," complete with a fake phone number. He carefully applied it to the side of the truck, covering up the logo that had been painted on the van. He switched the plates—stolen, of course—as well.

Now it was time to attend to other matters. The next step in the plan.

Chapter

6

I HAD BEEN AWAKE just long enough to take my morning shower, get dressed, and get a pot of coffee on before my cellphone rang.

"Raines," I answered.

"Robert, its Ashe. Turn on the news."

"The news? What's going on?"

"Get the news on. Oh, and I hope you're decent. We're coming in."

"We?"

Within seconds, the front door to my home, which doubles as the office of RDC Investigations, swung open. Ashe ushered two young African American women in ahead of him.

Both women looked to be in their mid to late twenties. They stood before me, their posture sheepish, with tears in their eyes. I had no idea what was going on, but I knew right away it couldn't be good. I rubbed my chin. "Ashe. You want to tell me what this is about?"

"Ladies, this is Robert Raines. Robert, meet Latesha Barnett and Tracey Montgomery."

I exchanged hellos with the two despondent women. I turned to Ashe again, said, "And what is this about?"

"Turn on the news," Ashe said.

Within moments, the local midday news filled the room. "… the circumstances are eerily reminiscent of a case from 2002 that rocked the entire city. Repeating, just this morning, three young African American girls aged eight, nine, and eleven, have been abducted from the Englewood area. As yet, the police have no leads…"

I turned the TV off. A wave of shock rolled through my body and for a moment, I felt sick to my stomach. That 2002 case, referenced by the news anchor, raced back into my mind and suddenly, I knew why those two women were here.

"Your daughters?"

Both women nodded.

Before another word was spoken, the TV and our cellphones began screeching. An Amber alert had been issued and was being broadcast statewide. My heart sank.

"I'm…I'm…so sorry. I take it you've spoken with the police?" I said.

"We have," Latesha Barnett said. "But—"

"Honestly, you're going to want CPD's resources on this," I offered. I hoped my voice was as soft and understanding as

I wanted it to be. "What about the fathers? Are they in the picture?"

Both women responded no.

"All the more reason to let CPD dive into this, they'd make sure that—"

"It's not my girl's father," Latesha Barnett said sternly.

"How can you be so sure?"

"He never wanted anything to do with her. After I got pregnant, he just up and left without so much as a G.F.Y. and we never heard from him, again. Ever. I've raised her, by myself, without any help, or a dime from him. And I never wanted anything, either. No way it's him."

"It's not my daughters' dad either," Tracey said. Her voice trembled with emotion as she continued, "He died five years ago; murdered not three blocks from our house. His case is still unsolved. And seeing as how the police have done nothing about that, I don't have much hope they'll do anything about this."

"Besides," Ashe said. "*He* called them."

"Who?"

"The kidnapper," Tracey Montgomery added. "He called us both. Only his call to me went to my voicemail."

I swallowed hard. "Can you play it for me?"

Tracey took out her cellphone, put it on speaker, and pulled up the voicemail message. *"Hi Ms. Montgomery, your daughters' kidnapper calling. Yes, you heard right. I've taken your daughters. How else would I have your number? Nice of you to store it in Layla's phone under, MommyLovesYou. I won't waste any time by telling you don't go to the police, but I will tell you this, if you want to see your girls again, you'd do well to reach out to RDC Investigations. If you can hire them, that is. I hear they've worked wonders for the wealthy. I wonder if they'll do the same for you. Call them up and see. If they play their cards right, they'll get your daughters back safe and sound. If not, what's the going rate for funerals these days? I'm sure you're asking yourself, why you? Don't. Your little girls are just a means to an end. Hire the RDC. See if they can save your daughters' lives. Ta-ta!"*

His voice was calm throughout the entire message; jovial even. He established credibility right away by quoting things Ms. Montgomery would know to be facts. And in the midst of all that, he taunted us. I couldn't believe my ears. Not only had some asshole recreated one of the most heinous crimes this city has ever seen, but it seemed, by the voicemail, that he did it on a lark. It was just a game to him. And for a reason very specific to him, he made sure it would land at our feet.

"I don't know what your fee is, but I don't have much money, Mr. Raines" Tracey said. Her voice trembled, and tears rolled down her cheeks.

"Me either," Latesha chimed in.

Both of them wore the pained expressions you'd expect of any parent facing their current circumstances.

"Robert," Ashe said, his jaw tightened. "We're taking this case."

I could only imagine what this did to him. Ashe wasn't one to see colors, but there's no way this didn't hit home for him as a black man himself. He wasn't around for that 2002 case. But Dale and I were, and it still haunts us. I don't want him to carry the same baggage we have. Being honest, I don't want to go through it again myself. But of course, I will.

"Ladies, it just so happens we have a special going this month," I said. "You got a dollar?"

Both women exchanged confused looks between each other, then turned to me and nodded.

"Then you just hired yourselves a couple of detectives."

Chapter

7

I DON'T KNOW HOW much our agreeing to take on the case of these missing tender-aged girls did to soothe their mother's collective psyche, but after a few tense minutes, they both seemed to calm a bit.

Tracey had been the most upset. Not only were her two daughters missing, but during my initial line of questioning, she'd brought up the fact that their father was murdered in their area a little over five years ago now. The case remained unsolved. And for that, she still harbored resentment against the CPD. "We're just black and from Englewood," she said. "Nobody cares about us. They didn't solve that one. Why would they solve this one?"

The hurt in Tracey's voice was unmistakable as she continued on and recounted the night her husband was killed. He was a pillar in the community. A good neighbor, a mentor, and coach of a boys' basketball team at the local youth center.

He'd gone three blocks from their home to the neighborhood corner store. He was there for a pack of cigarettes, to drop ten dollars on the Power Ball, and grab a carton of eggs, along with bacon, for the next morning's breakfast. It was the middle of summer, and a nice night out. So he had walked. She'd thought nothing of the fact he wasn't back home within the ten minutes he'd figured it would take him. Maybe he saw a friend along the way, and had stopped to chat, is all she'd thought.

But ten minutes turned into twenty, which then quickly turned into forty. It wasn't long before there was frantic banging at her door. She had wondered why he'd be knocking that way, even if he'd forgotten his keys. There was nothing in her mind that prepared her to see one of the neighborhood kids, a good boy, George Kinney from two doors down, a player on her husband's team, crying and in an all-out panic on her porch.

The first couple of times he tried to relay his message to her, she couldn't understand him. It was only the third time she'd made out the words, "Charles is dead. They shot him." Her world had been a spiral of unanswered questions, grief, double-shifts, and her daughter's homework ever since.

The official story of *wrong place, wrong time*, and *robbery gone bad*, offered little comfort.

Today's helping of bad news only rehashed old memories of promises unfulfilled by the law. She was hurting. She was angry. By my count, rightfully so. And she was more than willing to let me, who had the same face as every cop she'd ever talked to, know about it.

I didn't have to pull any records of the investigation into her husband's murder to know that more than likely, anybody from the neighborhood police were able to interview suffered from the three d's. *Didn't see shit, didn't hear shit, and didn't know shit.* That's the code of the streets. But that fact holds little comfort when the bereaved are looking for the "system" to bring them closure. And in Tracy's mind, it justified the doubts she had now. I couldn't say that she was wrong.

Ashe pulled her to the side and, after about ten minutes, he'd successfully talked her down off that ledge. Afterwards, the women took us through the girls' routine. Layla, the oldest of the three, always marched the two younger girls off to school. They took the same route every day.

After Latesha, following the instructions of the kidnapper, phoned our service and got hold of Ashe, he put a call into a former partner of his from the 7th district and got the lay of the land as it stood this morning.

"Around 8:36 a.m., a call came in to 911 about gunshots being fired on the same street the girls were abducted from," Ashe said. "There was a single male victim reported, but shortly after the ambulance made the pickup, they were ambushed. The EMTs and the male victim were found dead."

"No way that's a coincidence," I said.

"That's right. The shooting victim saw something. He quite possibly could've ID'd the kidnapper."

"And they all paid for it. He'd already gotten away, but decided to take great risk to be sure."

"That tells me he's a professional. Trained." Ashe concluded.

He'd know. There had been a lot about his past that he couldn't share, but during one of our conversations, Ashe had let me know that after the time he spent in both the marines and on the SEAL teams, he'd also worked for the CIA. While he never discussed mission details, I gathered enough to at least have a grasp on some of the things he's seen. If he thinks this is the work of a professional killer, which usually meant a mercenary, he knew what he was talking about. The only question that remained in this situation was why.

"And ruthless," I added.

"I know about the girls from 2002. Everyone around here does." Tracey Montgomery spoke again. Her voice was strained. "I went to the same school as the girls that went missing back then. I remember my mother praying every day that those girls would be found alive." She shuddered as tears streamed down her face. "I couldn't even imagine what those families went through then. And now, it's me going through it."

"Wait," Latesha chimed in. "You...you don't think...he's going to—"

"No." I knew where her mind was headed and cut her off as quickly as I could. "I don't believe this man has that type of interest in your daughters."

"Then why?"

"As he said in the message, they're a means to an end. We don't know what game he's playing just yet, but you can believe we'll do our best to find out. And bring your girls' home."

Chapter

8

AND JUST LIKE THAT, our other active cases—two divorce investigations and an insurance fraud claim—were on hold. This took precedence over any and everything we had going on.

After roughly another hour talking with the mothers of the missing girls, Ashe saw that the women got home safely. They had provided as much insight as they could under the circumstances.

It was tough asking them questions, seeing the pain in their eyes. Pain that suggested they had no idea if they'd ever see their daughters again.

When Ashe returned to my place, he filled me in on what he'd gotten up to while he was out. After making a few phone calls, he'd found that CPD had canvassed the area where the girls were taken from. The canvas produced no witnesses, but one of the pod cameras in the area caught the abduction. A couple hundred bucks got him a copy of the footage from a *friend* in the Office of Emergency Management and Communications (OEMC). That's just how the department works. With the right connections, and a little palm grease, you can get what you need.

Ashe produced a thumb drive and queued up the video. The pod cam had captured a white cargo van as it pulled onto the block where the abduction occurred. The driver stepped out, setting up orange traffic cones as if he was on some legit business.

"Look at that," Ashe said.

As I noticed how the man continually used the safety helmet to keep his face shielded, I said, "Our boy knows where the camera is."

"Solid trade craft."

Fast-forwarding a bit, we spotted the three young girls, the daughters of Latesha Barnett and Tracey Montgomery, as they neared the van. The sight of the man hopping out with a black ski-mask on, left me feeling hollow. He assaulted the three girls with what appeared to be a stun-gun, and quickly hustled all three of them into the back of that van.

"He's fast. No wasted motion," Ashe said through gritted teeth.

The pod cam also captured the shooting of a neighborhood resident who had raced out of his home. As much as I respected citizens who will get involved and try to intervene when wrong doing happens in their neighborhoods, this poor man had stepped into the path of a wolf and unfortunately, got devoured.

A few minutes later, just barely in view of the pod cam, we see the same white cargo van which, earlier had sped off, nearly have a head-on collision with the ambulance that arrived for the good Samaritan. Even though we already knew that we were watching the last seconds of those men's lives, it still left me in shock.

Ashe shut off the video, rubbed his chin, and said, "Well, what do you think?"

"Victimology doesn't tell us much here, the kidnapper pretty much said so himself in the voicemail."

Ashe nodded in agreement.

"And what kidnapper tells you who to contact?"

"Normally, their instructions are what not to do. *Don't go to the police. Don't involve the FBI.*"

"Right, but he advised specifically that they reach out to us, which tells us more about him than his victims do."

"Somehow, this is personal for him," Ashe said.

"And he knows a little of our history. Otherwise, what are the odds someone kidnaps three young black girls from Englewood and then tries to get us involved?"

"He's done his research for sure."

"And for whatever reason, he has an axe to grind with us."

"Well, let's help him sharpen it. He wants us, then let's see where we fit in his game, and then give him every reason to regret it."

I agreed.

"I've got something I want to check out, I recognize the logo on that van. It's from an energy company on the south side. Just curious if it was stolen or an elaborate ruse. If it was stolen, Six Eight will know."

Puzzled, I said, "Six Eight?"

"Yeah, local shot caller. Connected. Has his hands in a bit of everything. Had a few run-ins with him back when I was in the gang unit."

"Why is he called Six Eight?"

Ashe arched his eyebrows and said, "Because he's six-foot-eight."

"Makes sense." I held back a chuckle. "While you're doing that, I'm going to go see Dale. Best he hears about this from me."

Chapter

9

Paris, France

JUST AS SOON AS thirty-year-old Sophie Bisset, a pretty, petite, yet buxom and curvy brunette, entered her spacious Montmartre apartment, in Paris's 18th arrondissement, her cellphone rang.

She didn't have to think hard about who it was on the other end either. It had been a long day already, one that had seemed would never end in fact. And now, this call would keep it going. In the circle that Sophie ran in, she'd gotten a reputation as a miracle worker. A facilitator that repeatedly had got things… *facilitated*. Only one problem with being seen as a miracle worker. People are always expecting miracles.

"Yes," she answered.

"Well, what did he say?"

"Good evening to you, too, Mr. Duchamps," Sophie said curtly.

"Apologies my dear, I did not mean to be rude," Aubrey Duchamps said. "Please, do forgive me. Now, what did he say?"

"He said he's unavailable after this job is completed. But the good news is, he's on schedule. We should have the package in a matter of days."

"That's it?"

"He also said he's sorry, although I didn't get the impression that he was," Sophie said, and let out a giggle.

"Unbelievable! What is it with this, Mr. Keyes? How can he turn down my money?"

"His motivations go beyond money."

"I'll bet they do." Duchamps paused. "Have you tried offering something more, shall we say, enticing?"

Sophie let out a heavy sigh. "I may be in your employ, Mr. Duchamps, but I'm not your whore," she scolded.

"No, of course not, my dear. I'm merely suggesting you take, shall we say, a different, approach? Did you not say you and Mr. Keyes previously—"

"Yes, we did, but that was different."

"You see, this is an angle we could play."

"What do you mean by *we*?"

"My dear Sophie, if you can get Mr. Keyes to do this next job, you would not be working for me. You'll be working with me. As my partner."

One thing had been clear to Sophie since she'd worked for Aubrey Duchamps—a wealthy French financier—the man was always negotiating. Always trying to play an angle. When you had ambitions as audacious as his, that was a necessary skill. She admired that about him. If he's successful, there's a boatload of money waiting at the end of this particular rainbow.

Duchamps was a visionary, but needed a man like Keyes to see to the execution of that vision. To get a man like Keyes, he needed her to facilitate.

Sophie had been successful to this point, but as she'd known, Keyes could be stubborn. And whenever the man was off on one of his damned fool excursions to "prove" himself, he could be downright disagreeable.

But Duchamps had a point. There just may be an angle to be played here. One, in fact, that she could play for herself, if she could move the pieces on the board where she needed them to be. Being Duchamps's partner sounded just fine. But she had ambitions of her own. So, for now—

"Partners? That sounds wonderful, Mr. Duchamps." Sophie said, doing her best to sound genuinely interested.

"Please, call me Aubrey. Now, about Mr. Keyes?"

"As you said, I can try to entice him by other means than just money."

"How can he resist? I know I myself could not. You are extremely beautiful, Sophie. Any man would—"

"Keyes isn't like any man, but thank you for the compliment. I'll do what I can to get him on board. And in the meantime, you and I will need to come to terms on an arrangement."

"Of course, my dear. Of course."

Sophie ended the call. Her mind began working overtime. She may not have the kind of money that Duchamps has, but she has twice the vision. And it occurred to her she needed to have an edge to work her plan whether or not Keyes agreed. After all, as Duchamps said, even he couldn't resist her.

Chapter

10

Chicago, IL

"Say that again, Bobby."

Dale's face went ashen. For a moment there, I thought his heart had stopped beating. His voice came out in a near whisper. Like the wind got knocked out of him. I felt terrible even bringing Dale this news. He'd already had a lot going on, taking care of his wife after what they'd been through. Dale didn't need this helping of bad news lumped on his plate. He's been getting served all veggies, no desert. But how could I not tell him? He and Millie had taken a break from watching the news—something about shutting out the outside world while she heals—so I knew he'd be unaware. But regardless of the impact, Dale had to know. After all, this was a part of his past too.

So, standing in the middle of his kitchen, I repeated those horrible words. "Three young black girls, exact same ages as our victims from '02, have been kidnapped from Englewood."

Dale stared at me in disbelief. I'm sure his mind was racing, but words weren't finding their way out of his mouth. This was a bad trip down memory lane. Dale slumped in the high-backed kitchen chair he was sitting in. I figured I'd better sit down myself. This already was harder than I'd figured it would be. He answered the door all smiles when I'd arrived. My stomach knotted watching his reaction.

Dale got up from his seat, went to into one of the cabinets and produced two rocks glasses. He poured two fingers of Four Roses single barrel into each and returned to the table. We downed the glasses in a single gulp. There was no denying it now. No matter how much it hurt, we were back into it.

We talked about the old case and the emotions we, along with the other officers working back then, had gone through. During the course of that investigation, some of the guys had even become physically ill, given that many had kids the same ages as the victims. It was frustrating as for a while, far too long, in fact, we couldn't figure it out. But we were determined not to have an Atlanta Child Murders situation on our hands. We pressed on and eventually got our man. However, it still wasn't a happy ending as our victims never made it back home.

"I can't believe this," Dale said. "How does this happen again?"

"Well, there is one glaring difference this time."

"What's that?"

"The kidnapper reached out to the mothers. Told them to hire us to find the girls." I queued up a copy of the voicemail I'd taken from Tracey Montgomery's phone.

Dale listened intently as the calm voice informed the mother of two of her children's plight. And took a few digs at us in the process.

"Hire us if she can? You catch that?" Dale said.

"Yeah, jumped out at me right away."

"So, this guy knows our history. Our involvement in the old case, and what we're doing now."

"Same conclusion me and Ashe reached."

Dale rubbed his chin. He appeared to have found some wind, and the color had returned to his face. "So, the question becomes, now that he's got our attention, what does he want? And just how close to the original case is he going to take this?"

"Well, unlike Mr. Davison, this man's interest is us and not the girls. But while I don't think he has any designs on them sexually, if we don't get to those girls soon, I don't believe he'd have any hesitation taking their lives."

Dale agreed. "Collateral damage," he said, echoing the sentiments of the kidnapper.

I walked Dale through what the video Ashe and I watched earlier had to say, and shared my preliminary profile of this mystery man. He was patient. The way he'd lain in wait. He was also meticulous, using the elaborate ruse with the utility vehicle and the workman's getup. He'd been planning this for some time. And he was well prepared. When his moment came, he pounced.

"Boom! He had all three girls in the van in a shot. No hesitation, including when he shot the neighbor. The guy came outside, and our man went full-tilt in a heartbeat. His mind was already made up about what he'd do."

"You said he waited for the ambulance. Took the time to kill the paramedics just to make sure the other guy was dead."

"Ballsy or stupid?"

"Definitely ballsy. Almost thrill-seeker reckless. But stupid, no," Dale said.

I nodded in agreement. "The more I think about it, even though he had to know he was putting himself at risk, he remained calm, accomplished his task, and got away."

"His tone during the voicemail, leads me to believe he doesn't rattle easy. Staying around to ensure the death of a potential witness was a risk, but a calculated one."

It was like old times. Dale and me bouncing ideas and opinions back and forth off each other. We'd have this guy figured out in no time.

"I wouldn't be surp—"

"Dale?"

Millie's voice called out from the living room. It snapped us both back into *their* current reality. This wasn't eighteen years ago. While we'd been going on about the past and this mornings' events, she'd been sitting quietly on the sofa watching TV. The moment was over.

"Just a minute, dear." Dale called out. He looked at me.

"No need to say it. I wasn't trying to drag you out of the house for this, just felt you should know about it. Ashe and me, we can handle it. We'll keep you in the loop."

"Thanks, Bobby. I'll help in any way I can. It'll just have to be from here."

"You get back to taking care of Millie. I'll see myself out." I headed for the backdoor off the kitchen.

"Uh, Bobby," Dale said.

"What's up?"

"I have a bad feeling about this guy. He's dangerous. You and Ashe be careful with this one."

"I don't figure we'll be able to appeal to his better angels."

"Exactly. This guy doesn't have any."

Chapter

11

THE SOUTH SIDE POOL hall had seen better days, but most of the buildings in Englewood had. The area had been divested years ago. There had been success stories through the years, even though the community was largely a food desert, its residents living at or below the poverty line. And of course, it had more than its fair share of gangs, guns, and drugs.

That's where Anthony "Six Eight" Williams fit in. He always made sure there were plenty of each. He was a rare breed, not quite an "old head," but not young either. Yet he had the respect of both. He had connections with drug cartels so he could always get product or guns and didn't care who he supplied them to. He was equal opportunity that way. That came with a certain level of respect in the neighborhood. And Six Eight seemed to know everything that was going on in Englewood.

That was exactly why Ashe dropped in for a visit.

"How about a game?" Ashe said as he walked in. He had to yell over the gangsta rap lyrics emanating from the Klipsch speaker system. Probably stolen. The artist was opining something about how easy it was to make money and kill. Ashe wasn't sure. He tuned it out rather quickly. Except for the bass. There was lots of bass.

The place was empty, save for three young men hanging out in a back corner, seated at a table, talking amongst themselves. Each man had lengthy dreads visibly sprouting from beneath the knit skull caps they wore, along with matching black puffy winter coats. Though the winter wind had to be sending a chill directly up the crack of their asses, they still wore their jeans well below their waistline. The weed the men smoked left a heavy, distinctive smell hanging in the air.

"Tables full, man," Six Eight called out. He lowered the volume on the Klipsch. Even while sitting down behind the bar, he still looked every bit his full height. Not only was he a tall man, he also was easily a biscuit shy of four hundred pounds. His round face curled up in an uneasy frown at his visitor.

Ashe feigned a look of disappointment. "Is that any way to treat an old friend? That hurts my feelings."

Six Eight crossed his arms. "Old friend? You don't remember? Man, you shot me."

"In the leg," Ashe said and continued over to the bar. "If we weren't friends, my aim would've been a lot higher. Besides, that was what, four years ago?"

"Six. And I still got a limp." Six Eight stood up from his bar stool, his head nearly clipping a light fixture. "But it don't matter, cuz we ain't got nothin to talk about, homie, so you can turn your ass around and head right back out that door."

The young men in the back turned and rose from the table. One reached inside his puffy coat.

Ashe's right hand slid inside of his Navy style peacoat and instinctively found the butt of his Smith and Wesson M&P .40 caliber pistol. He had it drawn and leveled in the same motion. "Today's not the day you want to play that game, fellas. Get those hands back on the table where I can see them, or you'll all have matching holes in those pretty coats of yours."

"Gone with that bullshit, Ashe. You ain't even got that badge no more."

Ashe's eyes narrowed. "Tell me something, chin-less. Knowing me the way you do, you think that will make me more or less likely to rip your head clean off? Now sit your big ass down."

Six-Eight plopped all of his near four-hundred-pound frame back on his seat behind the bar, then nodded over at the young smokers. Their faces kept the hard stares, but they returned to their seats as well. Hands planted firmly on the table.

Ashe turned his attention back to Six Eight. "I've got a few questions. You give me what I want, I'll be on my way and your boys can get back to *playing pool*."

Six Eight groaned. A pained expression crossed his face.

The code, Ashe thought. *No snitching*. The big man wouldn't want to appear to be doing that very thing in front of the three young knuckleheads. "Look, I'm not trying to jam you up. I wouldn't even be here if I didn't think this may be important."

After a moment, Six Eight shook his head, then said, "I'll tell you what, man. I need a favor."

"You need a favor?"

"That's right, baby, that's how this works. You come in here wanting something from me, I'm gone need something in return."

Ashe raised an eyebrow. "And what's that?"

"You still got friends on the force, right?"

"One or two," Ashe deadpanned.

Six Eight leaned in close to Ashe, and whispered, "Well, if any of your former associates in blue would be kind enough to check out a house on the corner of 58th and Lowe, east side of the street, they might find a large assortment of illegal weapons, a couple keys of weed, and about a hundred bricks of heroin. Sounds like a nice bust. Turn some cops into heroes. And some serious jail time for somebody."

"Let me guess. You're giving up your competition?"

"Nah, man. I'm just a concerned citizen doing his part."

"I'll see what I can do," Ashe said. *Apparently, the code has been modified. No snitching unless it helps you personally.*

"All right. Cool," Six-Eight said, and nodded his head in approval. He sat back and said, "Now, what do you want?"

"You heard about that kidnapping this morning?"

Six Eight put his hands up and turned his gaze to the entrance. "Man, I don't know nothing bout that. Far as suspects go, that line forms on the other side of that door. You know how I get down. I ain't never did nothing to hurt no kids."

"Other than selling them that poison, right?"

"Whatever. I don't know about no kidnapping, though."

Ashe thought for a moment, then said, "You heard anything about someone stealing a work van from IEG? Anything like that?"

"No, I ain't heard…wait a minute. Slo-Mo. Yeah, Slo had been around here the past few weeks talking about this dude that came up to him asking about borrowing one of the vans from the company he worked for."

"Borrowing?"

"Yeah, he was supposed to get five grand to let some dude borrow his work van for like four hours. I thought he was full of shit, but he swore up and down dude flashed him with the cash and he said it was a done deal."

"Did he say who this dude was? He mention a name?"

"Nah, no name. Said it was some white dude, only, he wasn't really white. I just figured he meant some Arab. Don't get too many white boys over here in the hood flashing that kinda cash."

"Tell me about Slo-Mo," Ashe said.

"He slings for me on the side every once in a while. A little rock, weed, or whatever the situation calls for, but he works full time for the gas company. Anything more than that, you need to talk to the man himself."

"When's the last time you heard from him?"

Six Eight rubbed his chin, and after a moment, said, "It's been at least three or four days. He was supposed to slide on me Monday, had a little package for him. But he never showed."

Chapter

12

Six Eight, after his initial hesitation had been more than a little forthcoming with an address for Jerome "Slo-Mo" Watkins— affectionately dubbed so, according to Six Eight, because of the man's stilted speech pattern—he even gave up the man's mother's address.

His sudden verbosity, whether borne in exchange for having a house raided, a desire to get back to his day-to-day business, or that he thought he might get shot again, either way, left Ashe with the distinct impression that the man wanted him out of his establishment, and fast.

That was good. There really wasn't any time to waste. Ashe felt the faster that he could start putting things together, the better odds those missing girls would have.

Jerome's address was in Chicago's Roseland neighborhood. The area earned the nickname "the wild 100s," because of the rampant gang violence that plagued the area since the 1980s. Ashe parked in front of the apartment building of Jerome Watkins on 115th Street and Michigan.

The sidewalk and courtyard of the property was unshoveled. After carefully make his way to the door, Ashe pressed the buzzer for Watkins, and waited.

There was no response.

Ashe buzzed again and waited another minute before fishing around in his inside coat pocket and producing a pair of picking tools. He leaned in close to the door, using his body to shield his hands as they went to work, quickly manipulating the lock. After hearing a familiar click, he opened the door and made his way inside, proceeding to the third floor, apartment three.

He listened outside the door for a little over a minute. He detected no sound coming from inside. No voices, running water, television, footsteps, or snoring. Not a peep. Ashe again went to work with the picking tools and had the door creaking open in seconds.

"Mr. Watkins?" He called out as he crept inside. "I'm a private investigator working with the Chicago Police Department." While that last bit wasn't true, Ashe had found that it helped to calm people's nerves if they'd discovered he took the liberty of letting himself into their homes.

At least, that usually worked.

However, he was met only with silence.

Ashe went for his .40 cal, but after advancing about six paces inside the apartment, knew he wouldn't need it. The stench that greeted him was overwhelming. Even though most of the windows in the apartment had been left open, the cold winter air was nowhere near enough to hide the smell of decaying flesh that hung heavy inside the apartment.

After clearing the living room and back bedroom, Ashe made his way into the kitchen where he found the body of a black male face down across the kitchen table. The victim, from Ashe's vantage point, had been shot in the head. Single entry wound. Minus that glaring detail, the bloated corpse was a match for the description provided by Six Eight.

"Mr. Watkins, I presume."

The cavern created by the exit wound in the back of Slomo Watkin's head suggested the deed was carried out with a large caliber firearm. Blood, still tacky, had pooled on the table around the victim. Dried spatter colored the walls, along with a good portion of the floor, and baseboards. A bowl of Rice Krispies, obvious only because the cereal box sat open on the counter, had long since sopped up the milk and turned into mush. They neither snapped, crackled, nor popped anymore.

"Guess that explains why you never picked up that package from our buddy Six Eight," Ashe sighed. This lead had dried up fast. There were no obvious signs of a struggle, and no doubt that Watkins knew his murderer. He was comfortable enough to let the perpetrator in while he enjoyed his morning chow. *Poor bastard. Never saw it coming.*

Further examination of the kitchen counter yielded a most likely reason. "I'll be damned," Ashe said as he caught sight of an unsealed envelope, full of cash. He didn't bother to count it, but would lay odds it added up to five thousand dollars.

Ashe exited the kitchen and peered around the living room. There were only three photographs out in plain sight. The larger of the three was framed and hung on the wall. The other two, smaller, five-by-eight's, sat atop an end table. Each of them was of Mr. Watkins and an older, somewhat heavy-set woman with a head full of gray hair and large bifocals. In two of the photographs, the older woman was wearing a nasal cannula, though they kept the oxygen tank out of the picture. In all three, they were both wore bright smiles and were sharing a warm embrace.

Maybe the woman was his mother, or grandmother. But there were no pictures of any children, or someone that might be a significant other. Either way, it appeared there was someone out in the world that would miss Jerome Watkins, and be heartbroken to learn of how he met his end.

Judging from those few pictures he could see, and those he did not, male hygiene products in the bathroom, and the general appearance of the place, Ashe was comfortable concluding "Slo-Mo" Watkins was a bachelor. The one good thing about that: there wasn't any further collateral damage. He lived alone and died that way.

There was nothing left for Ashe to do, so he made a call to CPD and kicked his find over to homicide. But no way was this a coincidence. Nothing would convince him it was. As he and Raines had surmised earlier, their man doesn't leave any loose ends.

That thought made Ashe shudder.

Loose ends are exactly what those girls are.

Chapter

13

FRANK GOODEN STARED AT the pile of bills on his living room table. They were enough to make him want to puke up the eggs and Spam he'd scarfed down earlier for breakfast. His stomach curdled and rumbled as he thumbed through the "late" notices for his maxed-out credit cards, and the final notices from ComEd and Nicor gas. He figured the same type of notice from the landlord was coming soon, it would be just be plain foolish to think otherwise.

And the hits just keep on coming.

The latest addition, though, to this growing collection, was a notice from his divorce attorney demanding payment. Considering how badly he'd been taken to the cleaners by the other guy, Frank felt he deserved a steep discount. He'd have been better off being represented by a team of monkeys, for all the good Lon Rosen, esquire, had done him.

Then again, what could he expect from a lawyer whose flyers were camped out in the men's room at a strip club?

Just how had things gotten so bad? Frank Gooden didn't have the time, nor energy, for that type of contemplation. It was a long story. Cutting to the chase, though, it was all Sharon's fault. His marriage to the former Mrs. Gooden was a mistake fifteen years ago. Letting her stay home while he worked was an even bigger mistake. Biggest of all, though, was letting Sharon manage the household finances, as the only thing she *managed* to do was run him right into the poorhouse. Not the place he thought he'd be at fifty-one years of age. At this time in life, when he's closer to the end than the beginning, he was hoping to be ahead of the game instead of behind the eight ball.

And to top that all off, she had won in court, and he now has to fork over nearly half of his paycheck to her in alimony. Ain't life just grand?

Like the fella once said, ain't that a kick in the head?

Frank walked into his bathroom and turned on the hot water. He reached into the medicine cabinet and retrieved his razor and shaving cream. The face staring back at him from the mirror looked every bit his fifty-one years, and then some. He glanced down at his gut, which protruded and pushed the waistband of his boxer shorts down. He lathered his face. He felt tired. Drained. It was like that most mornings. A commercial he saw the night before, about low testosterone in men his age, came to mind. The product being hawked by a former athlete labeled itself as some type of "man boosting formula." If there was one thing Frank Gooden could use, it was a boost. He made the first stroke along his face with the razor and gave serious thought to ordering a bottle or two of whatever the hell the baseball legend was selling.

Yet another issue, and he was sure, somehow, Sharon had something to do with that, too.

Probably the only trouble in his life, that he'd entertain the argument, wasn't Sharon's fault, was his gambling debts. Frank had been on the receiving end of bad beat after bad beat. The mother of all losing streaks. That wasn't anybody's fault. That's just the universe telling you it doesn't like you. Frank understood that, although he had to figure all it would take was one lucky break to turn things around.

That was what made the conversation he had a few weeks ago with a fellow gambler at the Four Winds Casino in South Bend, Indiana, so interesting. Initially, he thought the guy was full of it. How couldn't he be, right? But not only was the man well informed—about where Frank worked, and what actually took place there, and that alone, took some doing—but then the guy went and made an offer that was simply hard for Frank to refuse. And then there was the kicker—the *retainer*—his new friend had dropped in his lap. Frank had no reason to doubt that this guy was the literal answer to his prayers.

Frank Gooden finished his shave, wiped his face with a hot towel, and walked into his bedroom. He opened the top dresser drawer and staring at him was his second chance. Part of it, anyway. He removed an envelope and opened it. The stack of bills with the band around it totaled ten grand. Each and every time he counted it. Last night had made the seventh time. And there was more cash to be had. Lots more. Enough to change everything. It would be a chance to get back on top, his version of it, anyway, and crawl out of this hole of debt that the former Mrs. Gooden had left him in.

It wasn't like he'd be getting this money for nothing. No, sir. What the man was asking him for was serious. A serious ask that carried a serious risk, the money be damned. If he's caught, that is. But given his current predicament, how could he not take that risk? Especially for a reward that was commensurate.

He'd plotted and planned this thing down to the letter, and Frank was convinced that it could work. He just needed for his new friend to come through on his end. Frank would have the table set, his guest would just have to sit down, eat and clean his plate.

Frank put the envelope back in the drawer and shut it. He pulled his uniform out of the closet and began to get dressed for work. Retirement wasn't far off, and he'd much rather do it as comfortably as possible. Besides, he'd already spent too much time working too many hours for too little pay. Gooden glanced back over at the dresser drawer that contained the wad of cash he held in his hand. His mind was made up and there was no turning back now. He would accept the risk. He felt a rush of excitement well up inside him as he thought about the poker term "going all in."

That's just what he was doing, and maybe, just maybe, while he was at it, he could turn around all that bad luck he'd been having since he'd said "I do," all those years ago.

Chapter

14

Saturday night

BOTH ASHE AND I had spent all of Friday evening and Saturday chasing down any leads we could find.

We came up empty on all counts. The trail of the mystery man who'd kidnapped our victims had gone cold. As the families had hired us, it entitled us to briefings by the police. Even though we got the distinct impression, they wanted to keep us at arm's length. It seemed that our getting credit, along with FBI Special Agent Dakota Quinn, for saving Senator Aaron Dietrich's life, from a Chicago Police Officer no less, did little to endear us to our former brethren. In some circles, anyway.

Just the same, we'd learned the stolen Ford Transit work van belonging to IEG, had been found, burned. The good news, the girls were not inside. The bad news, forensics hadn't turned up anything useful. Not that we thought our suspect would've left any evidence behind.

As Saturday evening rolled around, I needed to recharge. Nothing clears my head like some good live jazz music. Ashe and I met up downtown at the Jazz Showcase; my favorite jazz club in the city.

The soulful playing of the Kevin Hill jazz quartet filled the auditorium. Ashe and I ordered a couple of drinks. We both took our bourbon neat. Ashe had Bulleit, while I had Maker's Mark. We found seating in the rear. Whether you end up in front or in the back near the bar, there's never a bad seat at the Showcase.

"So, how'd that lead you ran down the other day pan out?" I asked and then turned up my glass.

"Slo-Mo? He turned out to be a dead end," Ashe said.

"You didn't have any luck finding him, or he just didn't know anything?"

"No. He literally was a dead end. Found him in his apartment, slumped over a bowl of Rice Krispies. Somebody popped him a new asshole right in the forehead."

"You're kidding?"

Ashe sighed, sipped his bourbon, then said, "I wish. I can't shake the feeling that this is all connected."

I agreed.

Ashe continued, "Connected or not, what doesn't make sense, is this guy went through the trouble of setting up this kidnapping, having the mothers get us involved, and then he goes dark. We should've heard something from him by now."

"I'm thinking the same, and that has me worried. Not only for the girls, but because we don't know what this guy is up to yet."

As much as I needed to get out of the house and away from the situation, mentally I just couldn't shake it. The jazz and bourbon did little to help. Every time the music would capture my attention, the taunting phone call would queue up again in my head. Or the pained voices of the mothers. Even my promise that we would find the missing girls began to haunt me.

Ashe appeared just as pre-occupied as I was. We found moments where we could applaud the efforts of the men and woman that graced the stage this night, but our conversation kept returning to the matter at hand. How could it not?

We sat through four or five songs and maybe downed two glasses of bourbon each the entire time. We were both antsy.

"I'm going to head out," Ashe said. "Tomorrow, I'm going back over to OEMC."

"What do you have in mind?"

"Our boy has been careful covering his tracks. But maybe not as careful as he thinks. There's no way he was able to dump and burn the van without passing a pod somewhere, or a security camera or two along his route."

"I'd agree."

"If I can get a general idea of where he was coming from, I'll work backwards from there. We'll make the van the star of this search. Somebody's had to have seen it on his way to the dump site."

I said, "Sounds good, and I'll head over to the department and get any new updates. Say we meet up tomorrow around noon?"

"Noon's good. And Robert, stay alert. There's no telling what this nut bag is going to do next."

At the end of the day it sucked just to go home, but based on where things stood, it was all we could do.

Chapter

15

At about the same time that Ashe and Raines had arrived at The Jazz Showcase, Ishmael Keyes was parking a dark blue, 2020 BMW X5, procured for him weeks ago by Sophie Bissett, in the alley behind Spy Bar nightclub. It was a frigid night out. The weather forecast said something to the effect of it being nineteen degrees out, five factoring in the windchill. A steep drop from the day's *high* of twenty-five.

But the River North *party paradise* was still packed. People loved to party. Winter in Chicago didn't stop that.

Tonight, Keyes's disguise called for a dark gray Canali wool suit and long wool overcoat. He had to look the part. And play it. After tipping the bouncer at the door a hundred dollars so he wouldn't have to wait in line, he made his way inside. He felt eyes moving over him as he did so. He looked like *somebody*. It helped, of course, that he knew how to *be* somebody. That was all it took.

There had been a steady stream of women giving him the eye, passing by where he'd perched himself at the bar, and making small talk over the thumping bass from the bespoke sound system. Some women had even offered to buy him a drink. But it was the brunette with the dark brown eyes that fit what he was looking for.

Keyes watched her as she whispered and giggled at the table with her friends. The first few times they'd caught each other's eyes, she quickly turned away, only to turn back again moments later, seeking more contact. Gathering her nerve, no doubt. And then she made her move.

Her steps were measured yet uneven as she sashayed through the crowd. Most likely she'd been here a while. And most likely, she had already thrown a few back and was racing to the red light that was her limit.

Perfect.

"I see you're Mr. Popular," the brunette said, squeezing by two other women already in Keyes's space that had been making small talk for the past ten minutes. A bold move on her part. He liked that.

"Popular is my middle name," Keyes said with a smirk.

"I love your accent," the brunette said. "Where are you from?"

"All over," Keyes replied, this time offering a wink with his smile. He ordered a double shot of Remy Martin Louis XIII.

"Oh, my, I see you know how to live, too."

"Where are my manners?" Keyes said. "Would you like one? I'm sorry, what is your name?"

The two other women seemed put off by not being offered a drink, and left in a huff, mumbling something under their collective breaths.

"Denise," the brunette said.

"Well, Denise, I'm Ishmael. I see now that you're popular, too."

The two exchanged smiles. After the bartender delivered their drinks, they picked them up and clinked glasses.

"Do you live in Chicago?" Denise asked and sipped her expensive beverage.

"No, actually I'm just passing through. Here on business." Keyes emptied his glass in one gulp.

"Oh? That sounds exciting. What business are you in?" Denise said, and in an effort to keep up, downed her drink as well. She winced hard and patted her chest.

"A woman after my own heart," Keyes said. He smiled and ordered her another. "I work for an international acquisitions firm. I'm here to acquire rights to a rare item. And also close out a few accounts. Nothing exciting really."

"Well, how long are you in town?"

Keyes again gulped his drink, and watched as the petite woman also did the same, then said, "Just the next three days, I'm afraid."

"Awww…that's a shame," Denise said. This time, she motioned to the bartender for another drink.

Keyes chuckled and nodded "okay."

Denise flicked her hair, gave a seductive smile and let her left hand drop onto his. She ran her fingers along the veins in his hand. "You have to let me show you around before you leave. There's quite a few things to see in this city, if you have the right guide."

Keyes leaned in close and said, "That would be wonderful."

Chapter

16

DENISE GREW EVEN MORE flirtatious as their conversation continued. Keyes, for his part, ordered several more rounds of drinks, being careful to make sure she wasn't over served. She was already at the point, Keyes noticed, where she had to concentrate and pronounce her words slowly. He needed her to make some conscious decisions a little later. Even if she was only conscious of them in the moment. It wouldn't look good if he had to drag her out of the club in full view of everyone—even if everyone else was consumed with their own good time. Besides, it does no good to over water a plant.

But, knowing the fate lined up for her, he felt he owed it to her to make her last moments enjoyable. He didn't find the conversation all that engrossing, or interesting for that matter, though he faked it pretty well. *Enjoy yourself my dear. It's a shame, really, what's coming. A shame that it's necessary. Or is it shamefully necessary?* Keyes had to suppress a smile at the thought.

Oddly enough, it occurred to him that in this moment, this chance meeting with Denise almost reminded him of when he'd first met Sophie Bisset. While Sophie was more beautiful and without a doubt a lot more sophisticated, both women had a way of inserting themselves into a situation and taking it over. Of putting people at ease. If he truly wanted to get to know this woman, that really would've gone a long way. Alas—

"I have to get moving. There's a stop I need to make before calling it a night. How about you walk me to my car?" Keyes said.

"How about you give me a ride home?" Denise blurted out. "I mean…never mind. Besides, I came with friends," she protested, half-heartedly.

"So, leave them. I'll give you a ride home. Besides, you're my guide the next few days, not theirs."

"Well, when you put it that way. Let me get my coat." Denise smiled sheepishly, stood, and nearly toppled over. Keyes helped steady her, and she gave a flirty smile and licked her lips. "Oops! Now don't you go getting any ideas, mister."

Keyes smiled and arched an eyebrow. "I wouldn't dream of it."

Denise retrieved her coat and bade her friends good evening while Keyes patiently waited. As they headed out, he leaned in, lips just over her ear, and said, "My car is in the alley."

Denise frowned. "The alley?"

She didn't resist, however, as her new friend led her out of the club and around the corner to the alleyway. "I feel like I'm going to end up on a show on ID channel," she chuckled.

Keyes said nothing, though his grip on her hand tightened slightly as they walked further down the alley. Before the twosome approached his vehicle, Keyes quickly spun so he and Denise were standing face to face. He pulled her into an embrace and kissed her.

"Oh, my," Denise said, her head spinning. "Right by the dumpsters. How romantic." She threw her head back and let out a drunken snicker.

"Romantic? No. It is poetic, though."

"Poetic? Why poetic?"

Keyes leaned in and kissed her again, deeper this time. He pulled her in tighter to him, using his left arm. With his right hand, he fished around in his pocket and within moments, produced a three-inch serrated switchblade. He thumbed the knife open quietly. Then swiftly brought the blade up and jammed it into her inner right thigh. Denise shivered violently. Before she could scream, Keyes reached up and covered her mouth and nose with a gloved hand. He twisted the knife back and forth and then yanked it out with force. Denise's eyes went wide, staring in disbelief into the face of the handsome man with the sexy accent that she'd found so intoxicating. She slumped to the ground in a heap, next to the dumpster.

The femoral artery, as planned.

Keyes stared as red crimson gushed from her wound and stained the icy ground. She didn't have much time. Maybe a minute or two before she bled out. He removed one of his gloves and placed two fingers on his neck. He checked his watch. Sixty-five. *Not bad*, he thought, and took a deep breath.

Snow flurries wafted through the chilly night air.

Keyes got down on one knee and leaned in close until his lips hovered just over Denise's ear, then said, "It's poetic because twelve years ago, five women met their fate under circumstances similar to this one, right here in Chicago. Thought you might have heard. Just the same, this was never personal. Just another step in the game."

Chapter

17

GIVEN THERE WASN'T MUCH traffic on the roads, I'd made it home in just under thirty minutes. What little relaxation I'd felt earlier at the jazz club was long gone. My body was tense. I was exhausted and feeling somewhat defeated as we hadn't made a dent in this case over the last forty-eight hours.

It's almost cliché now to say that if you don't have a lead or at least a break in the case within the first forty-eight, that odds of success decrease dramatically. And the odds of a happy ending decrease tenfold. That's the nature of this beast. It always has been.

Tired though I was, I found I wasn't sleepy. I did my best to stop my mind from drifting back to 2002, and thinking about Tiffany, Lashonda, and Amada. And their families. After hanging up my coat and kicking off my winter boots, I found myself in my living room which, ever since my wife, Elena, left me, doubled as the office of RDC Investigations. By the two file cabinets in the right front corner was a stack of boxes. Six of them. Each of those boxes were stuffed tight with folders. Copies of my old case files from my time with the Chicago Police Department.

Most of those cases, ninety-four percent, had been resolved. Some even had, for all intents and purposes, a satisfying conclusion. There were others, however, that were less so.

That 2002 case fell into the latter category. I was tempted to call Dale. He understood my misery better than anyone regarding that case. I checked the time. It was too late to disturb him. Besides, Dale has his hands full taking care of Millie. I don't want to intrude on that and have him spend any more time away from his duties than he needs to.

Against my better judgement, I made my way over to the boxes and began rummaging through them. The third box from the bottom, the only one that didn't have any descriptions scribbled on it, contained what I was looking for. I flipped off the lid, opened the first file and there they were. The pictures of Tiffany, Lashonda, and Amada, taken during happier times. The families had provided us with the photos in the early days of our search. Their happy faces stared back at me from that folder, and I couldn't stop myself from thinking about what those faces looked like in their final moments. The terror and brutality that fell upon them brought tears to my eyes.

When I retired from the force, there were a few cases that haunted me. Some, because they were left unsolved, pursued as far as possible, but still unsolved. Which left me with feelings of failure and a sour knot in the pit of my stomach.

In fact, that was one of the primary reasons that after I'd left the force, I went back as a private citizen and combed through the department's files, looking for something I might have missed years ago. And I closed two cold cases, years after my first run at them. Those results led Dale and me to start our PI business.

Regardless of how it all ended, there were plenty of moments in my career where I knew, without a doubt, that I had done my job and I got justice and closure for those wronged. There were commendations and atta-boys from the brass. I'll always be proud of the job I did as a cop, and the way I served the people of my city. But there were some cases that left me with nightmares. A fact which became even more apparent as I thumbed through my files.

I took a quick break from the boxes, and the multiple files I had scattered across the living room floor, and headed into the kitchen. Despite my promise to myself on the ride home that I was done drinking for the night, I decided to break it. I poured myself a glass of Maker's Mark and pulled some leftover rib tips from the fridge and tossed them in the microwave. While the BBQ soaked up some radiation, I enjoyed the first sip from my glass. But I needed to get back with those files. Back with those ghosts from the past.

There were no similarities, beyond the neighborhood where our current victims were grabbed, between the two cases. Yet, it was always possible that there was a detail or two that could trigger a fresh line of thought, so I was on this ride for the duration. While I believed what I had said earlier when

Latesha Barnett had asked about this kidnapper's designs for their children—that he had no sexual desire for them—I had no reason to believe he didn't have the intention of those girls dying, just the same. But why hadn't he reached out to us? What did he really want? Without those answers, I was left thinking the worst.

I flipped through my old notes, continuing my stroll down memory lane, the memories were so fresh I could feel them, taste them. In effect, it was the fall of 2002 all over again.

Chapter

18

Late October 2002

BY THE TIME THE leaves had turned colors and began falling off the trees, we'd been stalled in the investigation of three young girls—Tiffany McNeal, LaShonda Jenkins, and Amanda Preston—that had gone missing from the Southside neighborhood of Englewood going on just about eight months.

Each had been taken, in separate incidents, on their way to school. As the calendar dragged on, the families and the city all had the same questions—*who would do this? How had they done it? Why? Is it going to happen again?*

As for the police, we had no answers. We were stymied.

My new partner, Dale Gamble, and I had been working together for about three months before we got rolled up in the task force the chief of detectives had put together in order to make headway in the case.

Dale and I had hit it off from the jump. We both had the same approach to police work, and our individual styles seemed to complement one another. He was into his custom-made suits, healthy living, and had a love for words that led to an extensive vocabulary. Me, I ate bacon double cheeseburgers, sometimes for breakfast, couldn't recall the last time I went to a gym, used ten-cent words, and my suits cost little more. Yin and yang.

The only drawback, he was determined to call me *Bobby*. I hate being called Bobby. It didn't take me long to figure out he got a kick out of that.

We had solved the first few cases we'd been assigned on an average of less than a week. But on the kidnapping, our luck seemed to had run out. Until one morning, when checking the tip line, which for months now had been dry as a bucket of sand—outside of a few calls from angry women swearing that their ex-husbands had done the deed—there was an interesting call.

The caller remained anonymous, but that didn't matter. Most of the tips we'd received to that point were left in the same fashion. It was the information itself that got my attention.

The man on the tip line stated that his daughter, aged ten, saw a man peeking into her bedroom window. He ran the man off, but it was what his daughter said afterwards that prompted him to call the line.

She had recognized him.

The janitor from her school.

And this man's daughter went to the same grammar school the missing girls attended. No way was that a coincidence. It was just the type of thing that we needed to check out. Dale and I hopped into an unmarked squad car, jumped on the Dan Ryan expressway, and made our way over to Garfield Elementary School on 60th and Racine.

When we arrived, we entered the administration office. It looked in need of a major makeover. The paint on the walls had faded in most spots from a bright sunny yellow to a dingy beige. Cracked and peeling.

Ms. Sheila Potter, a somewhat hefty, bespectacled, middle-aged black woman with streaks of gray running through her hair, greeted us from behind a desk with a smile that said she was happy to be there. "How can I help you, gentlemen?"

We took out our badges. "CPD, ma'am. I'm Detective Gamble. My partner here is Detective Bobby Raines."

I shot him a look. Dale smirked.

"Would either of you like a butterscotch?" Ms. Potter asked, saving him from my wrath for the moment. She pushed a glass dish that was sitting on her desk, full of the candies, toward us.

Dale continued. "No, thanks, ma'am. We're looking for a Mr. Davison."

"Mr. Davison? What are you all looking for him for?" Ms. Potter said, helping herself to a butter scotch.

"We just have a few questions for him, that's all." I said, not wanting to raise a panic.

Ms. Potter's eyes got wide. She adjusted her glasses and leaned across her desk to get a closer look at our creds. Dale and I both held our badges a little closer.

Satisfied we were legit, Ms. Potter said, "He ain't here. He called in sick today. Do you want me to get the principal instead?"

"That won't be necessary. But we will need Mr. Davison's contact information. Phone number, address, whatever you have for him."

Chapter

19

THE ADDRESS PROVIDED TO us by Ms. Potter from the Garfield elementary school administrative office, took us to an apartment building six blocks northeast of the school.

Ken Davison had the basement, or garden, apartment. We parked in front of the building and exited our police cruiser. A stiff autumn breeze kicked up, whipping leaves and dust from the abandoned lot next to Mr. Davison's place toward us. We descended the three concrete steps that led us down to the basement level and knocked on the door. While it took a moment for our knock to be answered, we could hear shuffling around inside. The third time Dale knocked and again announced us as police officers, the door creaked open.

Staring back at us was a middle-aged black man, bald and clean shaven. He had a thin, wiry, but strong looking build. He stood maybe five-foot-ten and went about a hundred seventy pounds and was dressed in a grey khaki uniform with Garfield elementary stitched on the front over the left breast. "Mr. Davison" was stitched right beneath it.

"Ken Davison?" Dale said.

"Yes. Who wants to know?"

I flashed my badge. "Chicago PD. I'm Detective Raines. My partner here is Detective Gamble. We'd like to talk to you, if we could."

Ken Davison's eyes blinked rapidly. "I'm…I'm really busy right now," he stammered.

"It'll only take a few minutes of your time," Dale insisted.

"If you're more comfortable doing this at our house, instead of yours, we can always take a ride to the station," I said.

I noticed Davison swallow hard. Thin beads of perspiration formed on the crown of his head. He thought for a moment, then said, "Uh, I got a few minutes. Why don't you two come on inside?"

"Thank you."

We entered his home. It was dim inside. There was a dank, almost mildew-like smell that hung in the air. Piles of old newspapers and junk mail circulars filled each corner of the living room. Half-eaten microwave dinners, plates, and silverware crusted over with the remains of days old meals littered the dining room table. I found it surprising for a guy that worked as a janitor. Obviously, he didn't bring his work home with him.

"Uh, have a seat, I guess," Davison said. He flopped down on his sofa. Piles of clothing covered every inch. I wasn't sure if it was clean laundry in need of folding, or dirty laundry in need of washing, but my money would've been on the latter.

I continued looking around his living room. Then something peculiar caught my eye. I turned my attention back to Mr. Davison. "You live alone?" I asked as I looked for a safe place to sit. Confident that there wasn't one, I added, "On second thought, I'll just stand, thanks."

Dale nodded in agreement.

"Yes. I live alone. Divorced. Twenty years now."

I continued my line of questioning. "You got any young kids? A daughter perhaps? Or a niece that comes to visit?"

"Uh…no. Nothing like that."

"Interesting."

Ken Davison's breathing had quickened. Those thin beads of sweat that had formed atop his head had gotten bigger and streamed down his face now. While it was warm in his place— the man actually had the windows closed on this tepid fall day— the perspiration was a telltale sign.

"You change your mind? Going in to work after all?" Dale asked.

Davison rubbed the back of his neck, looking back and forth between us, then answered, "Huh?"

"We were told you called in sick today. My partner is just referring to the fact that here you are, all dressed up for work."

"Oh, uh, yeah. I did. I got dressed but didn't feel good, so I called in. Guess I just ain't changed out my work clothes yet."

Dale said, "Fair enough. Where were you yesterday evening? Say, around six-thirty?"

Ken Davison did that thing again where he looked back and forth between the two of us, and after a few moments, said, "Uh, home, I think. Yeah, here. Maybe."

"You sound a little confused about that." I stared hard at him and held that stare for a few moments, then let it drift across the living room, over to the display stand, and that object that had caught my attention earlier. Davison's eyes followed mine, just like I wanted them to.

Again, he gulped.

"Do you know why we're here? Why we'd be looking to speak to you?"

"N-no. No, I don't."

"You want to try to take an educated guess?" I said sharply.

Ken Davison leapt to his feet. This time his eyes darted between me, Dale, and the display stand. "I think it's time you guys left."

"What do you think of that, Bobby?"

"I think Mr. Davison here still hasn't told us where he was yesterday, and I think we'd like an answer."

Ken Davison's eyes widened and his breathing quickened. "Look, don't you guys need a warrant?"

Dale stepped toward him, crowding his space. "We don't need a warrant to ask you a question, Mr. Davison."

"Well, I want you guys out of my home. I don't like how you're pressuring me when I ain't done nothing."

"There's a family not four blocks from here that would say otherwise," I said.

Ken Davison, for what had to be the sixth time since the conversation heated up, swallowed hard. His eyes darted over to the display stand and back. "What they say?" he choked out.

"You like peeping into little girls' rooms, Mr. Davison?"

"What? No!"

"That's what we're hearing, Ken. You were playing peek-a-boo in an eight-year-old's bedroom window. That's what you were doing yesterday. Or are you going to tell us you were lost and just going to ask for directions?"

"No! No! It wasn't me!" Davison's eyes again found their way to the display stand and back.

Dale turned his back to Davison, facing me instead. "I don't know, Bobby. He come across as a *short eyes* to you?"

"I'm not!" Davison's voice was shrill and cracked as he protested.

I shrugged my shoulders, said, "He damned sure could be."

"And that could fit with our other case."

"What other case?" Davison said, worried.

We both turned and looked at Ken Davison, dripping with sweat in his living room. "*The* case," we said in near unison. "Three young girls missing from right here in Englewood," I added.

"Oh. Yeah. That. I saw something about that on the news."

"I'll bet you did."

"Now, about yesterday evening," Dale started again.

"Listen!" Ken Davison shouted and pounded his clenched fists at his sides.

He was more than a little agitated. He was wound tight and ready to pop. Then he suddenly blurted out, "I ain't go near no little girls' room yesterday. And I didn't kill those other girls you talking about either!"

20

"Now, why would you go and say a thing like that?"

"What?" Davison said. A genuine look of confusion rolled down his face. "You mentioned the three girls. I was just saying—"

"Three *missing* girls!" I said. After a few moments, letting time and silence weigh heavy in the room, I continued, "No one said anything about them being dead. Let alone, murdered."

"Uh-oh, that's quite a mistake there, chum," Dale said.

Ken Davison went ashen and his knees buckled.

"We'll come back to that. There's still the question of what you were doing peeping into that youngster's bedroom last night."

"I already said—"

"Bullshit! You messed up, *Peeping Ken*! The little girl recognized you from school."

"Another mistake," Dale said. "That's what? Two now?"

"You thought you were invisible as you walked through those halls? You think the kids don't know what you look like just because more times than not, their apt to walk by you and not speak? Explain it to me, Ken. What made you think after peering into that child's room, you could just walk away? Where does that type of confidence come from?"

"Maybe it comes from having done it before. And gotten away with it," Dale said.

"*Thinking* that he's gotten away with it."

Dale smiled. "Or is it that all of you janitors look alike?"

"And when Daddy came to the window, the big bad janitor took off like a scared rabbit. That makes you a coward, doesn't it, Ken? Maybe even the type of coward that could hurt children, right?"

Davison said nothing. His gaze dropped to the floor. His janitor's uniform was a soaked mess.

"Come on, now, Ken. Don't go all taciturn and tightlipped on us now. You've had so much to say since we've been here," Dale chided.

"And there's one other thing I need to ask you about."

I walked over to the display stand, getting a closer look at that item that had caught my eye on entry, and ever since had been the focus of both myself and Mr. Davison. It was a decorative pearl hairpin, in the shape of a triangle. The four center pearls were colored dark blue. Amanda Preston's mother had described the hairpin many times, and in great detail.

Mrs. Preston had informed us, during one of her many interviews, that Amanda had a matching set, but the morning she went missing, she'd left home without one of them. I'd spent months staring at a photo of it and recognized it right away when we stepped inside Mr. Davison's home. I was betting he knew I recognized it, too.

I reached inside my sport coat's inner pocket and produced a plastic evidence bag. Using an ink pen, I shoveled the hair pin inside the bag.

It was almost possible to see the life leave Mr. Davison's body. His eyes seemed to sink into his face and his shoulders drooped.

"And this?" I held up the pearl hairpin at Davison's eye level. "How do you explain this?"

"I dare say that ain't yours, slick," Dale said. "Somebody remind me, I've lost count. Is that mistake number three?"

"I found it," Ken said, his gaze still fixed firmly on the floor. "I found it, cleaning up the school. That's right, it was on the floor of one of the classrooms."

"That's not bad," Dale said. He nodded his head up and down and smiled at the man who was clearly now our suspect. "Although, I'd love to hear you explain why you brought it home, and kept it. But, hey, it shows you're thinking."

The hairpin was, on its face, circumstantial, but we had the peeping Tom complaint, so that was enough to bring him in.

"I'm thinking, too," I said. "And what I'm thinking, Mr. Davison, is that on second thought, we will continue this conversation at our house."

Chapter

21

Once we'd gotten Ken Davison back to the station house, and in the box, it was all academic. In my mind, anyway.

I *knew* he was guilty.

And I knew we'd get a confession.

For a while there, he did his best to deny any involvement, spinning incoherent stories, that we quickly poked holes through. "If you expect us to believe that, you're nuttier than squirrel shit," Dale had said at one point.

Ken Davison continued his song and dance, and we danced along with him, keeping him talking—appealing to any vestige of decency that he may have held inside him. We tried relating to him, on any level, even discussing the sad state of affairs 2002 had found the Chicago Bulls in after their dominance of the 90s.

Rule number one of interrogations is, you get your subject to talk by pushing their buttons, not letting them push yours. We were finding all the right buttons to push. To put it simply, using a lesson I had learned in my first year as a detective, we humanized him. There was no point in telling him how evil we thought he was. That doesn't mean it was easy sitting in that interrogation room across from him, knowing what he'd done. There was plenty that I wanted to say. Plenty, Dale wanted to say. But we held our tongues. We peeled back the onion that was Ken Davison. And one thing I knew for a fact was even bad men like their mothers.

So, for a while, we talked mothers. After that, we delved into what it was like for him growing up a young black kid on the Southside of Chicago in the sixties. We talked marriage—we listened as he laid out all the reasons his had failed. After serving him a double bacon cheeseburger and large fries from Lucky's Pub near the station, we had reached near the thirteenth hour of the interrogation—and he broke.

"I did it. I hurt those babies," he said. "I'm so sorry."

Tears streamed down his face, and he shook and shuddered as the truth broke the damn of his conscience. Once he started talking, he couldn't stop.

Ken Davison explained how, that after his wife had left him, there was nothing to stop the urges that had driven them apart. He'd always had a taste—a predilection—for little girls. His first foray into child molestation, which our captain, who was leading the task force, had already pulled us out of the interrogation room and informed us, landed him in prison for eight years. So, this time around, after he had stoned up and decided he'd give in to temptation again, he was determined to avoid being told on, and sent to prison. This time his victims wouldn't leave his presence alive.

He detailed how he had stalked the girls, and, trading on the fact that they knew him from the school, lured them with various lies, into his truck, and took them off for himself. Eventually, during our conversation, he gave up the location of their bodies.

Later, we found a box of photos he'd taken and developed himself. Ken Davison had photographed every moment of their suffering. His memories—keepsakes—of the event. We'd also found a couple other trophies he'd taken, much like Amanda Preston's pearl hairpin. LaShonda Jenkin's Power Puff Girls watch, and Tiffany McNeal's gold charm had been added to his collection.

Although we didn't need it, as we had Ken Davison's confession, DNA testing would later match the hairpin to Amanda Preston. There was no doubt. He was our man.

Many of the theories that had crept up during the course of the investigation had a sophisticated predator preying on those girls. All along, it was simpler than that. It was someone they knew. Not a family member, or fellow parishioner, but someone those girls trusted nonetheless. There was neither skill nor sophistication associated with Ken Davison, as evidenced by his botched fourth attempt at an abduction. Sometimes, it turns out, luck even shines on the predator. Pure dumb luck in the form of a clerical error that led to his prior conviction not showing up during his background check when he applied at the school. Pure dumb luck was why he'd gotten away with his crimes for the time he did.

But once he'd met Dale and me, that luck had run out.

We solved the case. The nightmare that had disrupted the life of the city was over.

As we concluded our interview, Ken Davison looked at me, tears still streaming, with an expression that I took as genuine sorrow and confusion, and said, "Just how bad is this going to be for me?"

Chapter

22

Saturday night continued…

FOR THE RECORD, THINGS ended *very* badly for Ken Davison. Very much so. He was found beaten to death one morning, in the prison shower, as he awaited trial. It was impossible for word about what he'd done not to get out. He was, for lack of a better term, famous.

That aside, the prisoners in the Cook County jail weren't having it.

To this day, I don't know, nor do I care to, how Ken Davison ended up with the general population, as opposed to in protective custody. Another *clerical error* like the one that allowed him to get the job at the school, I guess. No one was ever held accountable. Not anyone that worked at the jail. Not any of the inmates. And after the mental damage Davison's acts had done to the city, the mayor, the state's attorney, the superintendent—the powers that be—just as soon moved on. I can't say I blamed them. I've wrestled with the casual, dismissive manner in which I'd viewed his death over the years. I've even prayed for forgiveness for it. But that doesn't stop me from feeling the same way even now: Ken Davison got what he deserved.

As I sat on my living room/office floor, with the same drink in hand, and the leftover rib tips which I hadn't touched, I regretted taking this trip down memory lane. Being reminded, in vivid detail by my notes and reports, of what took place back in '02, brought a wave of nausea over me. I forced the rest of the Maker's in my glass down anyway, savoring the whiskey burn. The tips would go back in the fridge, I no longer felt like eating.

My *trip* had made me think of my wife, Elena, as well. She was so supportive of me. When the media began tearing down all the members of the task force when that case had stalled, and we were becoming the story, she helped me keep my head on my shoulders. She kept me focused. Elena was good that way. Talk about being a match for someone. She knew me like a book, and same for me with her.

The beauty of our relationship, I'd always felt, was that she knew my shortcomings and my faults. But more importantly, she also knew how to handle them, and me. That was true from day one. She was the glass to my water; the form around me that kept me from going over the edge. Her voice alone was enough to bring me back down from a rage, and believe me, there were many rages back then. I wasn't what you'd call a hothead, but as she had so eloquently put it, "You have a temper, dear." She knew how to be a cop's wife. She got me through that case, and many more that came down the line.

But so much has happened since then, including her leaving.

After spending about thirty minutes with my files, I wanted to throw them into my fireplace and give them a final blazing sendoff, but I forced myself to continue looking through them for a few minutes more.

While there was no direct correlation I could see between Ken Davison and our current kidnapper, I wanted to immerse myself in every clue and thought that ran through my head at that time. Sometimes, that sort of thing can help. And at this point, I'd take anything I could get.

After my stomach settled a little, I managed another two fingers of bourbon, then realized I'd had my fill of both. The booze and the files. It was time to call it a night.

I gathered up all the files littered across the floor, and despite my earlier desire to put a match to them, I tucked them back into their unlabeled box. An interesting thought occurred to me as I slid the box back into the corner with the others. When we were hunting for the kidnapper, which turned out to be Ken Davison, we thought we were looking for the bogeyman. I had a similar feeling about the Street Life Killer. He was the scourge of the homeless community in Chicago for years before he disappeared, only to resurface in Louisiana at the same time Dale and I, in our new lives as PI's, were working the missing person's case of Cecilia McAllister.

Neither of them was what I had expected. To be frank, they were both less than, in terms of what I thought we would find.

Evil, yes, they were both that. But there was nothing exceptional about either man. Were it not for a break or two that went their way, they'd have both been caught much sooner than later. I can't remember where I'd heard it before, but someone once said, the devil has his miracles too. They were the beneficiaries. But this new guy, I get a whole different vibe from him. I'm left wondering what will he be like when I meet him face to face.

And I have no doubt we *will* meet face to face.

I headed off to bed with the realization there was one good thing that came from my impromptu file review. In order to be what these recently abducted girls needed, I needed to feel the angst, the anger, and raw emotion that I'd felt in those days. I needed it to get me sharp. Get me on edge. Which is where I will need to be if I had any hope of figuring this out. The memories in those files also served as a stark reminder that I didn't want to feel that way again. The only way for that to happen was to have a different outcome this time.

Chapter
23

ISHMAEL KEYES HAD WATCHED the man with keen interest for about twenty minutes, ever since leaving Spy Bar, and the grisly, though necessary scene he'd left behind in the alley. The tall, gangly man in the tattered coat had marched his way along Madison Avenue, braving the cold, begging the occasional passersby for change as he did so.

He wore a skullcap and scarf, and both looked to be in the same condition as the coat. It was obvious his winter gear wasn't up to par. Every few minutes he'd duck inside the entryway of one of the many shops and stores that lined the street, a blatant attempt to steal a few minutes avoiding the blustery night air.

Keyes surmised the man was homeless. A skid row vagrant with grand plans no larger than scaring up enough change to buy a cup of coffee and haunt some all-night diner to keep warm. Although the man most likely reeked of BO combined with whatever filth he might have recently slept in, he was perfect.

The man's present direction, heading west bound as he crossed Central Avenue, was leading him to the border of Oak Park and Chicago. That, too, was perfect.

Keyes had already performed his due diligence. He'd confirmed his quarry wasn't home. He cruised up Madison Street in his rental BMW. Once the man was within three blocks of Austin Boulevard, Keyes pulled over and parked. After a few moments, he got out and trailed behind the man, being cautious not to spook him. He observed as his shabbily garbed subject collected what amounted to a little over a dollar by the time they'd reached Austin Boulevard.

Keyes had seen enough. This was his guy. The right tool for the job. "Say, bub?" Keyes called out.

The man spun on his heels. "Hey brother, can you spare a buck?"

"I can do better than that," Keyes said. "But I need a favor."

"A favor? Whoa, man, I don't need a dollar that bad."

Keyes laughed. "Not that kind of favor, friend."

The man turned away from Keyes and walked away. "I'm all right, man, that's okay."

"I'll give you a hundred bucks," Keyes called after him.

The man stopped in his tracks. He hesitated, but turned around. He looked Keyes up and down, but after a moment, again begged off.

"So, what are you going to do, take the couple of bucks you have in your pocket and ride the bus all night?" Keyes said and pointed to the CTA bus terminal on the corner. Keyes studied the expression on the man's face. He appeared to be thinking. Which, in Keyes mind, meant he had him. The man was on the fence and just needed a nudge to climb on over.

"What's the matter? A hundred's too short? All right then, let's make it three." Keyes reached in his pocket and produced a wad of cash and then counted off three crisp hundred-dollar bills.

"What do I have to do?" the man asked, then blew into his cupped hands.

"I have an old army buddy that lives on this block, in that building there across the street. I'm in town for a surprise visit and I want to play a prank on him."

"Really? That's it?"

"That's it. We've got a friendly competition going, he pranked me good last time he came out to San Diego, now it's my turn. You can help me out and help yourself out at the same time."

The man rubbed his chin as he stared at the bills in Keyes's hand. Keyes shook them gently and watched as the faces of Benjamin Franklin did a seductive dance in the man's eyes. Judging by the man's sudden shift in body language, Keyes was certain that he'd landed this fish. "As a matter of fact, we can wait for him in my car, get out of this cold. What do you say?"

The man hunched his shoulders. "I don't see why not."

Chapter

24

ASHE EXITED THE I-290 expressway at Austin Boulevard, and turned north, heading home. His earlier conversation with Robert Raines still fresh on his mind.

The kidnapper had to be up to something, but his actions, or inaction to be accurate, since the abductions had made little to no sense. If he wanted to engage them, and went through the very public, and risky, effort of kidnapping the young girls, it only stood to reason that everything would be in play at this point. There should have been a demand of some kind. An ultimatum, even. Yet there had been only silence.

That, and another death.

By now Ashe was more than convinced that the murder of Jeff "Slo-Mo" Watkins could be laid at the feet of the girls' kidnapper. That made four deaths—that they were aware of.

No loose ends.

The words echoed through Ashe's mind as he continued down Austin. It all made sense. More trade craft. As he had concluded earlier, they were dealing with a professional. Ashe had the hope, however, that while on the way to dispose of the vehicle used in the kidnapping, the man passed by at least one of the city's pod cameras, unaware of its precise location, and therefore had his picture taken. Smug in his skillful ways, just maybe he let his guard down for just a few precious seconds.

That's all Ashe would need.

Tracking had always been one of his specialties. Finding those that didn't want to be found. It didn't matter if they were over in Afghanistan, Iraq, or here in the states. If he could pick up a trail, he could find anyone.

This time, however, he needed to work as fast as he ever had, given the stakes. Not that he didn't understand before, but now more than ever, he sympathized with Dale and Robert. He understood, in greater detail, the pain both of his friends carried around all these years after that original case. Not only did Ashe not want to carry that burden, that weight of guilt, anger, and despair, but he didn't think his two elders could go through that again.

Ashe brought his Chevelle to a stop just outside of his apartment building. It didn't take him long to clock the man that was wandering aimlessly up the block. He was tall, and his tattered coat, along with the beat-up gym shoes he wore in mid-winter, suggested he spent most of his time on the streets. But there was always a host of characters hanging out along the border between Oak Park and Chicago. The CTA line ended on the corner of Austin and Madison, so no real surprise. Even in bad weather.

Ashe made a habit of watching everyone. Not because he was paranoid, or even hypervigilant. Being aware of everyone around you was just a good practice to be in.

Aside from the tall man, Ashe eyed a man and a woman across the street, bracing against the wind as they waited for the bus, and then he headed inside. He'd barely made it to his apartment building lobby when he noticed the man in the ragged, dingy coat had walked in behind him.

"Ashe, right?" the grungy man said.

Ashe turned to face him head on. "Yeah, and?"

The man flashed a smile with his severely chapped lips, and said, "You saying you don't remember me?"

"Am I supposed to?"

"C'mon, man. Iraq. Afghanistan. You got to remember me."

Ashe turned away from the man and made his way up the first-floor landing. He stuck his key in his apartment door. Ashe turned back toward the man and said, "Listen, pal. I spent over fifteen years in the military. And while I met many people, I never forgot who I served with. Living or dead. Trust me, pretending to be a vet, ain't the way to go."

"Is that like, against the law or something?"

"Doesn't matter if it is, or isn't. But it's a sure-fire way to get me to shove my boot up your ass. No grease."

The man followed Ashe up the landing. "C'mon buddy."

"The next step you take will be your last one. Now—"

Ashe paused. This man he'd been exchanging this ridiculous banter with had been a distraction. One that he didn't see coming.

And I'm an idiot for not seeing it from a mile away!

The first word that came to his mind, he let out in almost an accidental whisper. "Shit."

Ashe twisted the doorknob with his right hand and went to cross-draw his Smith & Wesson .40 caliber with the other. The pain came lightening quick. He immediately recognized the searing heat from a bullet passing through him. The grungy man attempted to run for his life and ending up serving as a human shield. Running up the remaining steps, he collapsed into Ashe. He had been hit at least twice in the back, as bullets from a semi-automatic pistol rained in a rapid-fire fashion, shot expertly from just behind him in the doorway. While some shots missed, and splintered the doorjamb, enough of them found their mark.

Ashe felt a second-round pierce his body. *So much for that shield.* He dropped his .40 cal as he and about one hundred and eighty pounds of dead weight fell inside his apartment. There wasn't much choice now. If he wanted to live, there was only one thing he could do.

No matter how much it hurt.

Part Two

THE CLOCK IS TICKING

Chapter

25

Sunday morning

THERE WERE AT LEAST a thousand different things running through my mind after I'd left Ashe's place. A plethora of thoughts about what could've occurred and why. Each complete with varied scenarios as to how and differing opinions on who'd been behind it.

I'd been driving less than twenty minutes when my cellphone rang. It was an unknown number, so I considered ignoring it. It's rare that I ever answer those. Aside from that, the scene at Ashe's place had been too much to process. But out of habit—

"Raines."

"Is this Robert Raines?" the voice on the other end asked.

"Yes, it is."

"Robert Raines, the private investigator?"

There seemed to be genuine surprise, and almost a hint of satisfaction in the voice.

"One and the same. Who am I speaking with?"

"Someone who's admired you and your team from afar for a little while now. I liked the commercial, by the way. Production values aside, you guys come off as serious. Capable."

"I'm sorry, now's just not a good time. If you're looking to hire a private investigator, I could refer you to—"

"No worries there, Mr. Raines. I don't need a referral. And you're already working the case I want you on."

The tone in the voice quickly changed. There was a steeliness to it now. Giving off the vibe that the caller was in control. It wasn't hard for me to guess who I was talking to. A moment later, my mystery caller confirmed it.

"I want you to know the girls are fine. For now."

"I was expecting to hear from you sooner."

"Well, I had some things to attend to. Some preparations to make."

"You're not disguising your voice?"

"Meaning?"

"I'm surprised you haven't used any voice altering technology. Not on the call with the girl's mothers, or on this one."

"I like the sound of my voice," he said and chuckled. "Besides, I don't have time for that type of nonsense, and to be frank, I don't need to."

That answer was very confident. It fit with his actions so far. "Can I ask why you're doing this?"

"How do you stand the winters in Chicago? I've been to some cold places, but only visiting, mind you. You actually live here by choice. That's incredible."

His tone went friendly again, speaking to me as if there wasn't something more serious for us to talk about. But I pressed on. "Those girls have done no harm to you. So, again. Why?"

"You're right. They hadn't. But I had to do something to get your attention. And may I presume then, that I have it?"

"You do. By the way, who am I speaking to?"

"Don't worry about that just now. Besides, I've left clues for you to piece together and sort all of that out. If you're half as smart as your history and reputation suggest, this will be child's play for you, Mr. Raines. If you'll pardon the pun." The caller paused after his poor attempt at humor, then said, "Oh, and I am sorry about your friend."

"Excuse me?"

"Your partner, Ashe. I can tell you, he's dead. I put two, maybe three bullets in him." He paused again, letting that sink in for me. A moment later, he continued, "I have to admit though, based on the man's reputation, I thought he'd be a little tougher than that. A little harder to sneak up on. It's quite sad, actually."

"You sonofa—"

"Temper, temper, Mr. Raines. We've got more to discuss, so I'm going to need you to stay focused."

He was right. I needed to recompose myself. Regardless of what he'd just said about Ashe, and his apparent ambush, there was still the issue of the girls at hand. No matter how mad I was, and whether or not I believed Ashe was in fact dead, I still needed to do all I could for those girls. Besides, that's what Ashe would want.

I took a deep breath, and said, "Why don't you tell me what we need to do to get those girls home safe?"

"Glad you asked that, Mr. Raines. After all, not only are those girls depending on you, but so are their mothers."

It took everything in me to ignore his needling. I kept my voice calm. "I'm listening."

"The first thing you need to understand is this: those girls have seventy-two hours, and then they're dead. If you don't find them in seventy-two hours, that's another three little black angels you can kiss goodbye. You follow me, Raines?"

"I follow."

"Good. Here's a little hint to get you started. You might want to check in with your former associates in blue regarding a murder at the Spy Bar. No doubt you'll recognize the signature. As for the victim, she's got your number."

I had no idea what he meant, but I didn't let on. There would be time, *hopefully*, to figure that out.

"There's a pattern developing Raines. Follow the clues, and you just might save those little ladies. Otherwise, they're dead. And so are you. I may give a pass to your buddy, Gamble. Pity what happened to his wife. But I won't guarantee his safety. Especially if you fail."

I was taken aback by the comment about Dale. "You seem to know a lot."

"That's because I do."

Arrogant prick. But right now, he has the upper hand, so he can afford to be.

"May I ask you a question?"

His voice was glib as he said, "As long as it isn't about where the girls are, feel free."

"Why us? My team and me?"

"You caught my eye. You seem to be a worthy adversary. For men like us, that's all we want, right? So now, we'll see. The clock is ticking, Mr. Raines. Tick tock, tick tock."

"Okay. Fair enough. And if I may?"

"By all means."

"If you had faced Ashe man to man—"

"How do you know I didn't?"

"Because if you had, I'm sure he would've killed you."

"Yeah? Well. Maybe. Maybe not."

He hung up, and I set a timer on my watch. He said I had seventy-two hours to find those girls. If that psycho was right about one thing, it's that the clock was ticking. And I needed to get to work, fast.

Chapter
26

DALE GAMBLE HAD GOTTEN up at 5:30 a.m. Sunday morning. Most days he was up by five but allowed himself the extra thirty minutes today. While he viewed it as best that he got up as early as possible to tend to his chores while Millie was still asleep, on Sunday morning's, he allowed himself that little thirty-minute luxury.

He made his way downstairs to the kitchen after taking a brisk shower. He put on a pot of coffee and then got dressed. Thermal tops and bottoms along with flannel. He hadn't finished his shoveling duties from the other day and given the time that's gone past, it was going to be back-breaking work this morning. Piping hot coffee was sure going to hit the spot when he came back in.

Dale's boots crunched against the wind-hardened, icy snow. *That's what you get, Gamble. Should've finished this off Friday.* He rammed the tip of the shovel into the packed ice. It crunched and cracked. The wind whipped around him as a stiff, early morning breeze blew by. A few turns chucking frozen snow around had Dale winded. He felt the muscles in his lower back stiffen up. But he was the only one to do it. Sure, he could ask Ashe. The big man was always dropping by, looking to help. But not since Bobby had come by with the news that three young girls had been kidnapped from Englewood.

That fact changes things. Big time. Without question, they took precedence. Dale was only sorry that he couldn't be out there helping his friends in their search. While they could call him with any leads, questions, or concerns, and he'd do his best to help them make heads or tails out of whatever comes their way, it's not the same as being there.

Right now, though, he had to be *here*, at home. For Millie's sake. There was no way he could leave her. That was the price they paid for Ashe getting her back alive. A price, Dale reflected, that he—

It was still dark outside, except for the motion sensor light that had popped on when Dale came out, but something caught his eye. If he didn't know any better, and he thought he did, it looked like there was an envelope taped to one of his garbage cans. Again. Dale dropped the shovel and walked over to the trash cans. There weren't any impressions in the snow, but it was all ice now, so if someone had walked back here, they'd have left no trail behind.

As Dale got closer, he could make out that in fact it was another envelope. The person who left the first had to know by now that they had the wrong house. That whoever they were looking to prank did not live here. Dale first passed by the trash cans and peered over his fence out into the alley. Only he and the wind were out.

Dale returned to the trash can and ripped the envelope from it. It was sealed, same as the first. Dale opened it and removed the note inside. Staring back at him, again in that same child-like handwriting, but in blue crayon this time, were the words:

Are you sorry?

"Sorry I didn't catch you out here in my yard," Dale whispered. "That's about the only thing I'm sorry about."

It still had to be a prank gone wrong. It still had to be just some knucklehead not finding their way into the right yard, but all the same, it was becoming at least slightly annoying. As he'd done with the first letter, Dale crumpled it and tossed it into the trash can. It was best to put it out of his mind for now. He still had chores to tend to. The most pressing of which was clearing the backyard walkway before it became a skating rink. Worrying about these notes were not on the list. Not today. With any luck though, soon enough, he'd catch whoever it was, and read them the riot act for trespassing.

Dale went to pick up the shovel and felt a jolt. It made him jump. He had to laugh at himself when he realized it was just his cellphone buzzing in his pocket. He glanced up at the house. Their bedroom light was still out. That was good. It meant Millie was still asleep and wasn't looking for him.

Now the question was, who was calling this early, and why?

Chapter

27

DALE'S HEART SPED UP, just a little, when he peeped at the caller ID and saw it was Robert Raines calling. An unexpected early morning call—you didn't have to be a cop to know that those were rarely, if ever, good. He answered the call and put the phone to his ear.

"What is it, Bobby?"

The news shared by his friend chilled him to his core. So much so, he didn't even notice the early morning wind as it whipped around him. His knees wobbled a little, and he went and took a seat on his back-porch steps.

"Missing? Ashe is missing?"

"Yeah, and it sounds just as strange to me saying it as I'm sure it is for you to hear it. I just got off a call with a man claiming responsibility for it all. The mess at Ashe's place. The kidnapping. Everything. And he said something else."

110

"Well, you already opened this can, we might as well eat it all."

"He claimed Ashe is dead. And that he shot him three times."

"Impossible."

"After seeing all the blood in his apartment, I don't know. I just don't know. Our mystery man also laid this on me, too. He said the girls only have seventy-two hours left. If they're not found in seventy-two, then they're dead. He's playing some elaborate game, and right now, I've got to dance to his tune if those girls are to have a chance. I have to think it's what Ashe would want, too. So that's where my focus has to be."

Dale felt a tightness in his chest. "Bobby—"

"No. I'm not asking you that. You're right where you need to be."

"Well, what do you want me to do? What do you need me to do?"

"I don't know yet, pal. But for now, just take care of Millie. And stay home."

"In case he comes here, after me?"

"Well, we can't rule that out."

Dale thought of the letters. What he'd been ready to write off as a nuisance, an accident, he now saw in a different light. It all made sense now.

After a few moments of silence, Robert asked, "Something on your mind?"

"No. It's nothing. You're right. I'll stay home."

"Good. Keep your eyes open and your phone close by. If I need to run something by you or have an update for you, I'll call."

"Bobby? You have to find those girls. You hear me. You have to find those girls, alive."

"I'll do my best."

"I know you will."

It wasn't fair, and Dale knew that as soon as the words had crossed his lips. With all that was going on at the moment, it wasn't fair to put that type of pressure on his friend. But the words had to be said. Three little black girls that they didn't save back in 2002 demanded those words be said.

That was why he didn't tell Robert about the notes. The man didn't need that additional distraction on his mind as well.

After the call ended, Dale got up from the porch and made his way back inside. After locking the door, he went to the front hallway closet and pulled his Kimber 1911 .45 ACP, along with five extra magazines and ammo off the top shelf. He sat them on the living room table. Dale removed and re-hung his coat and then retrieved his Benelli M4 Tactical semi-automatic 12-gauge shotgun from the back of the closet. He grabbed three boxes of shells as well. Dale recalled it had been a while since he fired it, but one thing was certain—it always let everyone know what your intentions were. *Now this will ring some serious bells.*

As he began removing the layers he'd packed on to handle the morning cold, he heard Millie's voice call out to him from the stairs.

"Dale? Is everything okay?"

"Honey, what are you doing up?"

"I heard you rummaging around down here. Are things all right?"

"Things are fine, hun. I'm just taking the toys out for a cleaning is all. You go on back to bed, I'll wake you when I've got breakfast ready."

Dale hated lying to Millie, but after what had happened with Fallon Krieg, there was no way he could tell her that another madman might show up at their door. And this time, it's not a doped up borderline psychopath with a mean streak, but a professional killer. She already jumps at the sight of her own shadow. That news would driver her clear out of her skin. So, for now, everything was fine. It had to be that way.

As Dale saw it, if their new adversary wanted to show up at his door, let him. He racked a load into the M4.

This time I'm home. This time, I'm ready.

Chapter

28

AFTER HANGING UP THE phone with Dale, I called Lt. Andrews and then made my way to the 12th precinct. I needed to get on the fast track with this thing, and he seemed to be the best bet to make that happen. At least, I hoped.

I wished for a moment that I was still on the force with access to all the resources the Chicago Police Department has to offer. As it stands, I'm retired. Just a private citizen now, a private dick. But I figured to call in every favor owed to me to get in front of this. My experience with Detective Royce earlier this morning aside, I was at a point where I needed some co-operation. As the kidnapper had so succinctly put it, the clock is ticking. Every minute, every second was crucial, and I didn't care who I had to talk to, or what hoops I had to jump through. We needed to find those girls.

I needed to find those girls.

I arrived at the station at 6:00 a.m. It was still pitch black out. That's Chicago in the wintertime. The sun would probably make an appearance, or daylight at least, somewhere about seven, seven-thirty. I was glad that Andrews was already in. He had left the scene at Ashe's place shortly after I did. No point in going back home, he'd said.

As I approached his office, I could see that he was on the phone. I wasn't sure with whom, but he was listening intently. He motioned me in to take a seat as I approached. From his end the conversation contained a lot of "mmm-hmm's," "yes, that's right," with a few "yes sir's," in the mix. Which let me know he was talking to a higher-up. There was a pack of cigarettes sitting on his desk. His office, and the man himself, reeked of smoke and ash. Andrews's hand kept going back and forth, stroking the pack, and tapping his fingers as if playing a piano against the desk. I see that after *starting again*, he hadn't found his way back to *quitting again*, at least not just yet.

After a few more minutes, he hung up. "That was the chief of d's," Andrews said. "Look, I don't have any good news as far as getting you any access to that investigation involving Ashe."

"That's not why I'm here, Lu. It's about those three missing girls."

"There you're in luck. There's a task force being put together. You'll have access to their intel. Daily updates. We might even be able to—"

"He called me," I said.

"Who?"

115

"The kidnapper. He called me, not more than twenty minutes ago, now. It's not good, Dan."

"What did he say?" Andrews said, and his hand started inching towards the cigarettes again.

"He said I've got seventy-two hours to find them, or they're dead."

Dan slumped back in his chair. His hand retreated from the cigarette pack as if it had suddenly stung him. "Who is this maniac?"

"No idea, but he mentioned another murder, said it happened at the Spy Bar earlier this morning. He recommended I look into it. He intimated that this latest victim is a clue, not only to his identity but also to finding the girls. Another thing, Lieutenant. He took responsibility for the shooting at Ashe's place as well."

Lt. Andrews put up a hand. His face contorted in an uneasy frown. "Just a minute." He picked up the phone again and re-dialed the chief. I listened as Dan recounted the story I'd just laid on him a few minutes ago. I couldn't make out what the chief was saying, but again, on Dan's end, I heard a lot more "yes sir," and "understood, sir." After a few moments, Andrews hung up the phone.

"Well?"

"There's still enough of the old guard around that were either involved in, or remember that case from 2002, and what it did to the city. Hammerlich doesn't want to see that again. That call you got, changes everything. Any lead you want or need to follow, you've got access to. Doesn't matter the precinct, or department. Any resources we have, you have. Point is, we're all hands-on deck to find those girls."

"Good," I said, relieved.

"That task force I spoke of, they're meeting in two hours at CPD headquarters. We'd like you for you to attend."

"I can do that."

"You're about to be front and center with this thing, Raines. You up for that?"

Not the words I wanted to hear, but Dan was right. That phone call from the abductor had put me in the spotlight. I nodded my head "yes."

"There's one more thing," Andrews said. "And per the chief, it's non-negotiable."

"Oh, yeah? What's that?"

"He's assigned you a partner."

"What? No, that's not necessary. Besides, he can't assign me anything, I don't work here anymore."

"Well, he has."

"Then, in that case, what about Mac?" I said, referring to my old friend, Abner McNamara.

"Out with the flu. Listen, you get our cooperation, and it comes with a price. This is it. If something happens, it's going to happen fast, and he wants us to at least have one man on the ground with you, aside from the task force. He's going to be your new best buddy. Besides, what better option do you have? Ashe is…missing. And where's Dale?"

"Dale will be sitting this one out," I said.

"To my point. And you did say there's a clock on this thing."

It wasn't as if I needed him to remind me of that, but those words alone were enough to get me to let go of any reservation I had about working with a partner. While I'd come here seeking cooperation, this was about ten steps further than I was looking to go. But what would be the point in refusing? There was no way I could turn down making use of the department's resources and hope to find these girls in time.

"Fine, fine. I won't argue."

"Good, you'll meet your partner at the briefing."

"Fair enough," I said, and stood up to leave. "But first I want to check out that crime scene at the Spy Bar. It's not too far from here, so I should be able to swing by there and back over to HQ for the task force briefing."

"Raines," Andrews said.

By the look on his face, I already knew what he was going to say. I didn't want to hear it. I certainly didn't *need* to hear it. But, of course, he said it anyway.

"Whatever you do, find those girls, you hear me?"

"I'll do my best."

"Good luck."

Chapter

29

I MADE IT OVER to the Spy Bar in just under twenty minutes. The scene, over in the alley behind the club, was taped off, and still being monitored by a couple of squad cars and an unmarked. Two uniforms were standing in front of the yellow tape.

I pulled up and parked. I got out of my Tahoe and introduced myself to the uniformed officers. "Don't worry, we were told to expect you," an officer named Wiles said. He raised the tape for me to pass by.

Word had come down from the chief of detectives, and fast. I glanced at the sky. The first vestiges of daylight were making their presence known, along with a light dusting of snow. The wind wasn't swirling as hard as it was earlier, but it was still cold out. The morning air traced along the outline of my face as I made my way up the alley, near the service exit of the club. On the ride over, thinking about taking on a new partner—which meant I'd lost my previous partner—haunted me.

I had wanted nothing more than to look for *my* friend. And there was no way I could believe that he was gone at forty-three. But I could hear Ashe now, "find those girls, Robert!" Same as everyone else had said. So, I put that out of my mind and focused on what was in front of me. If our unknown subject, or unsub, was telling the truth, and the victim from this crime scene held a useful clue, I needed to find it. The sooner I could find the girls, the sooner I could turn my attention to finding Ashe.

I didn't need a flashlight, or the streetlights, for that matter, to tell me what had happened here. Just four feet away from the service entrance of the Spy Bar, right next to three big green dumpsters, was a patch of red, scattered in a haphazard pattern, though most of it was centered around what had been the outline of a body in the snow. Two detectives were standing by, taking notes.

"Coroner's already claimed the body," a heavy-set detective said.

"Hi, I'm—"

"Robert Raines. I know. I'm familiar. That thing with the senator, and Officer Elliot James. It was on TV. Word spread through the department. I'm Detective Brian Moore. My partner over there is Detective Spencer Forney. We caught this one, but got word from our sergeant a few minutes ago about you coming down."

I shook hands with both detectives. "Brian. Spencer."

Both men were taller than me, but at only five-ten, that's not hard for others to do. Wrapped up against the cold, it was hard to tell their ages, but I'd put both in their forties. Moore was the larger of the two men, his stubby fingers matching the heavy jowls on his face. Spencer Forney was much thinner. Physically, he reminded me of Felix Unger from the TV show *The Odd Couple*.

"I'm not so much familiar with your history," Detective Forney said as he pulled his coat collar up. "But I can tell you, this scene, the way that poor young lady was left on display. One of the worst things I ever caught." He paused, biting his lower lip. "The look on her face was pure terror. That's an image I have no problem admitting that it's going to take me a while to get rid of."

His partner nodded in agreement.

"We all have things that haunt us, detective," I said.

Their calm demeanor was in stark contrast to what I'd experienced in my early morning run-in with Detective Royce. Things are different just a few hours later. Then again, these are different men, altogether. It's not to say that they'd developed the same opinion of me as Royce had. In the aftermath of the situation with Walter Rand, word had filtered back to me that some officers blamed us, me in particular, for what happened with Elliot. As if that could ever had been the case. I loved Elliot like a son and hated what he got mixed up in. But the evidence led where it led, and things went how they went. Nothing I could do about that.

"What did you guys make of the scene?" I said.

Forney rubbed his chin, and said, "Well, doesn't look like our vic was brought here by force. No drag marks. Steps seem relatively even. She may have known her attacker. We're having the owner pull any footage from inside the bar, but when we arrived, she was splayed out right here, for all to see."

I said, "I'm betting she didn't *know* him. And this scene, has some shades of something I've seen before."

"Is that right?" Moore said.

"Just a preliminary guess."

"You saying you got familiarity with the perp on this one?" Moore asked.

"A little. Enough to know the victim was specifically targeted. For what reason, I don't know yet. Has the canvass turned up anything?"

"No purse or ID was found with the body, but uniforms are still checking some surrounding areas. It's possible the perp took anything she may have had with her. We hope to know more once we see any footage from inside the club. See if she was here alone or with anyone. That can go a long way towards identifying her."

"Did she have anything on her?"

"Anything like?"

I thought about that for a moment and realized I had no idea. My early morning caller hadn't been that specific. "A number of some kind? An object left on her person, or was there anything written on the body?"

"Nothing like that, that I saw, but I'd recommend seeing the coroner. There could've been something we missed on that aspect."

"Thanks, guys. I appreciate it," I said and made my way back to my SUV. On the surface, there was nothing in the area that seemed to match the information I was given in my phone call. Other than, once again, I recognized similarities to a case I'd worked years ago.

As I cranked up my Tahoe, a thought occurred to me. I called the lieutenant. I needed another favor.

Chapter

30

Layla Montgomery awakened and found herself blindfolded. Again. Everything hurt, and it was hard to move. Her hands, and her ankles, were bound, and something she could feel around her body, keeping her restrained. Luckily, she didn't have to move far to feel for her sister, Kayla, and their neighbor, Shameka. They were still together. All things considered, that was good. After all, she'd been told over and over again, "No matter what happens, you all stick together!"

So at least that much had been accomplished.

She noticed something else. They were on the move. They were in a vehicle, as she could hear the engine rev, and feel when the driver, their kidnapper, would come to a stop. This made at least the second time he'd moved them, by her count. If she could trust her memory that is. Her head had been hazy since the attack.

What Layla didn't know was whether or not Kayla and Shameka were okay. And she was too afraid to ask. Prior to waking up in this vehicle, and being on the move, she recalled, they had spent at least the past two days in abandoned buildings. The rooms they'd been kept in, had holes in the walls, and smelled bad. Her stomach curdled just now thinking about it. The stench had been so strong, that each of the girls had fits of choking and retching; so it stood to reason the places were abandoned. There were plenty of buildings like that in their neighborhood.

There was a battery-operated lamp that had kept the rooms lit at night. Their kidnapper had also left apple juice and graham crackers behind for them. Layla took charge of that. Given she had no idea how long they'd be away from home, she had to make sure their meager provisions lasted as long as possible. Something else she recalled was that they all had slept a lot. The lumpy mattress they'd shared aside, it seemed the two younger girls couldn't keep their eyes open more than ten minutes at a time, and she herself had trouble staying awake much longer than that, no matter how hard she tried.

Only once had the man that had taken them while they were on their way to school spoken to them. It was while they were in that first shitty apartment building with nothing but juice and crackers to eat. They happened to be awake when he checked on them. He called himself Mr. Keyes. He had smooth features, and almost looked like a man from one of the soap operas their mother watched, Layla noticed. He promised he wouldn't hurt them as long as they did as he said. Layla had mustered up the nerve to ask, "Are you going to touch us? Touch our private places?" To which Mr. Keyes replied, "No little lady, I am not. And as long as you, your sister, and your neighbor over there don't piss me off by trying to escape, make noises, or otherwise be a pain, I don't plan to touch you at all. Soon enough, this will all be over, and you'll all be safe back at home in no time."

Layla didn't know whether or not to believe the man, but to the best of her knowledge, so far, he'd kept his word. He was barely in the buildings with them, as near as she could tell. When he would arrive, he'd check in on them, see if they needed to use the bathroom, or needed more crackers and juice. She remembered Kayla speaking only once during their ordeal, saying that she didn't like graham crackers. But they had to do for the time being. And in that way, Layla reasoned, maybe it was a good thing that they'd all slept a lot. It kept them from being scared and hungry all day. They were only scared and hungry the few minutes they were awake, instead.

But now, they were no longer in either of those rooms and Layla didn't know if it was night or daylight out. She'd lost track of time. How long had they been gone now? The man had said they'd be back home soon, but it hadn't been soon enough. How worried their mothers must be. She imagined being able to tell their mothers how hard she'd tried. She'd tried for them to get away, but the man was just too fast and too strong.

Tears began streaming down her cheeks under the blindfold. She did her best not to sniffle, and not just because she didn't want their kidnapper to hear. She didn't want her sister and Shameka, should they be awake, to hear either. She knew if they heard her crying, they'd start crying too. They'd no longer believe the words she'd spoken to them—that they were going to be okay. She had to be as brave as possible, she thought, as she again nodded off.

She was the one in charge, after all.

Chapter

31

It HAD BEEN A busy night and early morning for Ishmael Keyes. It was a good thing he stayed in shape. The physical toll from this type of life could be as exacting, if not more, than the mental one.

But everything had gone to plan, and that was quite a feather in his cap. There was just one more thing he needed to do, before taking care of his business for Sophie Bisset and her employer. And that was getting his little angels tucked away again. It was like playing a shell game. *Where are the girls, now? No one knows.*

With the physically imposing Ashe out of the way, he didn't hold out much hope for Robert Raines finding the girls. Although, by no means, was this a done deal. The man has brains. Raines's history says so. *But we'll see just how sharp you are, Mr. Raines. We'll see if you were worth all the effort I've gone through.*

He still wasn't sure what, if anything, he'd do about Dale Gamble. That piece of this equation still hadn't been resolved.

So far, Gamble had sat this one out, as expected. Even Keyes felt something for the man and his plight. But, as he'd told Raines earlier, there were no promises being made one way or the other. Depending on how well other facets of his stay in Chicago played out would be the determining factor in Dale Gamble's fate. Keyes had been keeping an eye on him. No question, Mr. Gamble was still on the radar.

Keyes brought the BMW X5 to a stop on the city's south side, underneath the elevated tracks of the Green Line, just west of the Dan Ryan Expressway near the 55th Street exit. There were a couple of old shipping containers that rested roughly fifty feet apart, in an empty lot. There was no telling how long they had been there, but the one he'd chosen was perfect.

Much like the abandoned buildings, Keyes had scoped it out months ago. All three had gone unused, unentered, and unbothered the entire time he had been monitoring them. Even better, the entry to the container he'd staked as his own was shielded from the street, and any potential nosey onlookers, and the expressway. Facing against another abandoned property, he would have all the privacy he needed for his next step. Keyes shut off the ignition and hopped out into the fresh, untrampled snow. The morning air was brisk, and the sun had begun to rise. He had little time to finish his task, so he got right to it.

He removed a key from one of his pants pockets and unlocked both of the die-cast hasp padlocks he'd installed months before on the shipping container doors, and pulled one open. Keyes then backed the beamer up to the container close as possible. He opened the lift gate, and there, wrapped in drop cloths and blind folded were the three blind mice.

His little black angels.

He hoisted each girl up over his shoulder, one by one, and carried them deep into the container and set them down on an old mattress. A small propane gas generator had been running, emitting a low hum and keeping the temperature at about fifty-two degrees. Not the tropics by any means, but the girls were going to have to make do with that and the blankets he'd stocked inside.

The generator also powered an oxygen compressor that kept the air inside breathable. "Welcome to Shangri-La, ladies," Keyes said. He went back to the BMW, retrieved a pouch and returned inside. Keyes removed a hypodermic needle from the pouch. He filled it with ketamine from one of the vials also contained in the pouch. "A little extra knockout juice, but you ladies should be used to it by now, you've been drinking it in the apple juice the last couple of days."

Keyes injected several cc's into each of the children. Enough to keep them sleeping for a while. This time, there would be no apple juice and graham crackers. They would not need them, he thought, as he had no intention of freeing them from their bonds. No doubt, the little buggers would find their way to the container walls. A few hours of them banging and screaming would attract attention. And that would be attention that his plan couldn't afford.

Keyes checked the fuel level on the generator. There was enough propane for it to run another seventy hours.

Keyes made his way out, closed the door on the container and re-locked both hasp padlocks. He checked his watch. "Better hurry, Raines. As I said, the clock is ticking."

Chapter

32

After stopping off at White Palace Grill for an Ultimate Meat breakfast skillet which I washed down with a couple cups of coffee, I made my way over to the Chicago Police Headquarters building on Michigan Avenue, just off the corner of 35th Street.

I couldn't say that the throng of reporters camped out in front of the place surprised me. Given what was going on, that was to be expected. But at the center of that gaggle of hens was another blast from my past, and just like the memory of the kidnapping from 2002, this trip down memory lane was also unpleasant.

Speaking, or more like holding court, was Reverend Alvin Garvin. Garvin was the head of Christ the Savior Baptist church in Englewood. He'd first caught the attention of the city when he organized basketball tournaments in the midst of a gang war during the early 90s. He was an educated, well-spoken, charismatic twenty-seven-year-old at the time, with movie star good looks. The press said he favored Denzel Washington. I didn't see the resemblance myself, but I digress. Garvin had publicly invited members from each of the warring gangs to, in his words, "put down the guns and prove themselves with a jump-shot."

A lot of local politicians in the city council, and the police brass, laughed. I think the Sun-Times even ran an op-ed piece at the time lambasting the idea. But, to everyone's surprise— including my own—his brash plan worked. Tensions in those Southside neighborhoods cooled, and the tournaments drew large, peaceful crowds. Residents of the area and the local gang members all turned out and rooted on the teams, each filled with young teens who'd been at each other's throats—literally at war with one another. And there was not one incident reported, regardless of who'd won or lost the games.

While the good reverend hadn't solved all the ills of Englewood, the tournament, without a doubt, had been a success. Even though there's always been gang violence since its inception, to this day, during the summer months, whenever Reverend Garvin's basketball tournaments are going on, it's like the violence goes on pause. The people in those neighborhoods are able to let out a sigh of relief and enjoy a few weeks of peace.

After that success, Reverend Garvin became the voice of Englewood. Any slights, real or imagined, surfaced against his community, and he was front and center. Oozing charm and with that radio smooth voice of his, he'd become a media darling overnight, and it seemed at least once a week, one of the major networks in the city had a news van parked in front of his church to get the latest gospel. He spoke out against Englewood being a food desert, railed against the mayor at the time about his lack of interest in serving that part of the city. While it took years of haggling and vituperative press conferences among other soundbites on television, eventually, two big chain grocery stores opened locations in the heart of Englewood.

Another matter that had gotten Garvin widespread attention was our abduction case back in '02. He led the charge, accusing the police, myself and Dale included, of not caring about those missing girls as that case dragged on. He organized daily marches, and didn't miss an opportunity to have a microphone in his face as he picked apart everything from the racial makeup of the officers on the task force, to our methods, and I think even the way some of us dressed. It got ugly. He and I exchanged words once. Even going nose to nose. Not my finest moment. But with the pressure we were under, I had to release some steam somewhere. His face seemed like the perfect place.

Our little dustup had been caught on camera. That didn't play well for me or the department. While my wife had told me at the time that I looked good on television, she also told me that the city was not ready to see my temper on full display. I took the hint. Not only from her, but from the higher ups that forbade me from having any further contact with him. I had avoided the man like the plague ever since. Even after we closed that case and he wanted to make a show of reaching out to all the officers involved to *thank* us for our efforts, I wanted nothing to do with him. I applaud the work he has done for his side of the city. Any help in keeping the shit down to shoe level is always appreciated. But that was where any grace I had for his holiness ended.

I caught a good enough glimpse of Reverend Garvin, as his press conference went on, to note that while by now he had to be in his early fifties, he didn't look a day over thirty. Judging by the way all the reporters gathered around him seemed to ignore this morning's frigid temperature, hanging onto his every word, he hadn't lost any of that charm or his rapturous voice, either.

"Why are you here this morning, reverend? Is there any truth to the rumor that you're going to be running for mayor in next year's election?" a reporter asked.

Reverend Garvin smiled. "All in good time on that. All in good time. But the reason I'm here this morning, is because yet again, *we* find ourselves in the position that somehow people in *our* community always find ourselves in. And once again, the black community, the Englewood community, must rise up. We have to rise up and demand more. We have to demand better from the police, and from the mayor of Chicago. That's why I'm here."

Thankfully, that was all I'd heard from the good reverend before I ducked inside.

Chapter

33

I **WAS MORE THAN** happy to avoid the reverend and the throng of reporters out front. I'm not on the force anymore, but I'm still not in the mood for any of his rhetoric. I don't take orders from the brass these days and with my wife having moved out, her either. So, there would be no telling how any type of confrontation between us would go.

I made my way over to the elevator bank and took the first car up to the third floor. I entered the large conference room on my right and marveled at the number of bodies crammed inside. As Dan had said, they were all hands-on deck.

The first person I noticed was Mayor Gabriel Reyes. Seeing his face reminded me of Senator Aaron Dietrich. Now that the madness from his visit in Chicago last fall has subsided, his presidential campaign was ramping up. Our mayor has been promised a spot in Dietrich's cabinet should he win. If the polling numbers are to be believed, that seems increasingly likely. As such, the mayor has been wearing the look of a man going places.

Also, at the front of the room, standing alongside Mayor Reyes—who nodded at me as I entered—was Chicago Police Superintendent Edwin Chalmers, Chief of Detectives Earl Hammerlich, along with District Commanders Derrick Johnson and Peter Gugliema. That's a group of heavy hitters.

Some of the other faces in the room were unfamiliar to me, but in the past when I'd worked on a task force, it was comprised of officers from different departments or law enforcement units: Major Case, Vice, US Marshals, DEA, FBI, you name it. Whatever was needed to fill the bill. The same was true this time around as well. Not counting the brass, or myself, there were about ten law enforcement officers (or LEOs) in the room.

I recognized a few of the CPD officers, specifically Jimmy Oliver and Ted Bakker. Both had come on a few years before I'd left the department. As I continued to scan the room, there was another familiar face giving me a look of disbelief from along the back wall. US Marshal Damon Greene. He wasn't as long in the tooth as me; I put him about mid-forties by now, but he worked on the original task force with Dale and me back in 2002. I could tell some stories about him. He had a very unique approach to his job working with the Marshals service. He was a big fan of westerns and fancied himself riding into town on a horse. Spurs and all. He was good at his job and a lethal shot if anyone made him pull. I liked him a lot.

I don't think that I had seen him since that original case though. It was like that with a lot of the guys on that search. When we found those girls dead, I think we all felt we'd let everybody down. The young girls themselves. The families. The city. Each other.

I made my way over to him. We exchanged a hearty shake. "Robert Raines? I got word you'd retired. How the hell have you been?"

"You heard right. I retired almost two years ago now. Been doing some PI work, pass the time, you know."

"Nothing wrong with keeping busy," Greene said.

"But other than that, I'm good. How about you?"

"I'm doing all right. Had two more babies since I saw you last. Ten and Thirteen now. My oldest, Tamara, will be headed off to college in the fall."

"You and your wife never got cable?"

"Always found ourselves having to make up for lost time. No time for TV," he said, laughing.

"Wow. Just, wow. What's that make for you, five?"

"Six. I kept telling my wife, if we had another, the hospital would give us a free set of steak knives. She turned me down."

We both laughed before Greene continued, "What are you doing here?"

"I got invited."

"By the brass?"

"No. The kidnapper."

"You're kidding?"

"I wish I was."

"Well, either way, this can't end like the last time."

"No sir, it cannot."

The superintendent stepped up to the lectern at the front of the room, interrupting our commiserating. "I need everyone's attention," Superintendent Chalmers began. His dress blues fit tight, and unless I missed my guess, he was nearing sixty himself. He had less hair atop his head since I'd last seen him. Old age and this job can do that to a man. Especially in a city like Chicago.

"We all know why we're here," Chalmers went on. "We all understand what our mandate is. Three young girls are counting on us. Two grieving mothers, are counting on us. The city of Chicago, is counting on us. I expect swift, effective action. I expect these girls to be found, and the perpetrator apprehended. I expect, and we've promised, justice. Now, there's some new information that has come to light. That being the case, I've authorized a former member of our ranks, a retired brother officer, to participate in this investigation. Robert Raines, if you would."

I wasn't expecting the superintendent to yield the floor to me, but made my way up to the front of the room. Everyone needed to be aware of what we were dealing with. After introducing myself for those in the room that weren't familiar with me, I got right to it.

"The man we're looking for, is dangerous. He's cunning and calculating, as we've all seen by now from the video of the abduction, and the murders of the lone witness and those paramedics. He also ambushed a partner of mine. Another former copper, as some of you well know. But more importantly, he's put a clock on us."

There was a murmur that went up throughout the room. Worried glances stared back at me.

"I received a call this morning from the perpetrator. He's given us seventy-two hours." I checked my watch. "Which is down to just under seventy at this point. If we don't find those girls by then, he stated in no uncertain terms, they will die."

Chapter

34

ANOTHER MURMUR ROLLED THROUGH the conference room like waves crashing on a beach, before someone called out, "Are you certain it was him?"

I didn't see the face of the officer that posed the question, but responded, "Yes. Yes, I'm certain it was him. More importantly, I believe him. A tip line has been setup, and we will have to work every call that comes in on it, follow every clue, go down all potential avenues." I looked over the faces staring back at me. Everyone appeared locked in. Laser focused. "I've asked that my phone be tapped, so in the event he calls me again, we can try to trace him. We can't leave any stone unturned."

A hand from one of the men clustered toward the front of the room went up. "Agent Joshua Welker, FBI. Everybody feel free to call me Josh. Do you know why he called you?"

Agent Welker was on the younger side. Then again, compared to me, just about everyone here is. He went about six-two, and a solid two hundred twenty pounds. I would later find out that he and his partner, Agent Daryl Jenkins, were both on loan from the FBI's Hostage Rescue Team (HRT). That meant they were two of the best. Just what we needed.

"As yet, Agent Welker, no I do not. Not exactly, anyway. Maybe I'll get that out of him when he calls back."

"How do you know he will?"

"Gut feeling," I said. "As many of you are aware by now, the kidnapper had contacted the children's mothers, and goaded them into hiring my investigative firm, so for whatever reason, he wants my team involved, but he hasn't been kind enough to share the specifics just yet. But criminals like this, those with a master plan, have to share it. How else can anyone appreciate it? Trust me, he'll call again."

Another man raised his hand. "Andy Baren, Marshal Service. Did he offer up anything else? Make any demands?"

"Demands? No. But he made some veiled references and mentioned that there is a pattern developing."

"That pattern being?" Barren asked.

"Right now, this kidnapping is a carbon copy of a case I was involved in back in 2002. If you worked in Chicago around that time, you know about it. Marshal Greene, over there, is familiar. He was on that task force, same as me."

Marshal Damon Greene nodded his head in agreement.

"The kidnapper also mentioned during our call, that there is another victim, a murder victim this time, and he claims it ties in to our missing girls. And if I'm not mistaken, based on what I know so far, there may be some ties to the past in that one as well. I'll be running that down once our briefing is over."

"Then providing an immediate update to the team afterward," the superintendent said.

"That's correct, sir," I said. It was amazing. I'd been retired going on two years, and within ten minutes, I felt like I was under command again.

The superintendent continued, "Lieutenant Deckard from the fifth will head the task force, and will be everyone's point of contact. He'll handle all briefings with the media. All command decisions will flow from my office, to the chief, to Deckard, and updates will flow in reverse order."

I took a few more questions along the lines of the ones that had already been asked. *Why these girls? Why me and my team?* Questions that I had no real answers for. After which, I turned the proceedings over to the lieutenant in charge.

I'd known Lieutenant Sam Deckard by name and reputation only: a hard charging, hard-nosed cop that did his best to close cases. He was in his early fifties with plenty of grey streaks running through his hair. He stood six foot and was fit and trim, but looked average. The scowl he always wore on his face, though, suggested he was anything but. Word around the campfire had him as a prickly hard ass, but a prickly hard ass that got the job done. And to me, that was all that mattered.

"As the super said, we all know why we're here." Deckard's voice boomed throughout the conference room. "The men in this room, you're the tip of this spear. We'll have officers backing us up, helping with canvassing the neighborhood, answering calls. But it's the responsibility of the men in this room to get this done," he said, pounding the lectern with a fist. "Am I clear?"

We all agreed in unison with a "Yes, sir." The briefing adjourned a short time later, after Lt. Deckard had given everyone their marching orders for the day. As I made my way out, Chief Hammerlich approached me.

"Raines, good to see you again, though, not under these circumstances."

I agreed, and we exchanged a handshake.

"Did you notice your friend outside?" Hammerlich asked.

"As a matter of fact, I did."

"Just what we need, him out there chumming the waters. Getting the city in an uproar."

"Well, he's nothing if not predictable."

Hammerlich leaned in closer to me. "We can do without the spectacle, if you know what I mean."

"I believe I do. Don't worry, chief, while I make no promises, I'm not looking for a fight."

"Great. Sorry to hear about Ashe, by the way," he said. "Royce is a good detective. He'll get some answers."

It seemed like he meant it, his role in Ashe's dismissal from the force a few years before aside, so I said, "Thanks, chief." Besides, CPD's loss was mine and Dale's gain.

"Don't worry about cooperation, I put the word out to every officer working a case citywide. As long as those girls are missing, you have access to anything you need in order to find them. Anyone that doesn't cooperate had best polish up their resume and be ready to lean on whatever other skills they have."

"I really appreciate the support on this, chief." And I did. It felt a little strange working with him again after he and the mayor had suckered me into taking on that McClintock investigation four months ago.

Hammerlich continued, "Andrews explained our terms, correct?"

"Yes, sir. He did."

"Good. Let me introduce you to your new partner, then."

Chief Hammerlich motioned to the back of the room. A young police officer stepped forward. He was of average height, and looked to be no older than in his late twenties, at most, early thirties. He carried a look of determination in his eyes, like he had something to prove, as he approached.

"Officer Sean McCombs, meet Robert Raines. Raines, McCombs here is going to partner up with you on your end of the investigation."

McCombs extended his hand. "A pleasure to meet you, Mr. Raines."

I took his hand and did my best to be cordial as well. I still wasn't sold on having to take on a partner. Private investigations, especially ours, are run a little different from police work. I wasn't sure which side of the line this kid walked on, meaning, if need be, could he look the other way on something if it meant getting those girls back alive? I don't know what hoops our mystery man is going to have me jumping through to piece together the clues, as he'd put it, but given the guilt I've carried the past eighteen years from the original case, I'd be willing to stretch some things if I had to. This was going to be a bit of a process feeling him out, but I'd have to do it as quick as possible.

After the introduction, the chief excused himself, leaving me to get things started.

"McCombs, right? So how long have you been on the force, patrolman?"

"It'll be eight years come June. Hoping to make homicide and detective grade one day. But right now, I'm here to do the job, same as you back in your heyday, right?"

"Right. Just the same, I'm pretty sure you're wondering who it is you pissed off to end up on this shit detail, escorting an old man around the city while everybody else on the task force is gearing up to kick in some doors."

McCombs seemed taken aback. His brow furrowed, and after a moment, he said, "No, sir. Not at all. I'm just here to help in any way I can."

"Well said. However, I can see through you clear as looking out of a window. I'm a trained investigator. Don't lie to me, son. You think it's a shit detail, all right. I would too if I were in your shoes, but trust me, it's not. You've just been thrown into the deep end. We're about to see how well you swim."

Chapter

35

THE FIRST STOP I made with my new partner, after grabbing a much-needed cup of coffee that is, was at the county morgue. When I was informed by Detectives Moore and Forney, who were in charge of the Spy Bar case, that the body of their victim had already been delivered to the morgue, I called Lieutenant Andrews, who in turned called the chief of d's. My request was simple, I wanted none other than Maxine Cader on it.

Max, as she liked to be called, and I go way back. We worked a number of homicides together. Even if I were to guess fifty, I'd probably be low. There were many times when she had provided the "a-ha" moment during the course of an investigation. Simply put, she was one of the best damned coroners and forensics experts working in the city. Anywhere in the world, if you asked her. Being honest though, I thought she'd have retired long before I did, but I was glad to find out she was still on the job. Given the stakes, I needed her expertise.

We entered the exam room containing our Jane Doe. The refrigeration units, stacked three deep in a long row along the back wall, sent a short chill up my spine. A rush of chemicals assailed my nostrils. Ammonia, mostly. It had been a while since I'd been here. The scent made my young stud partner gag as well. My old friend greeted me with open arms and a warm, exuberant hug. She looked exactly the same as when I'd last seen her. Max had always been a tiny wisp of a woman, and that hadn't changed. But though she was tiny, she was a force of personality. Some would say an acquired taste. And they'd be right. Her hair had gone completely gray—which she still wore pulled back in a bun—and her glasses appeared a bit thicker, but other than that, same old Max.

"Robert Raines, as I live and breathe," Max said. "How are you?"

Her embrace had lasted for a few moments before I said, "I'm fine, Max. At least I was until you broke one of my ribs."

She laughed, took a step back, and looked me up and down. "You've lost weight. You were a lot more…plump, back in the day."

"Gee, thanks."

"Heard about that thing with Dale and Millie. Pass along my regards, will you?"

"Of course, Max."

Max turned her attention toward the door we'd just come in and eyed my new partner. "Who's the rookie?"

McCombs's chest puffed out a little. That *something* to prove I saw in his eyes earlier had returned.

147

"Ma'am, I'll have you know I've been with the department eight years now," he said.

Max didn't skip a beat. "And I'll have you know I have bra and panty sets older than you."

"Take it easy on him, Max. It's his first time meeting you."

"Same thing my ex-husband said the night of our honeymoon," Maxine chuckled.

"Which one?" I asked.

"Number two, I think." Max laughed again and winked at McCombs. "Relax tiger, I don't bite." Max turned her attention to the rear of the theater as the door opened from an adjoining room, and in walked a young black man, maybe mid-twenties. He was clean cut and wore the same scrubs as Max. "This here is James Jackson. I affectionately call him JJ."

"She only calls me that when she wants to annoy me, because she knows I hate it," James said. He shook both mine and McCombs hand, then picked up a clipboard and started scribbling on it.

Max shrugged. "Just the same, I'm grooming him, getting him ship shape as one day, all of this will be his," she said and made an exaggerated gesture with her arms.

"Just when are you going to hang it up, Max?"

"When young Jackson over there has me on one of these slabs, I think that'll signal the end."

"Perish the thought," James mumbled.

"Anyway, Robert, how's Elena doing?"

"So, word hasn't made it this far, huh? We separated."

"Separated or divorced?"

"Definitely separated. For now, anyway."

A wry smirk worked its way across her face. "Want me to perform the autopsy when it's over?"

"I wouldn't waste your time. The cause of death has already been confirmed."

"Well, who am I to make fun? Last time I got any action was during the Bush administration. And I mean the dad."

"Thanks for sharing, Max. While we're here, though, how about a cause of death on our Jane Doe?"

"Oh, yeah. Right. This wasn't just a social call. I have to admit, things were always more exciting when you were around Robert Raines."

"I don't know if that's a compliment or not."

McCombs smirked and said, "No comment."

Max motioned for her assistant, James Jackson, to open the refrigerator drawer that contained our early morning victim.

"Preliminary cause of death is exsanguination. Large wound in her left thigh. My money says her femoral artery was severed. Seem familiar?" Max said.

"Very. It's just like Shear used to do." My earlier suspicion at the crime scene was confirmed. Again, I had to reflect on the man behind this madness. His thoroughness. This MO matched a serial string from 2008. Martin Shear would lure women outside of nightclubs and sever their femoral artery. He was a well off, handsome, educated man, and that was why he raised no red flags to any of those women. When we caught him, he'd brazenly said that if we hadn't, he would've continued his sick exploits. But how does our kidnapper know about that case, and why did he decide to emulate it? He's already kidnapped the girls, and his comment about this woman having my number made even less sense now. I had no idea how she fit into his sordid game, or how she'd help me find our missing girls.

"Same thing I thought," Max said. "And she's a brunette. Shear's favorite. Figured, that's why you brought me in."

"Still no ID?" I asked.

"Well, I just got thrown into the fire. Haven't had time to suit up, yet. Give me a couple of hours, I'll have her finger printed, get dental records, even tell you her last meal."

"Fast as you can, Max. Meter's running on this one."

Chapter

36

THE SUN HADN'T BEEN up an hour when Dinah Miller's cellphone rang; roughly the same time that Robert Raines was speaking during the task force briefing.

She looked at the phone as if it were from another planet. When she recalled it was Sunday, that only made receiving a call this early, even more odd. Most of the people she knew, her father included, wouldn't be up for at least another hour.

Dinah stretched, then reached over to her nightstand for her phone. She didn't recognize the number and was happy to let the call go to voicemail. Dinah nodded off, falling back to sleep, hoping to finish the dream she was having, when her phone again danced across her nightstand, vibrating and ringing intermittently.

She eyeballed the caller id. It was the same number again. *Isn't there a law against telemarketers calling on a Sunday?*

She wasn't sure if there was, *but there ought to be if there isn't.* Dinah again let the call go to voicemail. After a few minutes lying on her back, staring at the ceiling, though, she realized there was no longer any hope of going back to sleep. She was wide awake and just going to have to accept that fact. Dinah got out of bed and hopped in the shower. As the water beaded off of her body, she thought about what she'd cook her dad for breakfast. It was a refreshing thought, given the troubles they'd gone through over the years. She'd always appreciated that throughout her struggles, he'd always had her back.

Dinah toweled off after her shower and slipped into her robe. She made her way into the kitchen, still mulling over what the morning's menu would be. There was plenty of thick slab bacon and sausage in the fridge. So maybe a two-meat omelet. Dinah peered out of the window over the kitchen sink, noticing that there had been a fresh sprinkling of snow overnight. After breakfast, she'd take care of that too. Since her father had lost the use of his left arm due to a war injury, that was a task, among others, that she'd taken on since her own recovery.

Then it hit her. She'd make a hearty breakfast, something befitting this partly sunny, yet cloudy, and cold winter morning. Biscuits and sausage gravy, with a side of grits fit the bill. Dinah combed through the kitchen cabinets for the ingredients she'd need to get the biscuits underway. As she began her preparation, she heard her phone buzz again. Law or no, this was just rude. She could just ignore the calls, but there's nothing like giving someone (in particular a telemarketer) a piece of your mind before hanging up on them.

Dinah marched into her bedroom and picked up her phone from the nightstand. Just as it rang again, she thumbed the screen. "Hello?" she shouted.

"Dinah Miller?"

It was a woman's voice. A woman with an Asian accent.

"Yes, it is, and you've got some nerve calling my phone this early on a Sunday morning! So, whatever it is you're selling, you can just stick—"

"We have a mutual friend," the Asian woman said, cutting Dinah off. "I believe you call him 'uncle'."

Dinah's blood ran cold. This call had gone from an annoyance to something that was not only odd, but left her with a bad feeling curdling in her gut. Needless to say, the woman on the other end of the line had her attention.

"Go on," Dinah said.

"He needs your help. I have an address for you to go to, along with a list of supplies you will need to bring. I will also tell you what route to take. Can you be ready to leave in ten minutes?"

"Yes, I can," Dinah said. She listened as the Asian woman ran down a list of items for her to bring, which caused even more concern. Dinah's hands trembled. But as the woman continued to speak, she composed herself, gathered the items, and dumped them into a duffle bag. After the woman provided a specific route for Dinah to take to her destination, they ended the call. Dinah peeled off her robe and tossed on a layer of thermal under garments and wool socks, before dressing in jeans and a sweater. She got her boots, scarf, hat and coat on and headed out the door.

Breakfast was going to have to wait.

Chapter

37

Paris, France

SOPHIE BISSET HAD BEEN working the phone all day, reaching out to various contacts. Many of whom she'd made through her years of *facilitating*. But this time around, she was the one in need of a favor. If she was going to launch this most ambitious endeavor, there were things she would need. More to the point, someone.

While she would have loved nothing better than to woo Keyes into working on this next *project*, she had to lay the groundwork for the possibility—more likely, the reality—that Keyes would take that vacation after his endeavors in Chicago. And that was just fine. For him. Keyes had long been one of the most sought-after assassins and espionage specialists. Sophie knew personally the amount of money he'd been paid just in the jobs she'd negotiated herself. Another thing she knew, Keyes was shrewd with his money. He made smart investments. It's why the man worked when he wanted and could live it up when he wasn't.

Sophie wanted to be in that same boat. She knew her bold plan would be the only way to accomplish that. Once Keyes secured the package, she needed to be in a position to do the same. She also needed an exit plan. Only then would she be free from working for men like Aubrey DuChamps. Men who no doubt appreciated the services she provided, yet somehow couldn't keep their minds from entertaining *other* ideas as compensation. As if their money and power somehow entitled them entry to her bedroom.

Sophie reflected for a moment on the time she'd first met the wealthy French financier, Duchamps. He'd been seeking assistance in securing oil rights in the Middle East. In itself, not nefarious. But given that the deal needed to be closed without the Iraqi Oil Ministry in the loop, and no official paper trail, and that a large portion of the oil pumped would be sold to a non-friendly nation like North Korea, it was a matter that required a delicate touch.

Through a recommendation, DuChamps hired Sophie to get done what he needed done. Easy work for Sophie. She made a few calls and had DuChamps's operation up and running and under the radar of the French and Iraqi governments within days. DuChamps was pleased. He kept Sophie on retainer ever since. While her fees were steep, the profits he'd been able to make off of the deals she'd helped to broker, far exceeded her price.

A fact not lost on Sophie.

Now there was another major deal to be brokered. DuChamps already had feelers out. Sophie knew she needed to be first. She dialed the number of a man who's contact information she'd received only minutes ago. The phone rang, and on the fourth, a male voice said, "Yes?"

"Sheik Amir Al-Assan? This is Sophie Bisset."

"Miss Bisset, your reputation precedes," Sheik Al-Assan said in his thick Arab accent. "I was informed by a mutual acquaintance that you'd be reaching out to me."

"Yes, sir. And thank you for taking my call."

"The pleasure is mine. How can I help you? Or, as I understand, you were planning to help me."

"You are aware that a certain parcel will be on the market, and, as I've heard through that same mutual acquaintance, you had an interest."

"It was my understanding that market has closed. Your current employer is looking to set his terms with an interested party in exchange for expanding his oil concerns in the Middle East."

"This is true. But there's a possibility that things won't go that way. I need to know if there's a different turn of events, whether or not you'd be interested in bidding for said parcel. It will be a fair and open bidding process. I can guarantee that."

Sheik Al-Assan cleared his throat. "*You* can?"

"Yes, sir. I can," Sophie said confidently.

"Then you have my interest, Miss Bisset. And if you were to acquire said parcel, I'd without a doubt bid on it. But, may I ask, are you aware of the number of enemies you'd be making for yourself if you were to effect such a change in plans?"

"I am aware. I'm also looking to mitigate that as well. As such, I'd like to ask a favor of you. One that if you grant, I'll be in your debt."

"Is this where the west says, the plot thickens? What favor is that, Miss Bisset?"

"I'd like for the bidding, and the exchange, to take place in your country."

Sheik Al-Assan let out a hearty laugh. "Why would I do that?"

"To help me weed out any uninvited guests. An added benefit is that on the off chance anyone outbids you, they'd still have to get out of your country with the package. Should they not make it, due to some unfortunate incident, and you acquire the package that way, well, in that case, it wouldn't have cost you a thing. Sounds like you'd win either way."

"When I said your reputation precedes, I didn't know just how right I was. I will consider your proposal, Miss Bisset. Thank you for the call."

"And thank you for your time, Sheik Al-Assan."

Sophie disconnected the call. Her heart was racing. She had to call in several markers, owed to her by some of her wealthiest and most important contacts, in order to get the personal number of the Sheik. Though she held her composure during the entire call, her pulse and blood pressure were on the rise the entire time. Yet, it went as well as could be expected. That brought a measure of calm to her in the aftermath. Her plan could work. It was ambitious, sure, but so was Sophie.

As ambitious and smart, if not smarter, than any man she'd ever worked for.

She made her way to her kitchen and took a wineglass from the cabinet. She opened a bottle of 2010 Chateau Mouton Rothschild. Sophie had always liked a good Bordeaux. She made her way back into her living room and sat on her sofa and enjoyed a sip. Things were taking shape. It was time to see where the most important piece on her board fell into place.

Chapter

38

Chicago, Illinois

Just past noon, Dale Gamble had finished shoveling the snow around his home. It took longer than he anticipated, but was the only task that could take his mind off of things. Several times while shoveling, he had to stop and wipe tears from his eyes thinking about Ashe. The latest update from CPD was the same as all the other updates had been. There'd been no progress. He was still missing and they had no new clues. But after lamenting that fact, Dale had to switch into protection mode. If the man who kidnapped these children had any thoughts of dropping by, well, Dale had a powerful single barreled answer for any question the man posed.

Things weren't supposed to go this way. None of what has happened over the last four months was supposed to. It had all been surreal. And if Ashe was truly gone, then that made this entire private detective endeavor a disaster.

Dale made his way back inside after walking the perimeter and checking the cars on the block. They had all seemed to belong. He knew that in his current state he was hypervigilant, but he didn't care. Everything and everyone were a potential threat.

Millie was again on the sofa, this time watching re-runs of *Without A Trace*. It had been one of her favorites during its original run, and now that it was on TV again, it was something that relaxed her. It also kept her occupied.

Dale could get up and do some things around the house without her continually checking for him. He used the time to position weapons at key points in the house. The kidnapper had already been by, leaving those notes on the garbage cans. Most likely trying to assess the place. Find a weak spot for entry. Dale considered the same thing and made sure there was a gun within reach should either area of the house be breached. Having that mentality was a tough way to get through the day, but it was necessary. At least until Robert calls him and says this latest shit-storm is over.

After Dale completed the defensive tasks, he joined Millie and took in a few episodes himself. He did his best to relax his mind and get lost in the adventures of Jack Malone and his crew. But his mind continued to drift back to those three missing girls and to Ashe. That was inevitable. But as much as he wanted to be in the streets with Bobby during this ordeal, helping him figure it out, and bring those girls home alive, a quick glance to his right and he knew he was exactly where he needed to be.

One thing that stuck out in his mind, that kept his brain ticking in overdrive though, was the second note. It made no sense. The first one, "I know," was just a dig. A way to get under his skin. But the second one, "Are you sorry," that almost seemed to have some texture to it. It was a direct question. Not that it mattered. The man was a master at playing games, and Dale knew not to let himself be drawn too far in. But still he found it hard to let go.

After a few more re-runs, Dale got up from the sofa and made an excuse to go back outside. He couldn't tell Millie the real reason, but it was time to patrol again. Dale wished he could convince Millie to go stay with her sister. Or out of town. Anything to keep her out of harm's way, but even though she was more than a bit jumpy, she was still a tough old bird and wasn't going anywhere. As much as he was against it, Dale liked that, and would do everything he had to in order to allow her to be where she wanted to be. In their house.

The crisp air hit Dale in the face as he stepped out on the porch. He zipped his coat as his eyes scanned up and down the street. The block was empty except for one man. He was about halfway up the block but making his way in Dale's direction at a quick pace. Dale unzipped his coat and reached inside. His hand caressed his Kimber 1911. He gripped the butt of the gun and maneuvered his coat so that his pull would be clean if he needed to draw. As the man's pace quickened, Dale walked down his porch steps. He no longer felt the cold. His vision went tunnel and the only thing he could see was the man with the drawn hood and black ski mask.

Dale's heart raced. This was it. It was about to go down. Broad daylight, balls out, ugly. Dale drew the Kimber, but before he raised it, he observed the man make a sharp turn to his right and race up the front porch steps of a residence two doors down. The man danced in the doorway, his weight shifting from right to left and back as he dug in his pocket for his keys. Within seconds, the man made entry and was gone.

Dale was all alone, again.

"Jesus," Dale said as he re-holstered the gun. He let out a heavy sigh of relief. His hand trembled a bit. He could feel his heartbeat continuing to pick up speed, pounding in his chest, and making a dull, but hard throbbing sound in his ears. The cold returned.

A false alarm. That's all. It was just a false alarm. This time.

Dale decided it was time to go back inside and watch more re-runs.

Chapter

39

THE MORNING HAD RUSHED by and the afternoon was well on its way. Before I came down with a headache from a lack of food, I suggested to my young partner we break for lunch. Portillo's always served a great Italian beef combination.

As we enjoyed our meal, it gave me an opportunity to dig a little further into Officer Sean McCombs. While he seemed to be personable enough, my earlier reservations about how he might react in certain situations still stood. Not that I wanted him to bend or break the law, but he may need to take a step back and turn his head while I do. Ordinarily, that would be the furthest thing from my mind. But this suspect we're after may have killed one of my best friends, and we have those three young girls to find. So, if it came down to it, I may just have to cross a line or two. I had always wondered how Ashe made those types of decisions and lived with them. Just in these last few hours thinking about it, I've learned what a burden that is.

"Can I ask you something?" McCombs said, shoveling fries in his mouth.

"Shoot."

"Where did they dig up that old fossil in the morgue?" He sipped his soda, and seemed to have a moment of enlightened reflection as he then said, "Uh, no offense."

I shook my head and smirked. "Relax, kid, I'm not sensitive about my age. Ol' Maxie *is* something else. But she's also good people. Word of advice, if you intend to work homicide someday, you're going to need thicker skin. And not just because of the things you'll see on a day to day."

"You saying her job made her that way?"

I took a bite of my combination and reflected on the years I'd known Maxine Cader. "No. I'm pretty sure Max was like that as a child."

McCombs and I both laughed. I continued, "The way she is, though, made her right for the job. But even she needs her distractions, and getting under someone's skin is her favorite hobby."

"I see."

"Where'd you grow up, officer?"

"West side of Chicago, just outside of Oak Park. We weren't the Huxtable's but my mom and dad both worked hard. They put three kids through college—"

McCombs cellphone rang. He excused himself from our booth and stepped a few feet away. I could still hear his end of the conversation, and it was apparent to me who he was speaking to.

"My wife," McCombs said when he returned.

"How long have you been married?"

"Ten years."

"Ten years, that's a good start. Congratulations."

"Thanks."

"With the ambition you have, kid, there's something you've got to know."

"What's that?"

"Being a homicide detective isn't something you do, it's something you are. And that affects the whole the family. Not just you."

McCombs stared at me hard, taking in what I'd just said. I figured he'd need time to digest it. I know I did the first time I'd heard the same thing.

After a few moments of silence, he said, "Heard you mention to Max earlier that you're separated. How long were you married, you know, before?"

"Forty-two years."

"Wow. That's longer than I've been alive. Any tips?"

"Yeah, she's always right. And always do what you say you're going to do, even if it's the impossible. Now that doesn't guarantee you getting to forty and beyond, but it can't hurt."

McCombs laughed. "Part of that should be easy, she already thinks she's always right. She's just waiting for me to board that train."

"Any kids?"

"Two. A boy and a girl. My son, Sean Jr., is six and my daughter, Angela, is three. I've got to tell you, the happiest days of my life were when those little rascals were born." McCombs started thumbing through his cellphone. He turned it around and showed me a photo. His wife and his two kids. All three of them smiling like the world has been all they'd ever wanted.

"Here. Take a look at those faces," he said, and switched to a photo of just the children.

"Beautiful kids you have there, officer. Beautiful." I just noticed something else in McCombs eyes. For now, it's replaced that "something to prove" look that I saw earlier. It was pure bliss. Speaking of his family, his kids in particular had him over the moon.

"Thanks, Mr. Raines. They are my world, that's for sure. What about you?"

"I had a son."

"Had?"

"He grew up, and like his old man, he became a cop. Unfortunately, he died on the job."

"Mr. Raines, I'm sorry, I didn't—"

"No, it's fine. You didn't know. Besides, it's good for me to talk about him, bring him up in conversation. He hadn't married yet or had any kids, but what I find is that, most often, I think back to the time he was the same age as your son. And how protective I was. And what I would've done if anybody tried to harm him. I'm sure you're that way about your kids," I paused and looked into the young officer's eyes. Here was test number one.

"My wife says I'm over-protective," McCombs said.

"No such thing. I don't mind telling you, these three girls we're looking for, I feel very protective of them as well. I looked into their mother's eyes and told them I'd help get those girls home. Anything I do, and I mean anything, is with that goal in mind. Are you with me on that?"

Officer McCombs slouched back in the booth. He hadn't taken his eyes off me or blinked the entire time I was talking. And I returned that unblinking stare.

"I am," McCombs said finally.

His gaze remained steady. His pupils didn't shift and his posture remained at ease. I believed him. "Our Jane Doe," I said, switching the subject. "What do you make of the fact that her ID was missing?"

McCombs shifted forward again. "It means her identity is important in some way. He wants us...you, to figure out who she is."

"That's what I'm thinking. He put me on to this crime, yet withheld her identity. So as soon as we figure out who she is, we can figure out how or why she fits into his game."

It wasn't the same as when me and Dale would sit and bounce theories and idea off each other over a meal or a glass of bourbon, but talking it out aloud, always helped. Just then my cell buzzed. "Raines." I listened for a moment. "All right, we're on our way."

"Who was that?" McCombs asked.

"Come on, kid. We've got an appointment with the fossil at the morgue."

Chapter
40

WHEN MAX HAD CALLED, she was giddy. Not because she took the situation lightly, or took pleasure in someone else's misfortune. No, she took pleasure in the fact that she had done her job. And did it well. I knew she had something substantial to tell me.

McCombs's and I arrived at the coroner's office in no time. If this lead was as hot as Max's tone had led me to believe, we'd soon have something for my new partner to report to his superiors. That was the deal.

We entered morgue exam room number three, but there was no sign of Max. Just her assistant, JJ.

"How's it going, JJ?" I said.

James Jackson frowned.

I'd forgotten just that fast he wasn't fond of that moniker. "My apologies. James."

"What can I do for you Mr. Raines?"

"Where's Max? She has something hot for us."

"Well, she didn't mention anything to me. Maybe it's just fake n—"

"Don't you dare say it, or I swear to God I'll pull out my gun and shoot you in the foot."

"Sheesh," McCombs said, looking to suppress a smirk at the same time.

I hunched my shoulders, said, "Of all the moronic, third grade terms to make its way into the American lexicon, I swear that's one of the worst."

Max entered the exam room. "Calm down, Dirty Harry," she said. "JJ, there meant no harm."

"My fault. Guess I haven't had enough coffee. I'm a little cranky."

Max chuckled and said, "Well, you and the Cisco Kid over there come and have a look at this."

McCombs went to respond, but I waved him off. As I had told him earlier, he had a lot to learn if he was moving into homicide. It didn't appear Max was going anywhere soon, so he'd better learn how to play along.

"What do you got for us, Max?"

"Quite a bit. I got an ID for you," Max said. Dressed in her safety garb—face shield, scrubs, and gloves—Max approached the body on the gurney and pulled back the sheet covering our victim. "And this one came with a surprise."

"A surprise?"

"Fellas, meet Ms. Denise Sicoulis. Dental records came in, along with fingerprints. And just so you know, Robert Raines, I had to make the guy running the prints promises in order to get the id back so fast. Weird promises, Robert. That guy has some spiders in his attic, let me tell you."

"Max!"

"All right, so you don't want to hear about my dating life."

I knew I shouldn't have been encouraging her, but I engaged. "Aren't you still married?"

"Not since husband number four left."

I sighed. "So, are you divorced or separated?"

"The jury's still out. Haven't heard from him in just over a year now, so he's either dead, or hiding."

"My money's on hiding," McCombs said.

Max shrugged. "You're probably not wrong, kid. Moving on. Our victim here is twenty-six years old, had fettucine Alfredo and broccoli for dinner, and also a blood alcohol level of point nine-five. Which would lead me to believe she was having a good time last night until she ran into your lunatic."

"Tox screen?" I asked.

"Still processing. I put a rush on it, so we should have it next year."

"Great."

"And you confirmed COD?" McCombs asked.

"Yes. As I said earlier, cause of death was exsanguination. He cut into her femoral artery. Really tore it up, using a serrated blade. She bled out fast right there in that alley."

Our perp had picked a very gruesome way for her to die. Fast, yes, as it only takes minutes to bleed out from a such a wound, but as Max explained, excruciating. Once again, he was rubbing my face in an old case, so far as I could gather, simply because it amused the man to do so.

Max leaned in over Denise Sicoulis, and with a gloved hand, propped her mouth open. "Now for the surprise." Max then picked up a pair of forceps from a nearby tray.

McCombs and I exchanged a confused glance.

I said, "Tell me you're not about to pull a butterfly out of there."

"No, Dr. Lecter, not quite," Max chuckled. She guided the forceps inside Denise's mouth and retrieved a folded-up piece of paper. "Ta-da. Just like a box of Cracker Jack."

"My God," McCombs whispered.

"What is that?"

"Told you things were more exciting when you were around. It's a note of some kind. Stuffed in the back of her throat. I almost missed it, but once I noticed there was something there that shouldn't be, figured I'd better get you on the horn."

Max opened the note, placing it on a separate surgical tray.

"What's it say?" I asked.

"Seven."

"Seven?"

"Yeah, just the number seven. That's the only thing written on it." Max flipped the note over, making certain she was right, then shrugged her shoulders. "Mean anything to you?"

"Not a damn thing. It's a number, okay. The perp said, 'she has your number.' But I still don't know what this means. Seven isn't important to me in any way I can think of."

"Maybe he's picking up where Shear left off, and saying she's the seventh victim," Officer McCombs offered.

"No. We stopped Shear after his fifth. Which poor Denise here wouldn't have been number seven, anyway. And Shear didn't leave notes or clues behind, so the MO diverts there. This is all our mystery man's game now."

Max sighed. "Well, I'm afraid our friend here has told us all that she's going to tell. I confirmed identity, and cause of death, which came as no surprise. And I found her one big secret, which, by the way, that note was pushed down her throat post mortem. Now is where the serious detective work begins, I guess, as I'm out of magic tricks at this point."

"Thanks, Max. If anything else pops, give me a call."

"Will do."

McCombs and I headed out of the morgue. I was more baffled than I had been earlier. The kidnapper called and explicitly put me on to this murder. So, it had to mean something.

"Any thoughts?" McCombs asked.

"No." I checked my watch. We were ten hours gone, and I was feeling the effects of having gotten up at just after three in the morning. I was a little tired and needed more coffee to get my mind working right.

"You go ahead and call this in to Deckard. Afterward, we need to talk to Detectives Moore and Forney. We have an id on their murder victim, it's time we start digging into her life."

Part Three

CAT & MOUSE

Chapter

41

DINAH MILLER HAD BEEN traveling all day. She glanced down at her watch. The early morning hours had given way to the afternoon as she followed to the letter the instructions delivered by her mystery caller.

As instructed, she had alternated between public transportation—riding the L and then the bus—before making use of two separate Ubers. What under normal circumstances would've amounted to a forty-minute trip, had, because of those specific instructions, taken almost five hours. She wasn't surprised though. As she'd been taught by her father and her "uncle," avoiding detection required countermeasures. And given the level of secrecy required in this instance, those countermeasures even needed to have countermeasures. But finally, she'd arrived.

Dinah Miller made her way up the front steps of a home that sat in the center of a cul-de-sac, hidden behind a snow-covered privacy hedge of European beech. The hedge surrounded the house on all sides and reached about eight feet in height. Between that and the snowfall, it was like stepping into another world, alone and away from the remaining homes, Dinah thought.

She sat the large duffel bag she had slung across her shoulder down on the porch, and knocked on the door three times, just as she'd been told. She waited a minute, then knocked three times again. A moment later, the door creaked open. Dinah hoisted her bag from the porch and walked inside.

The door closed behind her, and standing before her in the living room, was a petite, pretty, Asian woman, dressed in a black tank top and black yoga pants. "Dinah, it's so nice to meet you. My name is Seiko."

For Dinah, though, introductions would have to wait. "Where is he?" she said. Panic had crept into her voice. It was the same panic she had done a masterful job of hiding as she crisscrossed the city to the burbs, hopping from bus to train to ride share. The same panic that had rose from the pit of her stomach and almost made her puke from the moment she'd gotten that cryptic phone call earlier. There was no need to hide it any longer.

Seiko motioned her to follow. "This way. Come quickly. He needs your help." She led Dinah down a hallway.

"Is he hurt?"

As Dinah entered a back bedroom, she heard a familiar voice say, "A little."

"Ashe! Oh, my God! What happened to you?" Dinah asked, even as her eyes took in the makeshift bandages wrapped around his midsection and left shoulder which were soaked through with blood.

Ashe looked at his *niece*. "I had a little trouble getting out of the way of some bullets," he said.

Dinah's knees went weak. She noticed he was sweating. A lot. "You've got a fever," she said nervously.

"I think so, too. That's why I need you. Glad you finished nursing school, by the way." Ashe managed a weak smile.

Dinah approached the bed and looked him over. "I graduated a month ago. And I'm a nurse, not a surgeon!"

"The shoulder wound is through and through," Ashe said. "I only need you to remove one bullet. I can feel where it's lodged in my side. After that, you just need to patch me up. Should be a piece of cake."

"Piece of cake?" Dinah shrieked. She started pacing the room, looking back and forth between Ashe and Seiko. "I am not a doctor!"

"I don't need you to be."

"What if there's internal bleeding? Organ damage?"

"Listen. I need you to remove one bullet and stitch two bullet wounds, then you'll be on your way home."

"Why did someone shoot you?"

"Once you stitch me up, I'll be on my way to find that out."

Chapter

42

"YOU NEED TO GO to a hospital, Ashe. I don't have any anesthetics, other than a local. And I don't have anything for pain. You know I can't—"

"I know. That's fine. I'll go to the hospital after. I need answers first." Ashe coughed hard. "We're running out of time. Do you need me to talk you through it?"

Dinah jaws dropped. "Talk *me* through it?"

"Only if you need my help."

"I'm pretty sure it's you who needs my help," she said.

"Then you need to get to it, young lady. First, I need you to calm down. Take a breath. I know you can do this. I need you to do this."

Dinah stared wide eyed. She began sweating, and not just because she still had her coat on. Her voice quaked as she said, "I...I...don't know."

"It's okay, sweetie. It's okay," Ashe said. He struggled to sit up. "Leave your bag, I'll do it myself."

Dinah took a step back from the bed. Her eyes bulged. "What? No way. I can't let you do that."

"Then you've only got one choice," Ashe said.

Dinah nodded, said, "Okay. I'll do it."

Ashe sighed. "Good."

Seiko's eyes lit up. "Can I watch?"

After a moment, Dinah replied, "You can assist. Go wash your hands and then start unpacking my bag. Lay everything out on the bed."

Dinah left out with Seiko to wash her hands as well. She returned first to the bedroom. Dinah steeled her nerves and began peeling back Ashe's dressings. "What's this?" she asked when she saw a grainy, grey powder caked in the wounds.

"Don't worry, it's just Quik Clot." Ashe said.

"Quick what?"

"It's a hemostatic agent."

Dinah nodded. "Okay, got it."

"I always carry some. If I didn't have it, I would've bled out by now, or been in much worse shape."

"Amazing," Seiko said. "This man walks around prepared for someone to shoot him."

"I half expected it was you," Ashe said. He laughed, then immediately grimaced.

"Okay," Dinah said and took a deep breath. "Let's get started." She took out a syringe from her bag, removed the cap, and injected lidocaine around the bullet wounds in Ashe's shoulder and just below his rib cage on his left side. "Seiko, hand me the saline, please. We need to clean these wounds first."

Seiko fumbled over the items she'd sprawled across the bed, before her hand rested on the bottle of saline solution.

"Hey. Relax," Ashe said.

His voice was growing faint, which did everything but make her relax. Yet she handed the bottle over to Dinah. "Pick up that gauze. Now, as I squirt, you gently dab at the wound with the gauze, you understand?"

Seiko's eyes grew wide as saucers. Her face went pale. It was quite possible she didn't want to watch as much as she'd thought she did. But they were into now. No turning back.

"Relax. Breathe," Dinah said and doused the bullet wound in Ashe's side with the saline solution, clearing out the clotting agent he'd used. Seiko pressed down with the gauze.

Hard.

Ashe held in a groan, though it was still audible.

"Easy," Dinah said.

"I'm sorry."

"Tell him, not me. Now, go again, nice and gentle," Dinah said as she again squeezed saline solution over the wounds, dislodging clumps of QuikClot. Seiko, using a lighter touch, kept up, clearing the debris.

Dinah took a step back. "I'm going to remove the bullet first. If I hurt you, I won't forgive myself."

"You won't hurt me. You can't," Ashe said. He motioned Dinah closer, and then took her hand and pressed it against his side, near his lower back, above his left hip. "You feel that?"

"I do."

"That's the bullet."

While she hadn't had extensive training in any surgical procedures, Dinah had seen a few done, and with Ashe determined to talk her through this operation, she was confident she could make it happen. She had to. For him. She owed him, after all.

"Seiko…hand me the scalpel."

Chapter

43

By no means was the "surgery" easy on her, or her patient, but Dinah got through it. She'd extracted her first—*and God willing, last*—bullet. Quite the accomplishment, considering she had no formal training. Or a license. Ashe gritted his teeth through the pain and kept her calm, and Seiko, though she shook and trembled the entire time through, provided at least adequate assistance.

After the last stitch was sewn in, Ashe passed out. The two ladies, after applying bandages, made their way out of the bedroom and into the living room. The sun had gone down, and the wind howled outside. It had been quite the day.

"You were incredible," Seiko said. "You should be surgeon, not nurse."

"Thanks, Seiko. I have to take it one day at a time. Someday maybe, but I'm just glad I could help Ashe."

"Your uncle, yes?"

"Yes, but not by family ties. He and my dad are best friends. They served together in Fallujah. They've both told me stories about their time over there. My dad saved Ashe's life. Lost the use of his arm in the process, but he doesn't have any regrets. Ashe has been around since I was ten years old. He's always been there for both me and my dad. Even when I got in trouble, and was spiraling out of control, he was always there. He saved my life. So, that's how he became my uncle."

"Sounds like how we met. I was in trouble, too. I was escort," Seiko paused. "I am not ashamed to say. This night, three years ago, a man was beating me. Ashe came from out of nowhere. We have seen each other ever since."

"That sounds like Ashe," Dinah said.

"Then he save me again. I'm here now, because of some crazy man Ashe thought might try to harm me. Safe house. He called this a safe house."

"Oh wait, yes. I've heard about that…situation."

"May I ask, how he save you?"

Dinah took a deep breath. Seiko had been honest with her. So—

"My mom died when I was thirteen. With my dad gone, off and on, fighting in the Iraq War, I fell in with the wrong crowd. I started using drugs. To put it mildly, I lost it. I lost me. But Ashe, along with my father, kept fighting for me. No matter how many times I went down the wrong path, they followed me, and brought me back. Ashe, I don't know what he did, but, somehow, he got the dealers I used to frequent, to stop selling to me. That helped me turn a corner. But I just love and appreciate that he never gave up on me. And he never would. That's why I couldn't let him down today."

Seiko put a hand on Dinah's shoulder. "You are very strong woman. He talks about you all the time. Now that I meet you, I know every word he ever said, was true."

The two women exchanged a hug.

"Wait. You've been seeing him for three years?"

"Yes. Off and on."

"I've never known Ashe to see anyone that long." A smile crept across Dinah's face. "I think he likes somebody."

"No. Probably not."

"Girl, please. Listen to me, I know that man."

"I hope you are right."

Dinah smiled. "Let me ask you something. Has he always made you call him Ashe?"

"It's the only name I know."

"You want to have some fun?"

Seiko shook her head, giddy.

Dinah leaned over and whispered in her ear. Seiko laughed. "Serious?"

"Very. When he wakes up, take that for a spin."

The two women exchanged another hug. "You take care of him for me. And make sure he goes to the hospital when he wakes up." Dinah said.

"I will."

"I'm going to get going. It's getting late and I know my dad is worried about me. But I didn't want to call from here just because."

"Oh yes, I understand. Thank you for everything you did for Ashe. Thank you for being nice to me. Oh, and Ashe wanted me to tell you—"

"I know. Go straight home. No zig-zagging. Got that lecture before. Good night."

Chapter

44

ASHE AWAKENED TO QUIET and the soft white light of the moon that managed to creep through the partially opened blinds of the bedroom he'd been resting in the past fifteen hours. The last thing he'd remembered was Dinah pulling that bullet out of his side. Not too long after that, his world had gone dark. Until now.

He reached around in the dark until he found the lamp on the nightstand next to the bed. He clicked it on and saw the fresh bandages. As near as he could tell, the surgery was a success. He could feel the stitches along his lower abdomen, back, and shoulder. They were nice and tight. A swell of pride hit him, knowing that Dinah had done so well. Her work was evidence that she was following her dream, her goal. Evidence that she'd make it.

Ashe sat up in bed. His body still hurt, every muscle ached and throbbed. He didn't have to think long or hard about how he'd got that way. Coming home early in the morning, he had an inkling that something was out of whack. But he ignored that feeling, attributing it to the man that had followed him into his apartment building, pretending to be a veteran. He knew deep down that he should've seen through that ruse but he hesitated. He should've been prepared for anything. If the guy had grown a second head, it shouldn't have been a surprise.

Even though he was ready to throw the guy a beating for his efforts, he didn't trust his instincts that something was way wrong. It goes without saying there was a price to pay for that. Though it transpired in just a matter of seconds, Ashe's memory played the events back in his mind in slow motion: that first round piercing his shoulder. He remembered feeling the heat and the impact of the bullet as it entered the front side of his shoulder and exited out of his back, just below the scapula.

The man that he had been conversing with, the faux-vet, cringed and his face went cock-eyed in shock and terror. One thing was for sure, he wasn't expecting that. Whatever part he had to play in this mess. Ashe remembered the man stumbling, barreling into him to get away, instead making himself a shield as three more shots rang out. Ashe felt the man shudder as the bullets thudded into his body. One round went straight through his impromptu shield, striking him below the rib cage and lodging in his side. The impact made him drop his own weapon. It was all he could do to get inside his apartment at that point as more shots rained from the entryway.

After stumbling inside his place, Ashe heard his assailant's footsteps as the shooter made his way up the landing. There was only one thing Ashe could think to do, and that was to head for the window—and jump out of it. Not a great choice by any means. But it was that, or eat another bullet or two. And he'd already had his fill of lead by that point. His adrenalin was through the roof as he lumbered across the living room and flung himself through the window. It was a twelve-foot drop, amidst shattered glass, down into the snow. He felt nothing at the time, but that escapade explained why his ankles, knees, and back hurt him now. A passing cab ended up being his means of escape. A benefit that was twofold. One: it eliminated the risk of his attacker doubling back on him if he'd tried to make it to his own vehicle. Two: it kept his hands free.

In the back of the cab, he applied the QuikClot he carried. It freaked the driver out. But a little extra cash cleared any qualms the cabbie had about transporting a bleeding passenger. As much as Ashe didn't want to, he had the driver head straight for the safe house where he'd stashed Seiko Yoon just four months before. His on again, off again acquaintance had almost fainted when he stumbled through the door.

Ashe appreciated Seiko's efforts to make him comfortable. She watched over him until daylight, when he instructed her to call Dinah. Seiko had mentioned more than once while they waited for Dinah to arrive that she hated being cooped up in the safe house. Even though she understood there was possibly a threat against her life. But she was quick to add she was happy to be there for him in his time of need.

Ashe's thoughts were interrupted as Dinah's question from earlier ran through his head. "Who shot you?" *Who indeed?*

He'd already established that the man was a professional. *But why would he be looking for me?* A thought occurred to him and brought a scowl to his face. Ashe winced as he reached over and picked up his cellphone from the nightstand and dialed a number. This number wasn't saved in his contacts. This one, he knew by heart. On the first ring, a voice answered the call saying, "The nation's finest cleaning service."

"Go secure," Ashe said.

The voice came back. "Authenticate."

"Nine-echo-apple-seven-kilo-bravo," Ashe recited.

Moments later, the familiar voice of Colonel Ryan T. Harrison came on the line. "Keeping odd hours, aren't you? What can I do for you this time, Master Chief?" Harrison, Ashe's commanding officer during his service in the CIA's Special Operations Group (SOG), said.

"I just need to know, was it you?"

"You're going to have to be more specific, chief. Was it me, what?"

"Did you have someone try to kill me?"

"Come again?"

"You heard me. Did you send someone to kill me?"

"Chief, why in the hell would I do that? I've been busy trying to recruit you back into the fold. I've told you for months now, the CIA has need for your skills. Some of the boys I have these days can't make up their mind which side of the cross they want to be on. I need nailers, not hangers. And you were the best nailer I've ever had. So, to answer your question, I've got better things to do than send someone to *fail* to kill you."

Ashe weighed whether or not he believed the answer he'd been given. On some level, it made sense. And right now, that was good enough. "Well, somebody took a run at me this morning."

Harrison sighed. "Let me guess, now that you're at least figuring it wasn't me, you want me to see what I can find out?"

"If it's not too much trouble," Ashe said sheepishly.

"Fair enough, chief. And for the umpteenth time, my offer still stands."

"I'll keep that in mind."

"If there's any chatter, I'll be in touch. What are you going to do in the meantime?"

"Sort this out," Ashe said. He winced as he shifted in the bed. After a moment, he continued, "The man has already made two mistakes I can think of."

"Not making sure you were dead is one," Colonel Harrison said, filling in the blank. "What's the other?"

"He let me see his face."

Chapter
45

THE SPRAWLING TWO-STORY building made of glass and concrete sat on roughly ten acres of land just outside of unincorporated Lake County, some forty plus miles outside of Chicago.

Twelve-by-eight glass pane windows lining the first level, along the front of the building, allowed light from the facility to seep out into the night, illuminating the pitch-black landscape. The facility was wrapped inside a steel chain link perimeter fence that was at least twelve-feet tall on all sides. Razor wire was wound in angry loops around the top of the fence. Every three feet or so, the fence was decorated with signs that screamed *Warning! No Trespassing! Keep Back! Electrified Fence!*

There was plenty of evidence that not only did the electrified fencing work, but its warnings had gone unheeded. Several racoon and squirrel carcasses lay in varying poses of death along the length of it.

The man calling himself Ishmael Keyes had arrived at the facility just after midnight. He had parked his vehicle just about two miles away. Not so far that it would take him too long to arrive or make his retreat, but far enough to approach undetected. Dressed in white snow gear from head to toe, including his balaclava, he blended into the snow-covered landscape and into the night.

Keyes approached the fence and unslung the TRG M10 bolt action sniper rifle from his back. He opened the night vision scope, laid down, and sprawled out in the snow. Keyes peered through the monocle. He slowly scanned the length of the building from left to right in the scope's green tinted hue.

He didn't allow himself to think about his kidnapped charges or the plans he had in place for the remaining members of RDC Investigations. That was fun. This was work. And when it was time to work, fun and play had to take a back seat. Even if only for a little while.

Keyes continued his recon. Aside from the two guards standing post at the entrance that appeared in his scope, it was quiet out. Just as he'd been told it would be. There would be no employees on site, and for security, midnight is shift change. While shift change was run in an almost military like fashion, on Sunday nights, they were a little more relaxed. Tonight, most of the guards protecting this facility out in the middle of nowhere would be commiserating with one another in the bowels of the building. Some even having a few drinks. That was their Sunday night routine. Routine builds complacency. Having nothing to do allows the undisciplined to become lax. That information was obtained with cold, hard cash. A moderate investment in Keyes's mind. One that was going to make this job even easier than it should be. He was promised a fifteen-minute window.

It was time to get to work.

Keyes moved up closer to the fence, ignoring the security camera posts, and produced a pair of wire fence bolt cutters from his tactical belt. If he'd been seen on the camera's, the campus would've been flooded with security personnel. As yet, that hadn't happened. However, this was the moment of truth. Not only was the fence electrified, it was also wired to an alarm system. Even if he wasn't fried, ten pounds of pressure would set the alarm off. Keyes made the first cut.

Not tonight.

Those defenses had been disabled. He was good to go.

Keyes cut a straight four-foot-high line in the fencing. After sliding his M10 inside, he squeezed his way through the opening. With each crunch of his boots in the snow, Keyes was prepared to turn and run should an alarm sound. As he got within two hundred yards with no complications, any thoughts of not completing the mission were gone.

Keyes kneeled in a shooter's stance. He found one of the guards standing post in the scope.

Just as the man lit a cigarette, Keyes discharged a round from his suppressed M10 rifle, dropping him in an instant. Before the second guard could grasp what had happened, he too was felled by a headshot.

Keyes slung the rifle back over his shoulder and drew his sidearm, a suppressed Hechler & Koch .40 caliber. Keyes advanced on the building at a quick pace. He was minutes away from the prize and completing his mission.

His intel had been good thus far—as it should have. He had a man on the inside, after all.

Chapter

46

ISHMAEL KEYES REACHED THE front entrance of the Wynn Pharmaceuticals facility as the door swung open.

"It's about time!" Frank Gooden said through clenched teeth. "What'd you do? Stop for coffee? The whole goddamned security squad will be up here in the next five minutes."

"Well, maybe you'd better show me to the lab instead of sitting here jawing," Keyes said.

Gooden frowned, then turned on his heels to lead the way. The two men passed through long white walled corridors. Everything looked sterile. Their boots squeaked in unison as they scuffed along the freshly waxed floors. On either side of them were numerous labs, visible through long protective glass windows. Each lab, though empty of any personnel, was host to its own unique experiments in varying stages.

"Smart isn't it," Keyes said. "Hiding a chemical weapons plant in plain sight just outside of a quaint little town."

Gooden wasn't in the mood to discuss Keyes's musings. He grunted and picked up his pace. That didn't bother Keyes in the least. He liked chit-chat at times like these. It didn't matter to him if Gooden did or not.

After a few twists and turns, the men arrived at a lab marked Bio-Hazard Level 4.

"This is it," Frank Gooden said. He'd begun to sweat. He checked his watch.

"How long before anyone misses the two men out front?"

Gooden checked his watch. "They're due to radio in in about two minutes!" He kept his voice at a whisper, but it was strained and filled with panic.

Keyes thought of when he'd first approached Frank Gooden. That was after doing some homework on the men employed at the facility. Saddled with gambling debts and a coming out on the undisputed losing end of a divorce where his wife got everything but the state of Illinois, Frank Gooden stood out. He was an easy *in*.

The thought of pocketing a cool fifty thousand dollars for what would amount to little more than ten minutes of *work* grabbed Gooden's attention in an instant. It didn't take Keyes long to convince Frank Gooden to go along for this ride. Granted, the man decided to re-negotiate and drove his price up another twenty-five grand.

While the price wasn't what Keyes would consider expensive, it wasn't cheap either. But, for Keyes, Gooden was a means to an end. Given that Keyes could expense any additional expenditures back to Sophie's employer, he was fine with handing out cash. To a point. Ten grand in cash up front was enough to get the ball rolling with Gooden. They'd agreed that the remaining balance would be paid once the job was completed.

Gooden had performed well thus far. He had provided Keyes with cover to approach the facility by disabling the security cameras and disarming the fence, and giving him the intel for the perfect time to strike. *How do you reward someone for that?* Seventy-five thousand dollars or—

Gooden slid a key card in the reader outside the lab. After a beep, he entered a code on the keypad and opened the lab door. "You got a respirator?"

Keyes smiled. He unzipped his winter coat and pulled the respirator hanging around his neck up over his face. "Of course, I do. I know that even the air in that room can kill you."

Gooden nodded, and said, "The code to the reefer with what you want is six-eight-seven-seven. It's on the top shelf. That's courtesy of Dr. Spears. The man just can't stop himself from talking."

Keyes slipped inside and after passing through an ante chamber where he received a blast of high-pressured forced air, made his way over to the large refrigerator unit along the far wall. He punched in the code Gooden provided and heard the electronic lock release, then slid the unit open. Two clear vials containing a purplish liquid sat on the top shelf. Keyes reached into his tactical belt and produced a small plastic container. He popped it open, then laid the vials, one at a time, along the foam padded surface inside the container. He snapped it shut and tucked it away.

"Time's up!" Gooden shouted in a whisper.

Keyes closed the refrigerator door and passed through the ante chamber, and slipped out of the lab.

Gooden slid the key card in the reader again and entered the code, closing the lab door, and hustled after Keyes.

"Is any of this going to come back on you?" Keyes asked as he trotted toward the exit.

"No. I was able to get Jenkins's access code. It'll look like he shutoff the security systems and accessed the lab."

"Jenkins?"

"He's one of the men lying in the snow with a hole in his head."

Keyes smirked. "Smart. Sounds like you thought of everything."

"Except one thing," Frank Gooden said as they approached the exit. The hallways were still clear. They'd been successful. There was just one matter left to resolve.

"What's that?" Keyes asked.

"The rest of my money. My payment. When do I get it?"

Keyes turned, raised his .40 caliber, and said, "How about now?" He squeezed the trigger, shooting Frank Gooden right between the eyes.

Chapter

47

OFFICER SEAN MCCOMBS CHECKED the time as he parked his car in his garage. It was 12:30 a.m. He'd missed dinner with the family by four hours at least. He'd missed tucking the kids in and kissing them goodnight. It had been a long day, working almost double the hours he would've pulled on his normal shift.

If he ever makes detective grade, this could be a glimpse of what the future would hold. Many more late nights, many more nights without dinner with the family, and of course, many more nights of not being able to kiss the kids goodnight. It would be a new lifestyle that they'd all have to adjust to. But it's what he wanted. *Right?*

What was it that Raines had said about being a homicide detective?

McCombs sighed and exited his vehicle. He made his way into his house via the backdoor which sat off the kitchen. He closed the door behind him and turned the lock, and the kitchen light came on. He started.

"Finally made it home, huh, Lone Ranger?" Stephanie McCombs said.

"Hey, baby. What are you doing up?" Sean McCombs moved toward his wife and kissed her cheek. Her eyes were bloodshot red. It was long past her normal bedtime.

"The kids missed you at dinner tonight, and when it was time for bed, it took some time to put them down," she said.

The couple embraced.

"Sorry, honey buns."

Stephanie giggled at hearing the nickname he'd called her since they'd first started dating twelve years ago.

"It's just this case. Those girls."

"I understand," Stephanie said. She looked her husband in the eyes. "Do you think you're going to find them?"

"I do. I really do. This task force has CPD, FBI, US Marshals. It's a good group. So, yeah. I think we'll find them. But there's a lot going on with the case at the moment. The guy that did the kidnapping, looks like he's also good for a murder, too."

Stephanie gasped and released her embrace. She looked her husband over. "Are you being careful?"

"Of course, I am, babe. You know me. Besides, I've got plenty of backup."

"This guy sounds dangerous."

"Maybe. He's turning out to be busy, that's for sure," McCombs said. His eyes dropped. "I saw the body at the morgue. It was…it was tough."

"How are you holding up?"

"I'm okay. This guy they got me partnered up with, old school dude from back in the day. He worked the original 2002 case. And from what he told me about our female victim, looks like that one is similar to another former case of his as well."

"You're kidding."

"I can tell he's feeling it. Big time."

Stephanie helped her husband out of his coat and boots. "All right. Enough of that kind of talk." She went to the front hallway closet to hang his coat. She called back, "Dinner's in the fridge."

"What did you cook?" McCombs asked, foraging through the refrigerator.

"Mac-n-cheese—"

McCombs poked his head over the open refrigerator door. "Oven baked?"

Stephanie smiled as she walked back into the kitchen. "Sean McCombs. I know you know your wife will never make mac-n-cheese out of a box."

"That's my girl."

"There's fried chicken in there too. And yes, I saved you the big piece of chicken," Stephanie said, referencing one of her husbands' favorite Chris Rock jokes before he could.

Sean McCombs laughed. The day's events played through his mind as he studied the look on Stephanie's face. Trying to get lost in her features, hoping to wash away the day. That scene in the morgue was more than just "tough" as he'd said. It was flat out horrible. But he couldn't let her know that. She was worried enough about him to stay up late, waiting for him to come home. Would she be able to handle this daily? Could he?

He put a plate of fried chicken and macaroni and cheese into the microwave, still being sure to keep his expression, and his mood, light.

"Dad!"

He turned and his three-year-old, Angela, came racing toward him.

"What are you doing out of bed?" Stephanie asked.

"It's okay. Come here, sweetie."

"I couldn't go to sleep without saying good night to you, daddy."

"Awww, sweetheart."

He scooped her up into his arms and hugged her tight. Angela kissed him on the cheek. The sleep in her eyes was clear. Yet, she stayed up long enough, even fooling her mom, to see her dad. That meant something. The tight hug meant something. And the kiss good night damned sure meant something. In a word: everything.

Sean McCombs couldn't help but notice how fresh and innocent his baby girl smelled—uncorrupted by the world. Unsullied by the realities he faced on a daily basis. After sending her back off to bed, his mind was made up. He wasn't a homicide detective. He was Chicago PD through and through, but some things weren't up for trade.

It was an honor to be on the task force, and he was even more determined to help find those girls. But after that, he wanted things to go back to normal. He was determined he'd spend even more nights with his family at the dinner table.

"You hurry up and eat your dinner, mister," Stephanie said with a mischievous smile. "I didn't stay up this late just to kiss you good night."

Chapter

48

IT WAS MIDNIGHT WHEN Officer McCombs and I parted company. Forty minutes later, I'd pulled into my driveway. I was dead tired, having been up almost twenty hours straight. No easy feat as I approach sixty-five years of age. The only thing I wanted was some bourbon and some sleep. But I knew I wouldn't be getting much of either. Simple truth of it is, I couldn't afford to.

Two fingers of Blanton's and about five hours of sleep was all I could allow myself. Then I needed to be awake and working on this case. My mind was racing with thoughts of Denise Sicoulis, the Spy Bar murder victim. McCombs and I had been at the station for hours, sitting with Detectives Forney and Moore going over the video provided by the club. Our victim was first spotted arriving with a group of female friends. They drank and danced, and as Max had stated earlier, she was having a good time.

At one point during the video, we see the victim make her way over to the bar. She began talking to a man seated there. What was noticeable about him to me right away, was how he each time he moved, it was in a way that his face wasn't picked up by the camera. I knew this was our guy. It was the same behavior exhibited by the kidnapper, and it wasn't accidental. It was a skill. More of that trade craft Ashe had pointed out the other day. None of the angles he was visible from gave us enough for a clear ID.

Our victim and the mystery man had multiple rounds of drinks and engaged in conversation for almost two hours before we could see them getting up. The man made his way to the exit first, ducking through the crowd, still being certain to keep his face shielded, followed by Denise. And we all know what happened from there.

Watching the last moments of her life playing out on the video, I wondered what he meant by his statement to me on the phone. What role did she play, and what was the significance of the number seven, written on a note and tucked away in her throat? The only thing I knew is that it was significant. You don't go through that kind of trouble on a lark. After getting inside, I went through the exercise of taking off all of my heavy winter gear. That alone took five minutes. I went in to the kitchen, grabbed a rock's glass, and altering my plan, I emptied the last of my Blanton's bourbon in it.

I sat down on the sofa in the living room. Exhausted and alone with my thoughts for the first time all day, I immediately thought of Ashe and had to fight back tears while taking a sip of my drink. I needed to refocus. There had to be something I was missing regarding—

My cellphone rang. I looked at the caller id. The call registered as "unknown." It was *him*. I could feel it. I answered. "Raines."

"Long day for you? You sound awful tired."

"Thanks for the concern, I didn't know you cared."

"Sure, I care. To a degree," he said and chuckled. His laugh sounded like a hyena. I imagined his face, featureless save for a mouth full of teeth frozen in a Cheshire grin.

I had spent some time at Quantico, the FBI's training ground, working with their profilers back in the 90s. A lot of what I'd learned there I'd been able to put to use throughout my police career and then later, in my second life as a private investigator. I figured I'd try to put those skills to good use now. "Why are you doing this?"

"Didn't you ask me that already?"

"I believe I did. I don't think I got a real answer, though. Think you're in a mood to give one?" My tone was non-confrontational. I let my genuine curiosity come through. I was met with silence. It seemed I was holding the phone forever. I could feel the muscles in my right arm tightening. And then—

"Can I be honest with you?" he said.

"I'd like to think so."

"My daddy, and mind you, I was very close to the man, always told me, 'Son,' he said. 'No matter what it is you do in life, be the best at it.' He told me even if I was a janitor, to be the best janitor the world has ever seen. And well, look at me now. I am a janitor of sorts."

"That's how you see it?"

"Sure. Now mind you, my job is cleaning up messes, or sometimes, adjudicating situations for some powerful, and being honest, unsavory people. I ameliorate—you like that word? I know I do, but I deal with whatever situation they want for a price. While I do that, I entertain myself with very specific challenges."

"Let me guess, this time around, me and my team...we're the challenge?"

"I just want to be the best at what I do. You can understand that, right? You can't go around calling yourself the best if you aren't matching skills and wits with the best. I've got dossiers on you, your longtime partner, and your military friend. I know what you've done. The things you've seen and experienced. I know how good you all are. People who are the best. Make sense?"

"Actually, it does. Misguided though it may be."

"Since we're sharing, how about you, Mr. Raines. What got you started down your path?"

I expected he'd turn the tables and ask me something personal. No sense in lying. I was trying to build rapport. I cleared my throat and said, "Believe it or not, same as you. It all started with my father as well. Different reason, though."

"Do tell."

"My father was a drunk, and a gambler. He wasn't a mean man, by any stretch. In his own way, I guess you could say he was quite loving. But he had his vices, and they came first. So, even on evenings when he had to watch me if my mother was out, that wasn't going to get in the way of his drinking. Or his gambling."

"Interesting. I like him already. Please, go on."

"Long story short. I was with my father the last night he gambled. A man, angry or jealous at the amount of money my father had won that night, followed him back to our car, which he'd left me sitting in, and shot him right in front of me. He robbed him and then took off into the night. Right there and then, I knew I'd be a cop. I knew I'd hunt men like that. Bad men who inflict pain at will on others. And based on your actions here in my city, I'm hunting you, now."

"Yes. Yes, you are. And I'm hunting you, too."

Chapter

49

"**But it doesn't have** to be that way," I said, doing my best to sound sincere. "We can call this whole thing off, I don't mind. You seem like a decent enough fella." I hoped to appeal to something, anything in him, that might allow this to end with no further bloodshed.

"Do I now? And the murder of your friend, and our young socialite...just water under the bridge?"

"Yes. If you were to tell me where those girls are right now, and we get them back safe. If you do that, I'm thinking, well, I'm thinking you could just disappear." It was b.s., but I was hoping he'd buy it.

He didn't.

"I'm not an idiot, Mr. Raines. Please, whatever you do, don't make the mistake of thinking so. I'm not telling you anything. As I said earlier, you sound tired. You should get some sleep.

You've got a lot of work ahead of you if you're going to save those little ladies."

"I'm not too tired to figure out what you're up to and get those girls back home."

"How is that working out so far? Last I checked, those girls were still tucked away where I put them. Question for you, Robert Raines. What do you think their last thoughts will be right before they die?"

"What do you think yours will be?" I shot back. Our conversation, this game of cat and mouse, had turned.

"If that moment ever comes, I won't notice. I only think happy thoughts."

"Well, maybe I can ensure that moment comes sooner than later. Now that I know who I'm looking for," I said. It was a bald-faced lie, sure, but I needed to get control of the conversation and not let him push my buttons. Maybe do a little button pushing of my own.

"Is that a fact?"

"Yes. It is. I saw you on the video at the club where you murdered that innocent woman."

"You saw *someone* on the video."

"It was you, talking to the brunette at the bar. What did you have to slip in her drink to get her to want to walk out with you, anyway?"

"Don't be fatuous, Robert. I didn't have to slip her anything. That one was hot and raring to go. That's going to get her in trouble one day. Oh, wait. Ooops."

Sarcastic prick. "It's going to get you in trouble, too."

"The only thing you saw on that video was *a* man at the bar talking to the woman that ended up dead in that alley."

He was too calm for my taste. Joking about a murder. I decided to turn up the heat, hoping to get him to slip up and tell me something useful. "We got your face, pal, all over that video. We're on to you, you understand what I'm saying? It won't be long now before we come kicking in your door, and for your sake, you'd better hope those girls are still alive or so help me God—"

The man erupted in laughter. So much for my taking control of the conversation and him not pushing my buttons. In a word, I was pissed, and breaking my rule number one of interrogations.

"You are such a good liar, Robert," he said in between chuckles. "I'm impressed. If I didn't know any better, I'd actually think you had me, but you don't. That failure aside, did you at least find the prize hidden inside the party girl?"

"Seven?"

"Yes, seven."

"Any reason you think that number should be special to me?"

"Come on Robert, we all have higher expectations of you."

"We?"

"Yes, the girls and I. Oh, and their darling mommies."

"You're an asshole."

"Duly noted. You've got more homework to do. Put it together, Raines. I'm pulling for you, because then it would mean you're the adversary I was hoping for. If not, the little angels are paying for it with their lives. The clock is down to fifty-two hours. Tick Tock, Raines."

I could see I wasn't going to get much from him. Which wasn't a surprise. But my other goal had been accomplished. Keeping him on the phone.

"I enjoyed our conversation. Now, get some sleep, Robert. But not too much, right? You put it all together and maybe then we can talk about how you get those girls home."

As strange as it seemed, I believed him when he said he "enjoyed" our conversation. It's quite possible I wasn't the only one angling to keep the conversation going as long as possible. "One question before you go. I'll make it quick."

"Go on."

"Tell me, how do you know for a fact that we don't have your face on video?"

The man on the other end of the line let out another giggle. "You know what, Mr. Raines? I'll indulge you. The reason I know you don't, is because if you did, you'd have already kicked in my door."

With that, he hung up. I hit asterisk-three-two on my phone and was connected to the CPD tech team that set up the trace on my line.

"Was that long enough? Did you get it?" I asked. My heart was racing in anticipation until—

"No. No, I'm sorry, we didn't get it. It's like he was able to scramble his signal. I tried everything. Everything I know to try, anyway."

I hung up. That took the wind out of my sails, and now I felt even more tired than I had when I first walked in the door. I downed my glass of bourbon and headed for bed. I need all the energy that the next few hours can provide.

Chapter

50

FUNNY THING ABOUT SLEEP. It can lead to dreams. I've had some friends of mine say they dream every once in a while. While others have sworn that they don't dream at all. I've heard from a doctor or two that we only remember the dreams we have just before we wake up. So, it would stand to reason that if you dream early on when you fall asleep, you wouldn't have any memory of it. Maybe you'd believe that you don't dream at all.

I'm neither a doctor nor a scientist, but I know for a fact that I dream. All the time. Every night. No time off. Sometimes the dreams are wonderful. A vintage memory of happy days long past playing out in my subconsciousness. Sometimes, it's simply a random, but still happy event. But then there are other times. Times like tonight. When the dreams are anything but random and anything but happy. When the dreams are nothing short of nightmares.

If I had to guess, I'd say that my eyes had been closed no more than twenty minutes when the first one hits. I dreamt I was partnered up with my son, Robert Jr. and we're on that fateful ride. The day he was shot and killed on the job. I'm his partner and I've got no bullets in my gun. The shit is going down and I'm powerless to save his life. I can smell the gunpowder in the air. I can hear the staccato pop-pop sounds as his body is riddled with bullets.

Powerless to help.

I can only watch. Next, I can feel his body heave and shudder in my arms as he takes his last breaths. That coppery smell of blood is in the air. In my nose. My son's eyes are staring up at me, dull and cold, while his voice echoes from some far-off place asking, "Why didn't you help me, dad?" The feelings are so overwhelming and powerful that I wake up. I'm sweating, my breathing is labored. It takes maybe another ten minutes before my conscious mind can accept that it was just a dream. In reality, I was never there.

I never had a chance to help him.

That's what haunts me the most. Many a day I sat and wondered if in my sons lasts moments, he called out for me and I wasn't there. That has been the hardest hurdle for me to get over. It's one that I will never get over.

I calm down after a bit, lay down on my side, and drift back off to sleep. Just my luck, dream number two starts up. *Coming to a theater near you!* I'm back in Grant Park during last year's Democratic rally, and face to face with my son's former partner, Chicago Police Officer Elliot James. A man that I'd loved just like a son. And just as it happened in real life, I'm forced to watch as he takes his service weapon, puts it under his chin, and pulls the trigger. I see him in his hospital bed at the University of Illinois Hospital. Also, just like in real life when I visit him, he doesn't talk to me here in this dream either. Even though he left me with those tantalizing yet haunting words, "If you only knew what really happened to your son." In my dream, he wakes up, though. His eyes stare deep into mine. He repeats the words he'd left me with. When I ask, "What? What do you want to tell me about my son?" He flat lines. Another dream that startles me awake.

I re-adjust the covers and quickly turn my head back into the pillow. If I allow myself to come out of my sleepy-dazed-stupor, I know I will not get back to sleep. Regardless of the potential demons that await me, I head back in. I need the rest. I toss and turn for a while but eventually drift off to sleep.

As I dream this time, my wife, Elena is sitting beside me on our front porch. Her touch, her hand on mine, is magic. The weather is warm. It's summer. We're both younger, too. Maybe in our forties? That fact, and that there are two tall lemonades sitting beside us, should make my mind realize it's a dream and I should wake up. My forties are well in my rear-view mirror. And I hate lemonade. But I'm enjoying her company too much. Dream or not, this was more like it. I stay in this happy moment for as long as I can. For as long as my mind will allow.

After a while, it all just faded away.

Chapter

51

Monday

I STUMBLED OUT OF bed, almost crashing to the floor, when my alarm went off. Waking up off and on through the night, I might have slept a total of three hours. It might as well had been ten minutes. I was still just as tired as when I laid down. However, it was time to get back on the clock. No rest for the weary, as they say.

Aside from my disappointment in the CPD tech's failure to trace the call, I was also puzzled. My caller had said that if we had his image on video, we'd have already kicked his door in. What was he trying to intimate? That I knew him, or that he somehow knew me? I put that thought on the back burner and after getting dressed, headed out the door.

I grabbed a large cup of coffee from Dunkin' Donuts on my way in to police headquarters on South Michigan Avenue. The briefing room once again was packed with the officers assigned to the task force. Even his honor, the mayor, had returned. Guess he didn't want any second-hand updates. Not on this. Even if he had ambitions of serving in the White House, one foot was still solidly in Chicago. My new *partner*, McCombs, had arrived some twenty minutes before me. Eager beaver, that one. The first point of discussion for our meeting was the failed attempt to trace the call from our suspect a few hours ago, which Lt. Deckard addressed.

"While we were unsuccessful on that score earlier, we might be in luck," Lt. Deckard said as he stood at the front of the room. "The FBI has loaned us one of their communications techs. I suppose the feds have some toys that we in the city haven't come up with yet. As such, they've loaned us Agent Kyle Dixon."

A mid-thirty-ish looking agent, with a close-cropped haircut, sitting with his laptop open, pecking away at the keyboard, looked up. He raised his hand. "May I have your phone?" he said to me.

I walked over to him and handed him my cell, which he plugged into his laptop. In this moment, I realized it was a good thing that I'd let Dakota Quinn talk me into upgrading to a smart phone. I held back a chuckle, wondering what the tech would've thought had I handed him my old Motorola flip phone.

"I'm uploading a program to your phone which will dump all call information onto my laptop. Even if he's calling from an encrypted cell phone, I will mine the data received on my laptop, parse the packets and get an accurate location."

I raised my eyebrows. I didn't understand the technical mumbo jumbo, which only made me feel worse when Dixon explained he'd given me the plain English version. Just the same, I caught the gist of it. "I thought the FBI no longer had programs that do that."

"Do what?" Dixon asked without looking up.

"Monitor our phones. You know, doing the whole big brother thing."

Dixon shrugged. "We don't."

"Right," I said with a wink as Dixon continued to work whatever technical voodoo he was doing to my cellphone.

"Better get rid of that phone once this case is over," Marshal Greene hollered out, which drew a few laughs from around the room.

"All right, all right. Settle down," Lt. Deckard said. "We're going to canvass the same area as we did yesterday, this time working south to north from 73rd to 59th between Green and Winchester. Pair off in the same groups. We're not only knocking on doors, we're checking backyards, under porches, inside parked cars. Any and everywhere three small children can fit, I want your noses in it."

I turned my attention away from the lieutenant and back to Agent Dixon as he returned my phone to me. "So, how soon do we know if this program of yours works?"

"Just as soon as you get a—"

As if on some unseen cue, my phone began buzzing in my hand.

Chapter

52

"**WELL, HOW ABOUT THAT?**" Agent Dixon said.

I looked at the caller ID. It was an unknown number.

"Aren't you going to answer it?" Marshal Barren said.

I swiped the screen. "This is Raines."

"You sound bright eyed and bushy tailed. I was worried you wouldn't get enough rest and that you wouldn't be up to this. You've surprised me yet again."

I recognized the voice as that of my late night—or early morning, depending on how you view that sort of thing—caller. I put the call on speaker, giving the thumbs up in the room to everyone. We'd just hit pay dirt. I put a finger to my lips. A hush fell over the room.

"If you're as concerned about me as you say you are, why don't you come down to police headquarters. We could talk face to face, sort this whole thing out, and you can tell me where those girls are."

"Tell me something, Robert Raines. Be brutally honest with me. Do you really think I had to put a rufi in that young lady's drink to get her to leave the club with me?"

"Where's Layla, Kayla, and Shameka?" I countered. "You do know that's their names, don't you?"

"Am I on speakerphone?"

Everyone in the room held their breath at the question. "Does it matter?"

"I don't want to be rude," he said. His voice was still playful. "Rude?"

"I'd like to say hi to everyone listening in."

"It's just you and me," I said.

"Oh, please. You're not even trying to lie with that one. Last night you were so convincing. I'm sure someone else is listening in, working their balls off to trace this call. Otherwise, you have neither the resources or wherewithal to play this game with me, my friend."

"That's just it. This isn't a game to me."

"What's in it for me? If I tell you where they are." Our mystery caller sounded sincere. But I had no illusions of the sort.

Agent Dixon twirled his finger in the air and mouthed at me to keep him talking.

"Well, if you come on down to the station, and tell me where they are, I can arrange for some free coffee."

After laughing, he said, "Nice try, Mr. Raines, but I doubt I'll be doing that. I have other things on my agenda for today."

"Well, how about I sweeten the offer? We can throw in free room and board for life, no guarantees on cable, though."

"You can keep the coffee, and the room. I won't need them. I more of an exotic beach, vodka martini type of guy."

"I don't think there's much sand where you're going, but some cons these days make a mean toilet alcohol, I hear. Might get you through your day."

"Instead of making jokes, Mr. Raines, if I were you, I'd be trying to put those clues together. The clock is ticking on those little angels. It seems you forgot."

"I haven't forgotten."

"Good. Because you're not funny. I can tell you, right now, they don't think you're funny either. If this is your best material, what a riot you'll be at their funerals."

His tone had changed again, same as it had last night. He was jovial, playful even, in the beginning, and now once again his voice had taken on that edgy, in-control tone.

I put the call on mute and dropped a hard stare on Agent Dixon. "You intend to have us listen to this shit all day?"

"Almost there," Dixon said.

All the eyes in the room were on him. It seemed everyone had left their seats and crowded around us. Agent Dixon had spoken with an air of confidence earlier about being able to trace this call. It was time for him to put his money where his mouth was. Or look as much a fool as the CPD tech did earlier this morning.

"You still there, Raines?" the caller asked.

I took the phone off mute, and said, "I'm still here."

219

"Well, you'd better get moving. There're no timeouts in this game."

The call disconnected.

I leaned in over Agent Dixon. "Tell me you got it," I said.

A smile made its way across Agent Dixon's face. "Bingo," he said, and turned his laptop toward all of us congregated around him.

Chapter

53

"**Gear up!**"

It didn't take hearing Lt. Deckard shout to get everyone moving, but his command resonated throughout the room. Tactical gear was quickly checked, bullet-proof vests tightened, and watches synchronized.

"I need an extra AR mag," Marshall Barren yelled out.

Damon Greene tossed one from across the room. Barren snatched it out of the air and tucked it in his gun belt.

"You set?" Officer McCombs asked as he noticed me watching everyone else.

I patted the sides of my coat. "Got my Sig right here on my hip, and three extra clips. I'm prepared as I'm going to be." I looked around the room again. "Besides, if the shit hit's the fan, I'm hiding behind all of you guys."

We shared a laugh.

Deckard continued, "Now listen up. We're going to run this by the numbers, everybody understand? Officer Oliver, you've got the ram. Once we're on scene, I want to see that door in splinters. You got me?"

"Yes, sir."

"When we arrive on site, the Marshals will take the lead. They're first through the door, followed by CPD."

Both Marshals Greene and Baren echoed, "Copy that."

"Roger that, lieutenant," Officer Bakker chirped.

"Feds, you're covering the rear of the building. Raines and McCombs. You two are backup. Wait for my word, I'll radio if we need you inside. Otherwise, you're covering everyone's six, got it?"

"We got it, lieutenant," I said. I looked at my new partner. He didn't seem pleased to be bringing up the rear. His face said he had wanted to be first through the door. I patted him on the back with a firm hand. "All in good time," I whispered.

"Now, we don't know what to expect from this nut bag, so I want everybody to be ready for anything. Job one is to get eyes on those girls and get them to safety. Job two, all of you, and I mean all of you, come back alive. That's a direct order. Now, let's move out," Deckard said.

We headed out from the conference room that had been serving as our "command post," and made our way to the motor pool. We looked every bit the part of a posse, with the Marshals, G-Men, and the CPD officers, including McCombs, carrying long guns.

I had an extra bounce in my step as I followed McCombs to his squad car and hopped in. Once he fired it up, memories of my days on the force rolled through my mind. As much as I enjoy being retired, I hated to admit to myself that I miss this. But I do.

The radio cracked, and Lt. Deckard's voice came across. "No sirens, we're rolling in quiet. I've already got a call in to the state's attorney. Our search warrant will be signed and good to go by the time we arrive. We breach on my go."

The lead cars rolled out of the parking garage. McCombs looked over at me, smirked, and said, "Buckle up, old timer."

We rode fast, and as ordered by the lieutenant, without sirens blaring. The lead cars had their lights flashing in order to warn other motorists out of the way, but other than the occasional honking of police horns, which sound like a cross between an excited bull moose and electronic nails being drawn across a chalkboard, we were whisper quiet.

We were headed to an address on the south side that was a little more than three blocks from where the girls were abducted. Talk about hiding in plain sight. Our canvass took us through the same area yesterday. But there were some doors that were knocked on but not answered.

I stared out the passenger side window, watching the city roll past in a blur. As excited as I had been when Agent Dixon tracked our kidnapper's phone, my mind continued working overtime. Maybe it was what my wife had always called my *natural pessimistic nature*, but before I knew it, my head began shaking from side to side.

"What? What is it?" McCombs said.

"I don't know. I guess, with the way this all started, I wouldn't have expected him to be so easy to find."

"Easy? To track this guy, the FBI had to do something with your phone that I don't even know if we'll be able to talk about. Our tech guys couldn't do that, so I don't know that I'd call this easy. And besides, who cares? We get those girls back, we arrest him. Win, win. So come on, no bad vibes all right?"

He was right. I allowed myself to get caught up, thinking that anyone who could ambush Ashe had to be the boogeyman. That he'd be creeping around for months, wreaking havoc across the city before we ever found him. I had some big final showdown that played out in my mind, when more than likely, he was just a lucky prick that struck at the right time.

Well, with us rolling in hot, that luck was about to run out.

Chapter

54

By THE TIME OUR caravan of two police SUVs and two squad cars arrived at the address just off 59th Street, I had put any doubts or questions lingering in my mind to rest. I was ready. Focused on the matter at hand.

Whatever the man behind these kidnappings, and the murder of my friend, was up to, we could bring it all to an end in a hurry. We needed to get him in custody and those young girls back, safe and healthy. That was all that mattered to me right now. This was the best-case scenario. Our task force bringing him in removes the chance of me giving in to any desire to seek revenge.

It was another wintry morning in the city, and the block was quiet. Most of those that were braving the cold to go in to work today, along with children headed for school, were already off, or making preparations to do so.

"Okay, men. Just like I called it," Lt. Deckard said over the radio. "Let's hit it."

We exited the police vehicles. Officer Oliver retrieved the steel tactical battering ram from the rear of one of the SUVs and approached the target house, a brick bungalow. The front door didn't look as if it would take much more than a stiff wind to knock it down, as the wood around the door frame appeared rotted. There was plastic taped around the windows, an old heat saving trick, visible from the outside.

The two Marshals, Greene and Barren, with their AR's in the low and ready position, flanked Officer Jimmy Oliver as he made his way up the stairs. Deckard and Officer Bakker moved in behind them, in tight formation. FBI agents Welker and Jenkins moved around the rear of the house, taking slow, measured steps in the uneven, unshoveled snow.

"We're in position," Agent Welker said over the radio.

Deckard mumbled in a low whisper, "Chicago police. Search warrant." He turned toward us. "We've been announced."

"Noted," I said.

Deckard turned to Officer Oliver, and said, "Okay, do it."

Officer Jimmy Oliver reared back with the ram, shifting his weight and turning at his hips before thrusting forward in one violent motion, swinging the ram and bringing the door crashing down. After the door collapsed in, Officer Oliver slid back out of the way. Marshal Barren tossed in a flash grenade, also called a "flash bang." It exploded in a deafening roar and, as the "flash" in its name would indicate, a blinding light. The

Marshals moved in, followed by Lt. Deckard and Officers Oliver and Bakker.

"Damn it!" McCombs said.

"Easy, kid. Easy."

"I wanted to be inside," he said, stone-faced.

We could hear shouts coming from inside, calls to "show me your hands," and "don't move."

"Me too," I said. "But only because it's cold out here."

McCombs cut his eyes in my direction. I smirked at him. He returned the smile. His face softened a little.

"We all have a part to play. Some parts are bigger than others. Besides, there are no small parts, just small actors."

"What?"

I groaned thinking about the age difference, which became even more apparent just now. "Never mind."

After about five minutes, McCombs radio cracked. It was Deckard. "Agent Welker. How are we out back?"

"We're secure here." Welker's voice came across.

"McCombs? Raines?"

"Secure out front, sir," McCombs said.

After another couple of seconds of silence, Deckard came back over the radio. "Everybody come inside."

Chapter

55

I DIDN'T KNOW WHAT to expect when McCombs and I walked into that house. I stepped over the splintered door that Officer Oliver obliterated with the ram, hearing wood chips crunch beneath my feet, and couldn't help but wonder were the girls okay? Had we been in time? I was also eager to look their abductor in the eyes—best way to get the measure of a man—and let him know that he'd been beaten.

As I entered the living room, my heart sank.

My earlier conversation with McCombs played in my mind. *Didn't seem he'd be this easy to catch*, I had said. *Always follow your first mind, Raines. You're too long in the tooth not to trust your gut.*

I caught Deckard's gaze. And that of the Marshals.

"What the hell's this?"

"That's what we want to know," Deckard said. He turned when Agents Welker and Jenkins entered. "Agent Welker, meet

Mr. and Mrs. Walter Barlow," Deckard said, pointing at the frightened couple that were on their knees in their own living room. They'd been secured with zip ties—wrists and ankles—as the house was cleared.

"What the hell?" Welker said.

Deckard frowned. "That's been the question."

"So, there are no kid's here?"

"Oh, there are kids here, all right. The Barlow's. Their four tender age children are in the back bedroom. Not missing, but terrified after all this. And since this is the address Agent Dixon provided, think maybe he has an opinion on what's going on here?"

Agent Welker took out his cellphone and excused himself.

"He did this," I said.

"He? Who?"

"Our mystery man. I don't know how he did it, I just know that he did it. He's laughing at us right now. Just another angle in this sick game he's playing."

"Can somebody explain to us what is going on?" Mrs. Barlow stammered out through tears.

"What's going on, is that we owe you and your family an apology," Deckard said. "Bakker, cut them loose."

"What about my door?" Mr. Barlow said. His voice was as shaky as his wife's, and with good reason.

"I'll be expecting the federal government to pay for that," Deckard said.

Agent Welker came back inside. "The call was made by a cellphone that was connected to the wi-fi network registered at this address."

"I only got wi-fi last fall, to help the kids with their homework," Mr. Barlow said.

Agent Welker continued. "According to Agent Dixon, our man had to be close by to steal their signal."

"Meaning he was here in the area this morning."

"Well, whoever *he* is, he ain't here now, and quite frankly, I'd prefer you all not be. Take your guns and get the hell out of my house!" Mr. Barlow's voice had regained its vigor.

The family's indignation, and anger, was justified. Here they were, all planning to get their day started, and all of a sudden, their door is smashed in. A flash grenade explodes, no doubt driving everyone's heartbeats through the roof before the Marshals and cops come in with ARs in hand.

For as much of a screw-up as this was, we were lucky. Gun ownership is legal in Illinois. If you own a FOID (Firearm Owner Identification) card, you can legally own a gun in your home. Given the way we made our entrance, had Mr. Barlow thought his family was under attack and he went to defend them, this could've gotten real ugly, real fast. It has happened in other states, which led to some of them banning what's called a no-knock warrant.

This was deadly. The search for the missing girls, and their abductor, could've added innocent civilians as a casualty. It became even more imperative that we find this guy. Although, now I wouldn't bank on using the FBI's tracking software. Somehow or another, this guy's too smart for that.

We filed out of the Barlow home. I could hear Deckard promising to have the front door fixed within the hour. It was something he had to make happen. Once word of this gets out, and things like this always do, it would only compound the problem if, in the middle of winter, the family's door wasn't fixed.

I stepped out on the porch, followed by Officer McCombs, cursing under his breath.

"Easy, kid. Easy. This didn't go the way any of us thought it would."

"I thought we had him, Raines. I thought we'd be bringing those girls home today," McCombs said. His shoulders slumped and there was a vacant stare on his face. He wears his emotions on his sleeve. I was like that early in my career. Then I learned how to let the angst and disappointments from this job eat away at me on the inside. Like cancer. Neither is healthy, but the latter at least gives the appearance you're always in control.

"Listen, there's going to be highs and lows with this investigation. That's just the nature of it. Especially given the stakes with this one. We're partners, so, we're going to have to look out for each other through this thing. If you're down, I pick you up. If I'm down, you pick me up."

"And if we're both down?"

"Then we're both screwed," I said.

McCombs chuckled a little. That was a relief. "That's more like it," I said.

"Okay," he said, composing himself. "So, now what?"

"We came up empty here. So now, we get back to following the clues we already have. But first, I have a stop to make."

Chapter

56

"THE HOSPITAL?" OFFICER MCCOMBS asked when I had him come to a stop outside of The University of Chicago Hospital. "What are we doing here?"

"*We* aren't doing anything. I am. I'll only be about ten minutes, tops. Just sit tight." I exited the police cruiser and jogged across the street and almost slip in slush and ice as hopped up on the sidewalk. A sheepish grin spread across my face. After taking a quick look around, being sure no one saw that near disaster, I headed inside.

Same as I had done at least once a week since last November, I made my way up to the sixth floor. Down the hall, in the east wing of the building, in room 640, was the object of my visit. Laying still, in a coma, with tubes running in and out of him, was Officer Elliot James.

"How are you doing this week, Elliot? Making any progress? Thinking about opening those eyes of yours?" As expected, the only answer I received was the low hissing sound of the ventilator that pumped Elliot's lungs with oxygen accompanied by the steady blip-blip sound of the heart monitor. I looked over Elliot. His bandaging wasn't as heavy as it had been in the past, and the bruising and swelling of his head and face was subsiding. The catastrophic bullet wound he inflicted on himself, sending a 9mm round through his lower jaw and out through his skull, had done a number on him. Last I was here, one of the doctor's told me there was still no improvement in his brain activity. Still no hope he would awaken from this coma.

But his family still refused the pull the plug. So far.

Just how much longer would they be able to hang on? I'm sure it's a tough decision regardless of all that's swirled around them given his involvement in the assassination attempt on Senator Dietrich. You'd think they'd just as soon pull the plug and let the incident fade into history. Elliot and his exploits aren't front page anymore, but as long as he's alive, he's still a story. Which makes them one as well. But as yet, to their credit, they're still holding on. Holding out hope.

Just what do they think is going to happen if he wakes up? I've often wondered and have even come close to asking once or twice on the occasions I've bumped into the family at the hospital. Would he have any recollection of who they are? Or what led to him being here in the hospital in the first place? Would he remember me, even? Or my son. What good could come from him waking up? Especially if he does remember. For my own selfish reasons, I hope he does.

"I can't stay long today, El. Got pressing work to do. Three young girls are missing and we're working like hell to find them.

I just thought I'd come by and see you now, since I'm going to be busy for a while." I stood beside the bed and patted his shoulder. "You get better if you can, El."

I turned to head out, and Elliot's father, Steven James, was just arriving. I exchanged pleasantries with him, and all of those questions I thought I wanted to ask him and his family entered my head. Again, I take a pass on that and make my way out.

Chapter

57

AFTER OUR FAILED RAID/rescue, Lt. Deckard and task force, along with additional patrol officers, continued on with the original plan of canvassing the target area in Englewood.

While they handled that aspect of the investigation, McCombs and I caught up with the detectives on the Sicoulis case. They had already made the notification to Denise's family. A chore that I was more than happy to sit out. Armed with a warrant signed by a judge this morning, they were headed to the deceased's apartment. It only made sense that we tagged along.

Along the way, I placed another call to Lt. Andrews, checking for an update on Ashe. There wasn't anything new for him to report, so I had to get my mind back in the moment. McCombs and I arrived at Denise Sicoulis's address. Detectives Moore and Forney were waiting in their squad car out front. The four of us made our way inside her apartment building, and after showing the landlord the warrant, were let into her apartment. We didn't know what to expect. I was hoping for a clue that revealed what the number seven could mean. But what we found, none of us were expecting.

The scene in Denise's apartment was just as grisly, if not more so, as the one I'd seen when I walked into Ashe's place yesterday morning. There was a trail of blood leading from the door, streaking through the living room, as if someone had been dragged. Watching our step, the group moved through the apartment, weapons drawn. We cleared the house. We took our time, being mindful of any evidence we could disturb or destroy, and also, the possibility that there was someone in the residence we could encounter. The place was empty. Except for what we found in one of the back bedrooms.

The source of the blood trail.

We came across the body of another woman. A blonde this time. She was laid out across the bed, flat on her back. The covers were tossed over her in a haphazard fashion. Her eyes stared wide up at the ceiling, frozen in her last moments.

A quick look around Denise's apartment and it was easy to conclude that the dead woman on the bed was the same one that was in some photos that hung on the walls. A friend or roommate. I didn't have to check to know she most likely suffered the same fate as Denise.

Detective Moore squatted down near the bed, observing our latest victim. "Same guy?" he asked.

"Five will get you ten that it is," I said.

We paired off and went through the apartment; a more detailed search this time. It wasn't long before I came across a handbag in the living room. It had dried blood on it. Going through it, I found Denise Sicoulis's identification. Our guy had been here. That was for certain. He left her purse behind to make sure that we knew he'd been here. In the process, he removed another potential witness. Anonymity has been his friend. No way would he give that up. The poor girl never had a chance.

"Found an id on this latest victim," Detective Forney called out. "Name is Claire Stinman, and according to her driver's license, she does in fact live here."

Back in the bedroom with the body, Moore whipped out his cellphone and called in for the forensics unit. After he'd hung up, he said, "This just doesn't make sense."

"Nothing this guy has done makes any sense, if you ask me," Officer McCombs said.

"Actually, it does," I said, drawing all eyes to me. "If you can see things in a twisted, psychopathic sort of way."

"Oh, is that all?" Moore said.

"Think about it. Whatever his aim is with those children, everything he has done, the kidnapping and the murders have been meticulously planned, and flawlessly executed."

"You sound like you admire this hump," Forney said.

"Not at all. But everything I've seen told me he's disciplined. Well trained. Motivated. Whatever his plan, it means something to him."

"Whatever his plan is, I don't care. I know I'd like five minutes alone with him when we catch him," McCombs said.

There was a fire in his eyes. He'd passed any tests I had for him with flying colors.

"Amen to that," Forney said.

That was something I was banking on. The one thing our kidnapper didn't take into account. This is Chicago. We don't allow people to fuck with children and get away with it. We'll hunt him til the end. No matter what.

Chapter

58

THE FORENSICS TEAM ARRIVED and began combing through the apartment, photographing the scene and dusting for fingerprints. I was certain they wouldn't find any of his. He's not that careless. But in the interest of leaving no stone unturned, they checked anyway. As the team worked, my guest arrived.

I had put in a call to Max. I wanted her on scene to confirm cause and time of death. Although one of those things, I was certain I already knew. I wondered what ruse did our mystery man employ this time to charm his way through the door. At what point did he become a savage? The professional killer with no qualms about leaving bodies in his wake, and in the most gruesome way he could think of. I was curious about something else, too. This is the second body that our kidnapper had dumped on me. He said there was a pattern forming. Looking at the dead woman laid out on the bed, I believed I had that figured.

239

For what it was worth, I also believed I had a few things figured about our mystery man as well. Having seen pictures of both Denise Sicoulis and Claire Stinman prior to suffering their fates, I can say they were both very attractive young ladies. With model good looks. Most men would be intimidated by their beauty and hesitant to approach them. Those that did likely wouldn't get past "go," nor collect two hundred dollars. Based on this, I surmised our man was an attractive fellow himself. And charming.

Those two attributes allowed him to engage both women and not set off any alarms. He was comfortable speaking with them and instantly made them feel comfortable as well. It's why Denise allowed herself to leave the club with him, and why Claire allowed him into their apartment when he dropped by and spun whatever story he pulled out of his ass in the moment. He's good. He's played this game before. *What was it? A smile and a saucy line? He was enjoying drinks with Denise, making her laugh and smile. Her inhibitions were down. Easy prey for a pro like him. But what about Claire? What did he say to you, young lady? What magic spell did he cast to get you to drop your guard and open the door?*

Handsome and charming.

Those same traits served the infamous serial killer Ted Bundy well also. So much so, that even during his trial for murdering and assaulting several women, other women were writing him love letters and swooning as he sat in the court room.

"Raines," Max said as she entered, rousing me from the latest round of questions buzzing around my head like agitated bees. She looked over at McCombs. "Kid."

"You know Detectives—"

"Ernie and Bert? Yes, I do," Max said eyeballing Forney and Moore.

The detectives laughed. If you worked homicide, no doubt you worked with Max at least once. If you worked with her more than once, most times you ended up with a nickname. If it happened to be something you didn't care for, there were two things you could do about it: nothing and like it. Ernie and Bert appeared to be just fine with theirs. I honestly couldn't remember what mine was, and I wasn't going to ask.

"She's in the bedroom, Max," I said.

"Lead the way."

I took Max to the back bedroom with the body, with the remaining officers in tow. "Max, before you get on with your examination, could you first look inside this victim's mouth please?"

"Sure, Raines. Wait. Don't tell me there's another one."

"I don't know," I said.

Max gloved up and propped the victim's mouth open. She pulled a small flashlight from her bag and shone the light inside.

"My, my, my." Max reached back into her bag and produced a pair of forceps. "You sure do know how to pick 'em, Raines." She guided the forceps inside and after a few moments, pulled a folded-up piece of paper from inside the victim's mouth.

"You've got to be kidding me," McCombs said.

Detective Forney's mouth fell open and his eyes went wide. "What in the hell?"

"Another prize inside," I said.

Chapter

59

WHILE I HAD HALF expected there would be a note in this victim's mouth, it still came as somewhat of a surprise. A chill had run down my spine as Max retrieved it.

Max stared us all down after unfolding the note. "I don't think you're going to be any happier about this one than the last one," she said.

"What's it say?" I asked.

"Ten. It's the number ten written on it." Max placed the note in an evidence bag.

"Wait a minute," Moore said. "This is real? I didn't want to believe the rumor going around this morning. I figured it was all bullshit. I thought that...I don't know what I thought, but, this...this is crazy."

"Moore, you'll find I'm not one for hyperbole. When I said there was a note in the dead girl's mouth, that's where we found it."

Max continued with her examination. She removed the bed cover and straightened the legs of the dead woman, which revealed something else that I knew would be there. The gaping wound in her inner thigh that said all that needed saying.

"Well, this confirms my earlier suspicion, based on the amount of blood loss. Without a doubt, your vic here—"

"Claire," McCombs injected somberly.

"Yes. Well, Claire, suffered the same fate as her roommate. Death was caused by exsanguination brought on by severing the femoral artery." Max confirmed. "She's almost out of rigor, so I can approximate time of death around twenty-four hours ago."

"What's that on her face, Max?" Detective Forney asked as he leaned in close to the victim.

Maxine examined Claire's face. "Those white streaks, you mean?"

"Yeah."

"Those, detective, are tears. Looking at the damage your guy inflicted with his serrated blade, she was in a world of pain. I doubt she had as much alcohol in her system as her roommate did." "How can you tell that already?" McCombs asked. "Blood carries the scent of alcohol, Cisco, if it's present in the body. With as much as we have all around this room, trust me, if she had been loaded like her friend, we'd smell it. Another factor, it's warm in here. Her roommate was out in freezing temperatures. So, there were no mitigating factors. This one here was in excruciating pain every second until the end."

A silence fell over the room. The gaping, angry looking, purplish, wound in Claire Stinman's thigh attracted my eyes like a magnet to steel. Max's words echo in my mind. *She was in excruciating pain every second until the end.* This is madness.

McCombs got us refocused on the matter at hand, as he said, "Ten. Is that making any sense to you, Raines?"

"No, it's not. It makes less sense now than when we'd found the seven."

"So, what's seven and ten?" Moore said.

"Seventeen, Sherlock." Max laughed. "All right, all right. I'll leave the detecting to the detectives. I'm going to have the boys go ahead and get the body down to the morgue. I'll confirm t.o.d and the usual particulars. If she has any other surprises, I'll be in touch."

"Thanks, Max. Appreciate it," I said and then turned back to the detectives.

"Well?" Moore said.

"Well, what? Max is right. Ten and seven are seventeen. It's nothing."

"The man has called you twice. Think Raines. It's got to mean something," McCombs added.

He had that look in his eye again. And though his voice was raised, I didn't take it personal. Just like that case back in 2002, this was beginning to wear on all of us. Everyone knew those girls were missing. Everyone knew that with each passing moment, we were closer to losing them. And none of us on the task force wanted to live with that. Least of all a father of two.

I raised my hand. "All right, officer. I'm with you, believe me." This was where I missed Dale. We worked well off of each other, able to blurt out ideas, dismiss what was useless and focus in on what mattered. None of these guys was Dale, but they were all I had. "Let's start again. What's seven and ten?"

"Seven-ten? Right? If we're not adding the numbers, but putting them together, it's seven-ten. Does that mean anything?" McCombs said.

"Still, no. But I like the way you're thinking. Gives us another way to go. Let's start looking at the alphabet, any known cyphers that run numbers to letters."

"I'll get that started," McCombs said.

I liked his level of engagement. I regretted ever doubting him, to tell the truth. With Dale on the sidelines and Ashe… *missing*, he's exactly the type of guy I need to have my back. He was going to do his family proud. I was sure of it.

"We'll canvas the neighborhood," Forney said. "See if there's any video, maybe a neighbor has a home security setup, and caught our guy dropping off the purse."

Moore said, "While you're at it, Spence, be sure to get the uniforms to extend the canvas in a four-block radius around the home."

"Will do."

"One thing is still bothering me, though," Moore continued as he rubbed his forehead.

"Please share detective," I said.

"What's itching my hind end is this, our guy kidnaps your girls, and still has time to drop two bodies, totally unrelated to that crime. I just can't wrap my mind around why."

"Holy shit," I said. And there it was. An *a-ha* moment.

"What? What is it?" McCombs said.

"It's not two bodies."

Chapter

60

Reporters from all the major networks—NBC, CBS, ABC and WGN—had been filing into the main auditorium at Christ the Savior Baptist church for the past thirty minutes. Each finding their own space to have their camera crew setup, making sure they'd be close enough, able to ask whatever questions and capture whatever soundbites that came about today.

They'd each received an invitation from the headman himself. He had something to say. An urgent message that he wanted to get out was the way he'd put it, about the abduction of the three young girls from Englewood.

And if Reverend Garvin was looking to talk, Chicago media was willing to listen.

The cameras were setup, and the lights came on.

Most of the reporters, expecting the reverend as their only host, registered a look of surprise when they noticed the couple and their four children sitting in the pews. Reverend Garvin appeared from the back. He was dressed in a black Daniel George custom made suit. Tapered to perfection, it gave the reverend more the look of a movie star than clergyman. His custom-made alligator loafers completed the picture.

"Thank you. Thank you all for coming here. Before you bombard me with questions, salient though they may be," the reverend paused. Almost on cue, the throng of reporters chuckled at his statement. He then continued, "Allow me to introduce you to some of my parishioners. This is Patricia and Walter Barlow, and their children, four-year-old Walter Jr, and his three sisters three-year-old Lisa, nine-year-old Sherie, and Aisha there is eleven."

The cameramen trained their cameras on the couple and their children before panning back over to the Reverend.

"Now the reason I have brought you all here today, is because I received some sad, and shocking news this morning, about a travesty that befell this family. This family with a hard-working mother and father. Children that not only attend, but excel in school. A family that, even though they face the same struggle as most families in Englewood, they're determined to do things the right way." Reverend Garvin sighed before striding across the church in short, measured steps. The cameras followed his movements, and again as he returned, walking those same steps, to stand beside the family. Reverend Garvin raised a finger and looked upward. "When I heard their story, my soul ached. I said a quick prayer, and I knew right then, I had to have them share their story with the rest of Chicago."

Suzie Galvin, a reporter and from ABC 7, interrupted. "What happened, Reverend Garvin?"

"Suzie," Garvin began, that Denzel-esque smile spreading across his face. "I can understand your wanting to get right to it. And, as the bible itself expresses that God is not slow, but merciful, I, in my humble personage, will be merciful and swift getting to the point, after saying one more thing." The smile left the reverend's face, replaced by a far more serious visage. "If this family, were a white family, let's say living in one of the posher neighborhoods of Chicago—on the Gold Coast maybe, or perhaps in Lincoln Park—they would not have suffered this indignity."

The reverend injected another pregnant pause, making sure his words sunk in. He took a breath and began again. "This morning, at 9:00am, the Barlow's had the front door to their modest, God fearing home, bashed in by none other than the Chicago Police. No knocking, no announcing, just boom!" Reverend Garvin clapped his hands together for effect.

"In an instant, the door to their home was in splinters, men armed to the teeth stampeding through their living room, rifles pointing in the faces of an honest, hardworking couple and their children. And do you know why?"

A slight murmur rose from the reporters. It was Suzie Galvin that verbalized the question. "Why?"

Reverend Garvin reached inside of his suit jacket and produced a kerchief. He wiped his brow. "This atrocity was committed under the guise of finding those three missing young girls. That's right. The abduction that's been all over the news, this is how CPD is going about solving it. By harassing Englewood residents—innocent Englewood residents—once again, wasting time. How are we, citizens of Chicago, residents of Englewood, not supposed to believe this case will end up the same as last time?"

The crowd of reporters erupted. Each shouting questions for the reverend and the Barlow family.

"One at a time," the reverend said, and smiled. "One at a time."

Part Four

CRITICAL POSITION

Chapter
61

ASHE HAD AWAKENED FOR a second time. Daylight was already rolling into the bedroom. He reached alongside him, but the bed was empty save for him.

He could still feel the pain from Dinah digging around inside him with the forceps, but he felt better just knowing the bullet had been removed. His skin was tight from the stitches, but he no longer had a fever, or the chills. He felt much better. Ashe reached over on the nightstand for his phone. He hadn't received any new calls. The wait continued. It had been four days now since those girls were taken. Ashe wondered how Robert was faring. By now, the scene at his apartment had been discovered.

Don't let that distract you, Robert. Keep looking for those girls.

Ashe sat up in bed, and after a few moments gathering resolve, stood. He took a deep breath and exhaled through gritted teeth. Vacation was over. *Time to get to work.* Ashe worked his arms around in a circular motion, twisting his torso from side to side, determining what he could and could not get away with. His knees, ankles, and back were still sore. And while his range of motion wasn't the best, it would have to do. There was a man out there that needed his attention. A man that would not be happy he was getting it.

Ashe's cellphone rang. He thumbed the screen and answered, "Yes?"

"Sounds like you're already up and at 'em, master chief," Colonel Harrison said.

"I am. It sure is good to hear from you, sir," Ashe replied.

"I may or may not have good news."

"I'm listening, sir."

"As you know, at various times, different government agencies are tracking different individuals entering and exiting the United States. And then, there are a handful of individuals that manage to slip everyone's radar. We have some photos you can look at. See if you can identify your man."

"Send them through. I'm ready."

"You know something, chief? There seem to be a lot of favors heading your way of late. Tracking individuals. Use of a CIA safe house. But none have been coming back my way. You understand what I'm saying?"

"Fine. I'll owe you," Ashe said quickly.

"Secure message coming your way. After you go through them, if anyone pops, give me a call back."

Ashe disconnected the call. A few seconds later, his phone buzzed. He opened the secure message he received and began scrolling through the thumbnail images. The first two weren't familiar at all, but the third—

"Gotcha."

Ashe redialed Colonel Harrison. When they were connected, he said, "Third photograph. That's the guy."

"Interesting," Harrison said.

"Why?"

"We know him as Orjan Brevik," Harrison said. "Formerly linked to the Ukrainian Special Forces, although his parentage is of mixed origin. Some say Russian and Afghani, but that's never been confirmed. Anyway, after his time in the military, he freelanced. Became a mercenary. Engaged in murder for hire and espionage. He's worked for everyone from the Russian government, to the Chechens, the Taliban, global corporations, the list goes on. Anyone that meets his price gets a highly trained killer. He's good at his job too. Fifty-seven confirmed kills, though rumor has it the number is much, much higher. Got in the country on a fake passport, quality work though. No doubt, he's using another alias by now."

"Brevik? Why does that name sound familiar to me?"

"It should, chief. And this is why it's interesting. He was actually on your to-do list prior to you deciding to leave SOG. Guess a little unfinished business came back and bit you in the ass there, good buddy. You're lucky he missed. That's not what he's known for."

"Sometimes you don't hit the bullseye," Ashe said. "Happens to the best of us."

"Copy that, chief."

"I'm going to need everything you've got on him."

Chapter

62

AFTER FINISHING HIS CALL with Colonel Harrison, Ashe continued his stretching exercises. Once again, testing his limits. The bedroom door creaked open. Seiko entered. Her eyes bulged. "You're awake," she said.

"Unlike you, I can't sleep all day."

"I can only sleep all day if I'm with you," she countered.

Ashe frowned.

"How are you feeling?" Seiko asked.

"Like I was shot twice and had someone dig a bullet out of me," Ashe said. After a moment, he continued, "But better than I did when I got here yesterday morning. How'd you sleep?"

"I didn't. I kept getting up, watching you. Making sure you okay." Seiko looked him up and down. "You should still be in bed. Dinah said you need rest."

"You both did good yesterday. Thank you. Is she gone?"

"Yes. Went home last night. She said you still need to see a doctor."

Ashe continued his stretching, determined to find all of his limitations. "Add it to the list of things I need to do."

Seiko continued to watch as Ashe went through his routine.

"Could you bring me some water?"

Seiko laughed. "Sure, Cendalius."

Ashe's entire body went stiff. "What?"

Seiko laughed harder. "Your secret is out, Cendalius."

"You and Dinah had quite the conversation while I was out, I see."

Seiko's chest heaved up and down as her laughter reached a fever pitch. "I can't believe that's your first name. All this time, I wondered. And now I know. I like it, though. It's a nice name."

"Well, I hate it."

Seiko's face still carried a grin as she said, "It's the name your mom gave you. Cen—"

"Hey," Ashe interrupted. "You don't understand. Growing up, I even made my parents call me Ashe."

A serious look rolled across Seiko's face. "Your parents. You know you don't talk about them. Ever."

"Not much to tell."

"Are they still alive?"

"My dad is too ornery and stubborn to die, and my mom, well…she's a whole other story for another time. But to answer your question, yes. They're still alive."

"Wow. I just don't believe it," Seiko said, her face dropping into her hands.

Ashe rubbed his chin. "What? That they're still alive?"

"No," Seiko said, and again erupted in laughter. "I don't believe you had parents. I think you born in lab."

Ashe laughed. *That was actually funny,* he thought. "Oh, shut up." He returned to his stretching.

"I would love to learn about them," Seiko added and headed out to get a glass of water.

"Like I said, not much to tell," Ashe called after her. "Typical African American household. Well, typical if your dad was a lifelong military man. Ended his career as a full-bird colonel. He was much better at that job than being a husband or a father. My mother had her way of dealing with that, and it was a way that only benefitted her. But they loved me. So there, that's the Ashe family in a nut-shell. Happy?" Satisfied he understood his limited mobility, Ashe got dressed.

"Thank you for sharing," Seiko said returning with water. "It means a lot."

Ashe walked over and hugged her. "Listen, I know it's been hard for you, being cooped up here. I'm just trying to keep you safe."

"I know."

"Good," he said, then kissed her forehead. Ashe walked over to the bedroom closet and pulled out an oversized duffel bag. He sat it on the bed, opened it and removed a Desert Eagle .50 caliber handgun fitted with a laser scope and three boxes of ammo. He also removed a fixed blade knife and a bottle of pills. After plopping two pills into his mouth, he tucked all of his supplies into a small tactical bag before returning the duffel to the closet.

"What were the pills?" Seiko said and handed him the glass.

"Vicodin. Just in case," Ashe said and washed the pills down with a swig of water.

"You're going out? You haven't eaten anything." Seiko said.

"I'll grab something while I'm out."

"You're going after the man that shot you?"

"Damned right."

"Is he the same man that kidnap those girls you were looking for?"

Ashe thought for a moment. While he couldn't be sure, that wasn't out of the realm of possibility. "That's a good question. When I find him, I'll be sure to ask him."

Seiko sighed. "This man, he's dangerous, yes?"

"He is. He's made his moves. Now I have to make mine. We're in the critical position."

Seiko stared wide eyed. "You play chess?"

Ashe tilted his head to the side, smiled and said, "Apparently, so do you. We'll have to play sometime."

"That would be nice," Seiko said. "In the meantime, can you do me one favor?"

"Sure."

"Don't get shot again."

Ashe smiled. "I'll do my level best."

Chapter

63

THE OPERATION AT WYNN Pharmaceuticals, which doubled as an off-book US government owned chemical weapons plant, had gone like clockwork.

Ishmael Keyes had enjoyed the work. It was exhilarating, even if it was rather easy. Frank Gooden had been an interesting pawn, and Keyes respected his use of one of the other men at the facility as a cutout. That was a smart play. And now, with Gooden's death, the loop around the heist was closed. Permanently.

Not to mention saving sixty-five grand to boot.

Keyes had secured the package and got away clean, even if things had gotten a little messy on the way out. With his primary mission completed, Keyes was now ready to focus on the task at hand. The *true* prize.

He'd already taken care of the most physically imposing of the trio. The one called Ashe. Yet Keyes had been rethinking how that had unfolded ever since. Stalking and ambushing the man at his home, was expedient. And justifiable. But after doing his homework on Ashe and studying his history, he would have preferred to go hand-to-hand with him.

That would've been a real challenge.

And being honest, Keyes thought, *that could've gone either way*. There were just too many variables in that equation. A lot of moving parts. He simply had to enjoy the hunt and the takedown. *Although, there's nothing like hunting something that's hunting you back. Shame. Maybe in another life, Mr. Ashe, we'll have that adventure, going hand-to-hand and seeing who takes who*. Keyes smiled at the thought, and his mind flashed over a similar *adventure* with a foe he thought worthy.

He had been contracted by the Soviets to assassinate an up-and-coming political leader in the Ukraine. Vassily *something or other*. He didn't remember that guy's name anymore. But he remembered Vassily's head of security, Anatoly Moskov. Moskov was former Russian FSB (Federal Security Service), a Sambo champion, and a big bear of a man at six-foot-five and a husky three hundred plus muscular pounds.

Moskov was the trophy prize on that trip—a hundred-point buck.

After fulfilling the contract, and taking out the politician, he tracked Moskov to his home and confronted him.

Keyes remembered the look in Moskov's eyes as he explained who he was and what he'd done. He could feel the heat rising from the large man's body as his rage exploded.

The big Ukrainian had a five-inch height advantage along with a hundred plus pound weight advantage. He also had the anger advantage. He had a reason to want Keyes dead, and he seemed to put all of his advantages into his first punch which caught Keyes near flush. Keyes knew that if he hadn't anticipated and rolled with that punch, the big Ukrainian would've turned out the lights for him and then did only God knows what to him.

As it was, Keyes's equilibrium had gone squirrelly. He felt his knees buckle. But he evaded the next haymaker; it seemed as if Moskov had reached as far back as Romania as he loaded up on that one. Keyes sidestepped, parried the blow, whirled and delivered a powerful kick to the side of Moskov's knee. The sound of the man's MCL snapping filled the crisp mountain air. Moskov dropped to one knee and Keyes connected with a crushing elbow to his throat.

Keyes remembered Moskov staring at him with what looked to be shock in his eyes. A powerful palm strike to the face, driving his nose into his brain, ended whatever thoughts the Ukrainian had running through his mind.

Keyes smiled again as he reminisced. Even though that one punch Moskov landed had fractured his jaw and left him with a concussion, that encounter was fun. Moskov was a test. A test he passed with flying colors.

And he had every intention of passing this one as well. It was time to wrap things up. If Raines could put things together as he expected, then bringing this show to a close should be simple. He'd laid out a trail of bread crumbs. Now, he just needed the old clue hound to finish eating them up.

But first, before the next step in his plan, he needed to tend to the small matter of getting the BMW detailed. It had reeked ever since the night he recruited that street urchin to ambush Ashe. And he'd had enough. The smell reminded him of—

Keyes's cell phone rang. A smile stretched across his face.

Chapter
64

"KEYES," HE ANSWERED.

Sophie Bisset's French accent filled his ear. "What is that noise in the background?" she chirped. "What are you up to?"

"Believe it or not, trying to get BO out of my car!" Keyes shouted over the roar of car wash machinery.

"Do I even want to know?"

Keyes laughed, said, "Probably not."

"On to more important things. Is it done?" she asked.

"It is. As promised."

"Ce sont de bonnes nouvelles."

"That is good news, isn't it? And better news for me, will be confirmation of my payment."

"The transfer will be completed once our courier picks up the package. I trust you haven't changed your mind, and will not be delivering it yourself."

"Look at you, trusting your instincts. Smart. I've still got a few things to finish up here. And things are going well, thanks for asking."

"My employer suggested I try again. See if you'd reconsider. He even suggested we could use his villa in the Alps for two weeks before your next assignment."

"Told him about our little trysts, did you?" Keyes asked.

Sophie cleared her throat. "It came up during conversation."

"And you both somehow thought…"

"That such an offer might…win you over. That, and the fact there's a lot of money on the line here. You could charge double your usual fee."

"First off, you're good sweetheart, but not that good. Second, do I strike you as a man who needs money?"

"No. You don't need money. But you are an asshole sometimes, do you know that?"

"It's been mentioned recently. I told you before, everything has its place. That includes you." His harshness shouldn't surprise her, he thought. It's how he's always been. Just the same. "It's nothing personal, my dear. Let's just say the stars didn't align for us this time and leave it at that."

"That's a little better," Sophie said with a slight tremor in her voice. After a moment, she went on, "Just what is this ridiculous pursuit of yours? Why is it so important?"

"Sophie, my dear. I don't think you'd understand."

"Try me."

"Random acts," Keyes said.

"What? What are you talking about?"

"Random acts of life that no one see's coming. The thrill of how it all can end in a moment's notice. It's a rush like no other. That's my pursuit. Sometimes life ends because of who you work for, or because you're three little black girls living in the wrong neighborhood, or because you're a brunette, or just maybe because you made a commercial."

"Huh?"

"The law of unintended consequences, Sophie. That's all. I told you before, you wouldn't understand."

"And you're the consequence?"

"No, sweetheart. No," Keyes laughed. "I'm the random act."

Keyes ended his call with Sophie, confident in his decision, her additional offers aside. After patiently waiting for his vehicle, which had a fresh, almost floral, aroma by the time it was returned to him, Keyes headed south to pay a visit to the sleeping beauties. He had an idea. They were due for some fresh air. A break from the container. It was time to take them traveling again.

Whether or not it was prudent, he wasn't sure. But it was worth exploring. In a cruel twist of fate, he was eyeing a larger role the girls could play, making the failure of Robert Raines and his RDC Investigations team complete. And even more tragic.

Chapter

65

"So, which of you is it?" Mayor Reyes asked. He stood up from behind his desk in his City Hall office and leaned over it, staring up and into the eyes of the taller men assembled before him.

Police Superintendent Edwin Chalmers, Chief of Detectives Earl Hammerlich, and Lieutenant Sam Deckard all stood at attention. Silent. Their eyes shifted back and forth between them, unsure of what they were being asked.

"I want to know which of you is behind the campaign to make sure I don't win re-election next year." The mayor's audience remained silent. "Can either of you explain to me what I just watched on the afternoon news, not twenty minutes ago? Imagine my surprise as I watch a family being interviewed, saying they had their door kicked in this morning by CPD. Check that. They were very specific. By *my* task force!"

And there it was. Bad news travels fast. Especially when aided by the media.

"Sir," Lt. Deckard interjected.

The mayor's eyes narrowed. He held up a hand and said, "I'm not finished." He walked from behind his desk and put his hands in his pockets. "To make matters worse, who was sitting there on TV with the family, grinning like an idiot? Our old *friend*, Reverend Garvin. Ten-to-one says he's playing an angle so he can run against me next year." The mayor walked past the men and continued, "He's got political ambition, don't let him fool you."

Again Lt. Deckard spoke up. "Sir, I take full responsibility for the mix up this morning."

The mayor turned. "Mix up? That's what we're calling it?"

"That's what it was, sir. Our suspect called Robert Raines this morning. We traced the call, or rather, thought we did. According to the FBI's tech guy, the kidnapper used something called a sniffer attack."

Mayor Reyes's face went slack.

Deckard continued, "Now sir, I don't know what that means any more than you do. But the tech says it allowed our guy to hijack that couples wi-fi and made it look like their home is where the call came from. Under the circumstances, with those three girls missing, it was a good lead—our best lead—at the time. I felt we had to pursue it. Turns out that was a mistake. But that's all it was, regardless of the narrative anyone else is trying to spin."

Mayor Reyes frowned. "Oh, that simple, is it? Well, maybe you should've been on TV delivering the news, then."

"Sir, in all fairness," Chief Hammerlich began. "I—"

"Enough," the mayor said and waved him off. "What's done is done, and we are where we are now. My chief of staff, you all know Javier? Eh, maybe not, doesn't matter, but he's already working to clean this mess up. That's his job anyway, and boy is he going to be busy. Tell me, did we at least fix that family's front door?"

"We did, sir. I had a crew come right out, put up a brand-new door. Charged it to the feds." Deckard said.

"Good. And where are we with the investigation?"

"Raines and McCombs are following up additional leads left behind from that crime scene at the Spy Bar. The rest of the team and about thirty patrol men are out canvassing the area," Deckard said.

Mayor Reyes walked back over to his desk and sat down. He let out a heavy sigh. "I was an alderman sitting on the city council back in 2002 during that original case. All of us in this room were here for that. The shit-show it became as the investigation dragged on and on, seemed like the entire city was about to explode. We can't have that again."

"Agreed Mr. Mayor," the superintendent chimed in.

"And we can't have any more instances of police kicking in doors. Unannounced or otherwise. Unless we're sure, and I mean damned sure, it's the right door being kicked in."

"Understood," Deckard said.

"From now on, any decisions to get a warrant and make entry will run through me first, sir," Chief Hammerlich added.

"The only thing I want to see on the news from now on is good news," Mayor Reyes said. "The people in this city used to think Chicago just ran on its own. Like it went to bed same time as them, got up in the morning same as them, enjoyed a cup of coffee and went to work. That's what we called it, right? The city that works." Mayor Reyes stared out the window of his office, taking in downtown Chicago.

"And you know who convinced them otherwise? Who convinced them that to run a city like Chicago took determination and vision? Me. I convinced them I was the man that had that determination and vision to get things done. To get this city moving in the right direction. They bought it. Hook, line, and sinker. They voted me mayor." Reyes turned back around to his audience, and stared at Deckard. "And Lieutenant, that's exactly why I need you all to find those girls. Alive. Because I'm in charge. I'm el jeffe. So, if we don't find them, or if we kick in another wrong door, or God forbid, shoot an unarmed innocent civilian, come time for next year's election, I'm going to end up grabbing my ankles in front of city hall."

Chapter

66

AFTER MCCOMBS AND I raced out of the apartment of roommates Denise Scioulis and Claire Stinman, I made a call to the sixth precinct looking for my new buddy, Mark Royce. I'd gotten word that he was out to lunch, though dispatch would reach out.

McCombs and I were waiting at Royce's desk when he walked back into the station. He wore that same look of disdain he had a day ago when we met, as he approached me. I was prepared for whatever he was ready to dish out. There was a lot on the line, and I had the entire brass at my back. If he wanted to make this a turf war, I was more than ready for it.

"Listen, Raines," Royce said as he walked up to me twirling that damned toothpick in his mouth. I couldn't help wondering if it was the same one from yesterday morning. "I don't like you. I think you're a glory hound, and I got no use for glory hounds."

I rolled my eyes and said, "And I think you're an ass—"

"That being said, word came down from the top. They say I have to cooperate with you, and I will. Besides, if there's anything in this case that helps you find those missing girls, well, I can put any professional disagreements aside, for now."

"Great, so that means there'll be a later, then. I look forward to it. In the meantime, what were the results from the canvas at Ashe's place?"

"Canvas turned up nothing useful. A few neighbors heard what they thought were gunshots, at least three called it in, while others rolled over and called it a night. There was a blood trail outside the apartment building, but after a few feet, the trail disappears. No further sign. Even the footprints we were tracking from the building disappeared into a shitload of others, so it was hard to discern what was what."

"Any hits on his cellphone?" McCombs asked.

"Who's this?" Royce said.

"Officer Sean McCombs, meet Detective Mark Royce."

The two men exchanged a shake. "No hits on the known number for Mr. Ashe. I've still got units in the area, keeping an eye on his car and place, in the event he returns. In the meantime, we've widened the search radius in the area."

"The man we're looking for, is responsible for that scene, by the way, but we can get into that later."

"Hey, I'm here to provide whatever you need. Anything you can throw my way, I'm more than willing to take," Royce said.

"Trust me, we catch this guy, there's several units that want a piece of him. But I need to ask, who's working the John Doe you found at Ashe's place?"

"Ted Daugherty. I worked with him on a lot of cases. I don't think he's got to the body yet, but—"

"Get him on the line and tell him don't touch it. I want that body handed over to Max Cader."

Royce hesitated for a second, but I imagined he heard the voice of Chief Hammerlich mentioning polishing up the old resume, and he hopped on the phone.

I pulled out my cell and called Max.

"Hey Max, it's Raines. There's a John Doe down at the morgue, lead detective on the case is Royce. I need you to look at that body, and I mean now. Tell me if this one also has a prize inside."

Max excused herself to go track down the body at the morgue. I had a hunch I had been looking at this from the wrong end. Whatever Max finds would go a long way in determining if I'm right or not. In the meantime, it gave Royce, McCombs, and me a chance to talk. Royce seemed very supportive of me finding the girls, and I respected that. Whatever issues he felt he had with me he didn't allow them to get in the way of police work. He even apologized for his behavior at Ashe's place, not that he needed to. But I accepted the apology, anyway.

It wasn't long before Max called me back. "What do you got for me?"

"An eight," Max said.

"That's it? Just another number?"

"Well, if your guy is nothing else, he's consistent. But yes, that's it, just another number. If John Doe here is like the ladies I've examined, I'm guessing this is all he's going to give. Make something happen, Robert." Max's voice had taken on a serious tone. "Figure it out. Find those girls."

Oh, yeah. No pressure.

"Thanks, Max. I'll be in touch."

After I got off the phone, McCombs asked, "Well?"

"Eight," I said.

"Eight what?" Royce asked.

"The kidnapper has committed other murders," McCombs said. "In each of three cases now, the victims have had a note with a number on it shoved down they're throats. Seven, ten, and now, eight."

"What the hell does that mean?"

"We don't know. It's just random numbers, best we can tell. Added all together, it's twenty-five. Or take it as seven, ten, eight, it could be a key of some kind," McCombs offered.

"Key?"

"We've got a pair of detectives looking into cyphers, but it's—"

"Wait a minute. I think I've got it," I said. The thought had swirled through my head at light speed. Yet, I had already rejected it five times before realizing, based on everything that our perp had said, it made perfect sense. It was the only thing that made any sense at all.

"What are you thinking, Raines?"

"Something he said to me in the very beginning. She's got your number. So, the numbers we're finding are all related to me on a personal level, and I was looking at it wrong."

"How so?"

"Royce's John Doe was found first, not Denise. If we take the numbers in the order the victims were found, then we've got eight, seven, ten."

"What's eight, seven, ten?" McCombs asked.

I closed my eyes, still struggling with the thought. "Eighty-seven-ten."

"I still don't get it."

"My address is eighty-seven-twenty. If my theory is right, this is just a few doors down. That means the sonofabitch is on my block."

Chapter

67

WHAT DOES A MURDERER look like? I've pondered that question more times than I care to remember, and each time I have, the answer terrified me more and more. That's because the answer is: you, me, anyone. Everyone.

Murderers always have a face that family, friends, and acquaintances had seen daily, and yet were not aware of the evil, hate, or angst that resided behind the façade. They smile at us, say "hi" every morning and then one day—their murderous instinct pours out, leaving dead bodies in their wake. I just couldn't believe that was the situation I was staring down today. It didn't seem real.

"So, you actually know this guy?" McCombs asked over the wail of the siren.

He was behind the wheel of the squad car with the lights flashing full tilt as we raced over to my street in Galewood.

Luckily most of the city streets had been properly cleared and salted, although we'd occasionally hit slush and I could feel the back of the cruiser fishtail and begin drifting out of our lane before McCombs regained control. Detective Royce followed us in his unmarked, and I'd already called in to Lt. Deckard reporting our lead. Back up was on the way. We were close to putting an end to this madness. Close to rescuing those girls. This time, I could feel it.

"Yes. Well, no, not really," I stammered in answer to McCombs question. In fact, I didn't know him at all. I only knew *of* him. Living at 8710 on my block was a late-twenties something kid that had moved in not too long ago. Keyes. When I first met him, he had said his name was Ishmael Keyes. I'd always had a hard time remembering that. In truth, I went out of my way to avoid making small talk with him. Guess that's another drawback to being a cranky old man. Had I taken the time and paid attention to him, I might have sniffed him out long before he began hatching his evil plan. Then again, I've got enough going on in my own life. Maybe I wouldn't have seen this coming no matter what I did. At least I'll tell myself that.

"Which is it, Raines?"

"It's no. He's new in the neighborhood. Overall, quite type. I mean, he tried to be friendly enough, but there was nothing to bat any eyelashes about." I stopped myself from saying he "never showed any signs," or "I just can't believe it." If only I had the proverbial nickel for every time I've heard those words uttered.

"Regardless, he's got a lot to answer for. A whole lot."

"That's true, officer, but let's not get ahead of ourselves here. He may not be home, or he may be barricaded inside with the girls. We don't know yet. Let's get there and see about getting him in custody first."

"And if he happens to bump his head into something hard during the process?" McCombs said.

"I'll be sure to get him an ice pack."

McCombs chuckled, but his facial expression was stony. Hard as concrete. He was focused. It's funny. I thought I'd have to worry about him holding me back, but now, I've got the feeling I'd better keep an eye on him. Once the girls are safe, then all bets are off. But we've got to close that deal first.

This entire time Ishmael Keyes had lived in the neighborhood, I never once gave thought to what he did for a living. Or what he got up to in his spare time. *Age and apathy.* That's the only explanation I could come to as I continued to ponder this revelation. I retired from the police force. I wasn't asked to leave. Maybe subconsciously I had realized I was losing a step. Although, I don't think me from twenty years ago would've pegged this guy as a kidnapping-murderer. Still, I should've been able to sniff crazy on him. *Did he do all of this because I ignored him? Did my dismissal of him trigger some psychotic episode?* I circled back to the statement he made to me the first time we spoke on the phone, "I had to do something to get your attention." *Is this somehow my fault?*

My cellphone rang, putting the parade of questions marching through my mind on hold. It was Dale. "Dale! Good news. We think we've got him!"

"That is good news."

"You won't believe where," I said, and then walked Dale threw the clues that drew us to the residence a few doors down from where I live and where we host our office. He registered as much shock as I had.

"You be careful, Bobby. Like you said, you haven't crossed the goal line yet. And this guy's smart, don't forget that."

"You got it, Dale. How're things at home, how's Millie?"

"It's all quiet on this front. Millie's taking a nap, so I had a few minutes. Just thought I'd check in."

"I'll call you once we have the girls safe."

"You do that. That'll be a load off."

Chapter

68

I ENDED THE CALL just as we turned onto my street. McCombs killed the siren. I figured this guy had to be expecting us, but he didn't have to know the exact moment I was going to kick in his front door. And once we get those girls, he'd have to answer for Ashe.

"Get on the radio, see if we can get an ETA on that backup," I said and exited the squad car.

McCombs was out a few moments later. "Backup is six minutes out," he said.

I directed Detective Royce around to the back of the residence. "We'll hold for Deckard and the team," I said. He nodded in agreement and raced around back.

My phone rang. I pulled it from my pocket and glanced at the caller id. It was an unknown number. No doubt *the* unknown number. I answered. "Raines."

The man I now knew to be Keyes said, "I see you finally made it. I'm impressed. Tell me, were you surprised it was me?"

"I have to admit, I was surprised. Tell you the truth, Mr. Keyes, I'm still surprised, and I still don't understand why."

"Is there anything I could say that would make you understand?"

"I doubt it. As you mention it, right now, I don't care. But I told you we'd be kicking in your door."

"You did. But you didn't mention you'd be kicking in other doors along the way. Oh, yes. I saw the news, Mr. Raines. That poor family. How scared they must have been." He laughed that hyena like laugh of his again.

"Yeah, I'll bet you got a kick out of that. Playing more games, trying to cost more lives. How did they fit into your philosophy of challenging yourself?"

"They didn't. That was just me amusing myself. But you share in the blame, too."

"How's that?"

"I told you to follow the clues, and you ran off, trying to improvise."

"Well, I'm here now. So, let's make this easy. Come on out and tell us where the girls are."

"They're here. Inside with me. You're welcome to come in, because we're not coming out there. Your friends can wait outside. This party is for you and me. The door's unlocked."

I muted the call as out of the corner of my eye, I saw Officer McCombs making his way up the steps. "Wait for backup, they should be here any minute," I said.

I turned my attention back to my call, unmuting the phone. "The game is over, Keyes. You're caught. I played your game and beat you. Now give us the girls."

"Is that how you see it?" Keyes said. "I'll give you credit for figuring out the trail to get here, but how many bodies were you going to let me drop in order to leave those breadcrumbs. You played a good game Raines, but one of your employees is dead, another has become and in-home caretaker, and you, well you just come on inside and I'll tell you all about you."

My other line buzzed. It was Dale again. "Hang on, Keyes. I need to take this," I said and turned and walked over to the curb.

"Robert, is the bomb squad coming?" Dale said. His voice was frenzied.

"Bomb squad? Why?"

"Hey!" Officer McCombs called out from behind me. "I can see him. He's sitting in the living room. I can see him!"

I barely made out what McCombs had said, as Dale was talking in my other ear. "I just got a weird feeling. This guy has mimicked two old cases we've worked. Like you said before, he's done his homework on us. And it's not out of the realm of possibility that he was in town during that Simon Peters deal. I just prefer you be care—"

"McCombs, wait!" I shouted and turned back toward the house. "Get away from that—"

The force of the explosion lifted me off my feet and slammed me hard to the ground, and then the world went black.

Chapter
69

WHEN I HAD COME to, I was being tended by paramedics. My head swirled, and my vision was blurred, painting the world around me in a kaleidoscope of colors. The paramedics' voices sounded muffled, as if my ears were stuffed with cotton, or they were speaking from some faraway place. After a few moments, I could make out one of them asking me, "Are you okay?"

I nodded my head slowly for fear if I did it any faster, I'd black out again. It took a few moments for me to realize that I was on the ground in the snow, and for a moment, I didn't know where I was or why.

Then the cold, hard truth came to me.

We had tracked our missing girls and their abductor, Ishmael Keyes, to the house he owned on my block. I was on the phone with Keyes…wait, with Dale. Dale had called to ask me about—

I peered over the shoulders of the paramedics as they worked to get me to my feet.

There were multiple police, EMS, and fire vehicles on scene by now. Firefighters were hard at work, trying to put out a blazing inferno. The water from the hoses froze as soon as it touched the house, bathing it in a sheet of ice, while red-hot flames flailed out of the windows and danced along the roof. The roof of the house that *we* had tracked the abductor to. *We,* was me and Officer Sean McCombs. Bits of memory flashed through my mind. Him walking up the steps of that porch.

I told him to wait for backup, didn't I?

"Come on, buddy. Let's get you in the back of the bus, check you out, huh?" One of the EMTs said.

I let them walk me over to a waiting ambulance, supporting my weight on their shoulders. With each step, I tried to turn my head around and get a view of the house. It was engulfed. I didn't see any sign of Officer McCombs. "What about the people inside?" I asked.

"Say again?"

"Did they survive? Were they able to get the girls out of the house?" I demanded.

"That's the firefighter's job. It's what they're here for. We have to let them do their thing. Ours is taking care of you, all right?"

As they sat me down on the lip of the ambulance, I remembered that Detective Mark Royce was with us as well. I tried to find him through the crowd of first responders, but my head was still fuzzy. I may have looked right at him and not recognized him. As I watched that house burn, and the frenetic pace at which the firefighters tried to get it under control, I could only wonder what went wrong.

Keyes and I were on the phone. He said the girls were inside. *How did I not see something like this happening? I told McCombs to wait for backup, right? Is McCombs okay? And those girls, God, please tell me those girls are okay. They have to be.* I felt a tear streak down my face. I already knew the answer. It was amazing that I was alive. Anyone inside that house simply couldn't be. No one could have survived that. No one.

A paramedic flashed a penlight at my eyes, trying to get me to follow it with my pupils only. I saw spots mostly. Just the same, I said that I was okay. No way were they taking me off the scene. I'd be here until the end. Until that fire is out.

As my vision improved, I noted some of the brass gathered behind some squad cars: the superintendent, the chief of detectives, along with the district commander. I saw several members of the task force: FBI Agents Welker and Breslin, US Marshal Damon Green, and officer Bakker. It was a full house. Everybody had a front row to the disaster playing out. News crews had arrived, but CPD had the area cordoned off pretty tight. Whatever they were broadcasting, whatever facts they felt they knew, they had to tell them outside the perimeter. And that was just as well. If anyone had stuck a camera and microphone in my face right now, there's no telling how that would end up. But it wouldn't be good for them or me.

Lieutenant Sam Deckard, the task force lead, made his way over to me as the medics continued to check me out.

"Raines, what the hell happened?" he said.

"Now might not be the best time to question him, sir," one of the EMTs said. "He's suffering from a concussion. We're recommending he get checked out at Stroger Hospital."

"I'm fine," I said, and then turned to Deckard. "I…we… McCombs and I called for backup. We arrived on scene with… with, Detective Royce." I had to come to grips with the fact I wasn't all right. However, I still wasn't leaving. I slowed down. Took a breath. "I got a call…I think McCombs was on the porch…and, I…I don't know." I shivered a bit, and one of the medics wrapped a blanket around my shoulders. It dawned on me then, I had no idea how long I'd been down on the ground in the snow. "Have they pulled anyone out?"

"CFD has made two recoveries, so far. Both ours."

"And are they—"

"Royce will be fine. He's in worse shape than you, but nothing that won't mend. But McCombs…he didn't make it."

My heart sank. I thought of his wife and kids, their smiling faces staring at me from his cellphone the other day.

"Why don't you go ahead to the hospital, Raines. Get checked out. We'll need to debrief you after a doctor clears you. We need to know what happened here. What could've been avoided."

"And who to blame?" I said and looked Deckard in the eyes as best I could. "I won't argue. You can blame me."

"It's not like that, Raines. Listen, go—"

Lt. Deckard's voice, and that of shouting firefighters, was drowned out by the sound of the burning house collapsing in on itself.

285

Chapter

70

I **WOKE UP IN** the middle of the night. The clock on my nightstand said it was three-thirty a.m., which meant that I'd been asleep exactly an hour.

After spending several hours in the hospital, being examined and treated for the concussion I sustained after the house of Ishmael Keyes blew up, I cabbed it home. I felt about twenty miles south of miserable, so I reached for my favorite numbing medication, bourbon. It didn't work. Not after all I'd seen and lost yesterday.

Officer Sean McCombs's family had been at the hospital. I offered my sincere condolences. I'd only known him just over a day, but I grew to like him fast. This was beyond a nightmare. His wife, Stephanie, though her eyes were bloodshot red from crying, put on as brave a face as she could. There was a line of CPD personnel that each took their time with her, passing on heartfelt well-wishes. His two children, Sean Jr. and Angela, were inconsolable. I couldn't find any words I thought would help, so as more officers stepped up to speak, I tried to find the exit.

That was when things took a turn for the worse.

The saying, *bad news travels fast*, has never been truer than in these days of cable news, cellphones, and social media. The pit in my stomach that already had felt like it would eat me from the inside and swallow me whole, grew bigger as Latesha Barnett and Tracey Montgomery entered the ward. They had followed the line of police officers, is what they'd said, when I asked how they found me. And they were not alone.

None other than the good Reverend Alvin Garvin had accompanied them.

A television crew wasn't far behind.

"Is it true?" Latesha asked.

"Is it true what they're saying on the news? That the man who took our babies was in that house?" Tracey added.

"That's why you were there, right? Because he was there."

Their questions came in rapid fire fashion.

"We believe so, but—"

"What about our girls? Were they in there, too?" Tracey asked.

"We don't know that yet," I told the grieving mothers. "We don't know that they were in that house, and—"

"Don't lie to us!" Latesha Barnett shouted.

It seemed everyone on the ward, doctors, nurses, the other officers all stopped in their tracks. We were the center of attention, and to drive home that point, the cameraman turned on his light. The camera was hot—catching the end of Ms. Barnett's rant.

"You already lied enough when you promised you'd bring our girls back home!" She added as the two distraught women strode off, arm in arm.

I didn't think it was possible for me to feel any worse.

I was wrong.

"I knew when I heard that this man was involved, that this was the most likely outcome we were facing," Garvin turned and said into the camera. Loud enough for me to hear, of course.

Once again, it was 2002. But there's a big difference this time. I'm not on the job. I don't have repercussions from the brass to look forward to for engaging in what was surely about to be a mistake on my part. But I was beyond pissed. Beyond reason. And I damned sure was going to engage. "Excuse me," I said.

"You heard me!" Garvin snapped back, being sure the camera stayed on his good side.

"I'm afraid I didn't," I said and walked toward the reverend. I stopped just short of going nose to nose with him. "Would you like to repeat it?"

Garvin smiled. "Absolutely." He turned and faced the camera head on. "This is how serious the Chicago police department took our missing black babies in Englewood. They were so serious about finding them, that they let this man, who is no longer even a cop, by the way, take the responsibility. The last time that happened, when he *was* a cop, those girls died! And now the same thing has happened today. This is how the black community is treated in this city. It starts from the mayor on down."

My fists tightened. "Are those new glasses you're wearing, reverend?"

"In fact, they are."

"Nice. Fancy. Would you mind taking them off, please?"

"Why?"

"Because I don't want to break them when I break your face!"

"All right, that's it! That's enough!" Lt. Deckard said, arriving just in time before I let my temper get the best of me and clock the reverend on camera. "Okay reverend, the sermon is over. Don't you have something better to do, like fleecing your congregation for another Cadillac?"

"What did you say to me?" Garvin said, indignant.

"You heard me," Deckard said. The scowl on his face even made me pause. "You and the camera crew, out right now."

At Deckard's words, several of the rank-and-file officers made their way over and escorted the news crew, and Reverend Garvin, out of the waiting area.

My anger at Garvin aside, I couldn't feel any smaller thinking about the angry mothers that had torn into me first. I understood their anger and frustration, and what could I say? At this point, I don't have any answers. Whether or not the girls were in that house or why this all happened, I had nothing for them, so the mothers were left to think the worst.

I know I did.

As I tried to fade into the background after that little dustup, Lieutenant Deckard approached me. "You all right?" he said.

I told him the time wasn't right for a debrief, and that we could talk first thing in the morning. I was surprised he agreed. Then he laid another bomb on me.

"So far, CFD has only been able to recover one body from the rubble of that house. An adult. Maxine Cader has custody. She'll let us know what she finds out."

"But…was there any sign of those girls?"

"Not yet. But if they were in the basement of that house… well, it's going to take some work getting to them given the collapse. The fire department knocked off for the day but will be back at it tomorrow with excavating equipment. Right now, it's just too early to tell. I'm sorry."

The fact CFD knocked off for the night told me all I needed to know. They're no longer conducting a rescue operation. It's a recovery. A recovery can wait one more day.

"I'm sorry, too," I said.

"Come on Raines, let me get you out of here. You're a bourbon man, right? How about I buy you a drink?"

"Not today, lieutenant. Going to have to take a rain check on that."

"Okay. Rain check then."

I shook hands with Deckard and made my way out of the hospital. I was living my worst nightmare. I never imagined things going the way that they had. I hailed a cab, and during the ride, I called the only person in the world I felt could sympathize. I was in luck. Dale could talk. I understood everything going on in his home life, so if he hadn't been able to, I would have been left to deal with the aftermath on my own.

I needed him more than ever.

Chapter

71

DALE HAD TALKED WITH me the entire cab ride from Stroger Hospital to my place, keeping me company, and trying to keep me level.

"It just doesn't make sense, Dale."

"None of this has from the very beginning."

"There was nothing about him that suggested his endgame was suicide, and what about the time limit? He gave me seventy-two hours. We were just at thirty-three hours when it all went to hell." I remember slamming my fist against the seat, getting the cabbie's attention. After apologizing, I returned to my call.

Dale had done his best, saying everything I needed to hear like, *it's not your fault, you couldn't have known, you told the kid to wait for backup*. Yet, none of that had brought me any comfort, and I couldn't accept it.

By the time I'd gotten home, I had planned to drink (against doctor's orders) until I either passed out or found a place that offered me a little comfort. After four drinks, I found I would get neither. Interrupting my booze cruise, Lt. Dan Andrews, my former CO, called. We didn't speak long, but he hit the high notes, same as Dale had. It's not my fault, he told me. I did my best. It took everything in me not to yell that my best wasn't good enough. Not last time. Not this time. But I held it in and the call ended without me making things worse.

I thought of calling Elena, but every time I picked up my phone and scrolled to her name in my contacts, I found myself putting it back down again. Continuing to take on cases after I'd retired from the police department, was why she left me in the first place. I had made that choice to continue, in essence forcing her to take the only path she felt she could. It wouldn't be fair of me to expect her to console me and tell me that things would be okay. Being honest with myself, this was the type of thing that she wanted to get away from, and she'd succeeded. I didn't dare try to pull her back into it—

And then my phone rang. It was Elena. Amazing how that happens sometimes. You think of someone long and hard enough and next thing you know—

"Hello," I said.

"Are you okay?" she asked. The sound of her voice was soothing. In three seconds, she'd done me more good than the acetaminophen given to me by the doctors and the booze combined.

"Honestly, I don't know how I am."

"I'm so sorry about those girls," Elena said. "The things they're saying about you on the news…"

"I can only imagine. But, given how this all turned out, maybe they're right."

"They are not right. And I don't want to hear you say that again, Robert Randolph Raines."

In the past I'd never liked when she used my full name. It always meant I was in trouble with her. But this time, it felt good.

"I already know that you did your best to get those girls home alive. There isn't a man in the history of the CPD that's been more devoted to that job, and to the people of this city, than you."

"Thank you. I needed to hear that."

"It's going to be tough, but you'll get through this. And I'll help you get through it. If you want me to."

I was stunned. Things had been thawing between us of late, but this was the biggest olive branch extended yet. "I really appreciate that," I said, trying to hide my shock. "I still can't believe what happened. We were so close to bringing those girls home. I guess I just didn't see this coming. I couldn't read his end game."

"If you had to guess, how many people have you saved during your career?" Elena asked. It seemed her voice grew more and more soothing as she spoke. "How many people have you made things right for?"

"I…I don't know…I'm not sure."

"The point is, more than you lost. You can't save everyone, Robert. I know you'd like to, but we both know that's not how life works."

She was right. If there was one person in this world, I would've saved if I could, it would've been our son. But like she said, that's not how life works.

"You're right."

"I know I am. You looked good on TV, by the way."

I gasped. "They aired that, huh?"

"They did. As for Reverend Holy Pants, between me and you, you should've bopped him good. He earned it for what he had to say."

I smiled. It was good knowing she was in my corner and she was right. Again. Reverend Garvin had earned a crisp five across the lips. After a few more minutes, we finished our conversation. Then again, I was alone with my thoughts, and the ghosts of those girls and Officer Sean McCombs.

Chapter

72

Around eight that evening, FBI Special Agent Dakota Quinn, my May-December fling since my separation, and dear friend, called. Word had made its way around. The case was already drawing national attention. *Kidnapper dies in fiery explosion—what about his victims?* I believe was the story she saw on CNN.

Quinn was off on assignment, so she didn't have a lot of time to talk. "But I wanted you to know I've been thinking about you," Quinn said.

"Thanks, Dak. It's good to hear your voice."

"Is the other news true?" she asked. "About Ashe?"

"You've heard about that?"

"Do I have to remind you I work for the FBI?"

"No. You don't. Right now, it seems so. We haven't found a body yet, though." My voice cracked. My emotions welled up and formed a lump in my throat and my eyes watered. I did my best to get myself back under control. "But that's still an open case."

"Robert, I'm so sorry. I know what he meant to you."

"Thank you."

"Are you alone?" Quinn asked.

"Just me and a little bourbon, hanging out. Making quite the pair."

"You shouldn't be alone right now. Have you talked to Elena?"

It stunned me to hear Quinn mention my wife. It's rare that she does, but even being hundreds of miles away, she was worried about my well-being. Regardless of what it took.

"We spoke earlier," I said.

"Oh?"

"She's very supportive, but I'm going to spend the night alone," I said.

"I understand." There was a bit of relief in her voice. "Well, as soon as this assignment is over, I'm coming to Chicago."

"Thanks, Quinn. I appreciate it."

"You take care, Robert Raines."

Hearing from Quinn helped. A little. It also added to my overall confusion. I know I'd give my right arm for Elena to come home, and yet, I can't deny the connection I've developed with Dakota Quinn over the past year plus. Just the same, right now, there wasn't much of anything that I could think of that would soothe my mind. After that call ended, I was back at the bottle. There was an old stale cigar I had been keeping around my place. When I bought it and tucked it away, it was to be for a celebration of some sort. Nothing cigar worthy ever materialized, and based on today, never would. It was just another distraction. I wasn't even dissuaded by the number of times I coughed and hacked at the smoke generated by the stale tobacco. My mind would go blank for a moment or two until I could breathe again. When it cleared, I'd take another puff.

This was my routine until I dozed off around two a.m. I thought I might be able to close my eyes and get some sleep, so I headed for bed, nodding off around two-thirty. An hour later I was awake again.I tried to go back to sleep, but found I couldn't. I watched some *Law & Order* re-runs on cable, and a few infomercials, until the sun made its appearance. The official signal of a new day.

I got out of bed, made breakfast and then turned on the news. Worst mistake I could have made. The house fire was the lead story, and I found my name being mentioned more than Ishmael Keyes. That's never a good sign. All that good will from working with Quinn and saving the senator some months back was gone. Now I had bungled the rescue attempt, got a Chicago Police officer killed, and another wounded. What was that line in that movie about living long enough to see yourself become the villain? Wasn't expecting that I'd see that so soon.

I turned off the news. But it gave me one good idea. I decided that I'd brave the cold and go visit Detective Royce in the hospital before meeting Lt. Deckard for my debriefing. Imagine that, just two days ago I wanted to punch this guy in the face. Now I wanted to visit him to make sure he was okay, and maybe just to see if he blamed me too.

My cell rang. The number belonged to the county. "Raines," I said.

"Good morning, Robert."

It was Max. Even her tone was dim. Things were really in the toilet if Max Cader was subdued. "What do you have for me, Max?"

"Confirmation. The body pulled out of that fire. Dental records were a match. It was Ishmael Keyes."

Chapter

73

Tuesday

"IF YOU WEREN'T FAMOUS before, you sure are now," Mark Royce said, and laughed as I entered his hospital room. I was still reeling from the gut punch Max Cader's news had been, so his barb barely registered.

"Let's see if we can get a nurse to give you an injection for that sense of humor. Maybe something on the lethal side," I replied.

He clicked the mute button on the TV in his room. He'd been watching ABC 7. The caption on the screen said, *Abductor killed, same fate for his victims*? At least this time they had the decency to frame it as a question instead of stating it as fact.

"How are you feeling, Royce?"

"According to the docs, if I had been standing just ten feet closer, you'd be asking my ghost that question."

"So, how are you feeling, Royce?" I said again.

"Well, right now I'm on enough Percocet that I don't feel the pain from my broken arm, punctured lung, fractured leg, or the concussion. I guess I'm good. I heard you took a knock to the noggin yourself."

"Yeah, concussion they said. Just a slight headache now, is all. Say—"

"Save it," Royce said. "I heard you clear as day tell the kid we were waiting for backup. I don't blame you. And I don't blame him for not listening to you, either. We all wanted to get in there and tear that guy apart and save those girls. Nobody saw this coming, I don't care what the talking heads on the TV say. Or that damned preacher, or whatever he is. You got me?"

"I got you." His words surprised me, but I appreciated them all the same.

"Let one of them strap it on every morning and hit the streets. See what they think then."

I nodded in agreement. Police work, *good* police work, is easy to arm chair quarterback. But oh, so different if you're in the middle of the action. The eye of the storm.

"Did they find those girls?" he asked.

"So far, only one body has been recovered from inside the house. Max called me this morning and confirmed, dental records say it was Ishmael Keyes. I hear CFD is going back out there with some big-time equipment, properly go through the wreckage, see if they can find the girls."

"I been up all-night praying, Raines. Praying that those girls weren't in there…even though…"

"Even though, we know they were," I said. My voice cracked, and I wiped my eyes quickly.

"I don't want to be a part of this. I don't want this to be my history. They might be spewing your name all over the news, but I was there too. I guess I had visions of a parade and a medal from the city for finding those girls."

"Who's the glory hound, now?" I said with a smirk.

"Guilty," Royce laughed. After a moment, his face contorted and became serious. "I heard…that…McCombs had a family," he stammered.

"He did. Wife and two kids. Both young," I said.

Royce's head sank. "Could've been me," he said.

"Could've been all three of us. As much as this sticks in my craw, I can't overlook the fact that we were lucky."

"Yeah, lucky," Royce said.

The sound in his voice didn't convince me. He didn't believe that for one minute. Neither did I. "Look, I just wanted to check in. See how you were doing," I said, and turned to head out.

"Thanks, Raines. Don't let those jerks on TV get you down. You worked that case, worked it well, and don't you forget it."

"Thanks, Royce. I appreciate that."

"Oh. One more thing."

"What's that?"

"Want to hear something funny?"

I grimaced, then said, "Sure, why not. Cheer me up."

"I left a patrol at Ashe's place, you know, in case he turned up, seeing as we were looking for him."

"They saw him?"

"No. They didn't. But they called me this morning just before you got here."

"And?"

"His car is gone."

"Stolen?"

"Could've been. But patrol was sitting there the whole time. I read his military jacket. The parts that weren't redacted and that I could actually get my hands on, anyway. Could be something. Could be nothing. But either that car thief had mad ninja skills…or…"

I nodded and walked out. I didn't want to get my hopes up, but it was the first thing I've had to smile about all day.

Chapter

74

My EXUBERANCE FROM DETECTIVE Royce's news didn't last long. If Ashe was alive, wouldn't he have contacted me by now? I couldn't dismiss that question even as I prayed that, in fact, it was true. There was a part of me that had to hold on to that hope, though. For one, I *needed* my friend to still be alive, and two, in the face of everything else, what would I do if I couldn't believe that?

I wrestled with those questions as I bought myself a cup of coffee at the White Palace Grill. I decided I'd stay close to police headquarters as my debrief was about an hour out. If I'd had gone home after visiting Royce in the hospital, there was no way I would've come back out. I felt that lousy. Despite my conversations with Elena, Quinn, Dale, and Detective Royce, there wasn't any way of feeling better about this. Three little girls died because I wasn't good enough. Just like last time. Sure, members from the task force had reached out over the hours and expressed that this was on all of us, again. But I didn't see it that way. I couldn't.

I was glad that Dale was at home with Millie, though. There was no way he could've handled being involved with this. Not with what he's already got going on. Not that there's a such thing as fair in situations like this, but that would've been especially cruel. Don't get me wrong, he's hurting too. He's hurting for those families and he's hurting for me. But he's at least somewhat insulated this time around. This failure is owned by Robert Raines alone.

"Another coffee, hon?" the waitress who'd been taking care of me asked as she saw my cup had gone low.

"Please," I said, wishing for a splash of bourbon to go with it.

After she'd refreshed my coffee, I reflected on Ishmael Keyes. What possibly could've motivated him to do this? What did he hope to gain? I still didn't have any idea how or why the suicide angle came into play. I stared into my cup of coffee. The answers weren't in there.

I thought about skipping the debrief with Deckard. The way this has hit the news, the reputation of RDC Investigations was already in the toilet. I'd be lucky to get divorce setup jobs tracking loser husbands down to twenty dollar an hour motel rooms that smelled of cheap cigarettes and stale cum. Why cement everything as official by going on the record?

As I finished my coffee, I nixed the idea of skipping it. My sense of duty wouldn't allow it. Besides, I never ran from anything in my life. No point in starting now at an age when running is the last thing I need to do.

"Excuse me," a young woman seated at the table across from me said, waving her hands to get my attention.

"Yes?"

"Aren't you that guy on the news?"

"No. I'm not."

"Yeah! Yes, you are," her male companion chimed in, snapping his fingers, getting the other patron's attention. "You're the guy with the girls and the house, that whole thing!"

"Did you have to go in guns blazing and end up shooting those girls?" the woman asked.

Great. Now I'm being reviled for something that didn't even happen. I dropped the cost of the coffee and a tip on the table and stood up to leave. "You two have a good day," I said. I had somewhere to be.

Chapter

75

"No priors, right?"

"That's what I said, Raines. Ishmael Keyes had no priors. Based on everything we dug up, he was a model citizen. The few people we've been able to talk to so far that knew him described him as nice. Friendly. Worked a steady nine to five as a computer nerd. Made about a hundred fifty k, lived alone, and paid his taxes. He didn't even get parking tickets. We're talking to his family now. They didn't see this coming either. By all accounts, he was clean. Until this," Lieutenant Deckard said.

I was the one being debriefed, but I seemed to have more questions for the lieutenant than I had answers. I got the impression that got on his nerves, just a little.

He rubbed his eyes, then said, "Tell me again, when you arrived on scene, what happened?"

"As I stated before, in route, we called for backup. When we arrived at Keyes's residence, McCombs, Royce and myself approached the house, but I advised we were waiting for backup. I sent Royce around back just to cover the perimeter."

"Leaving you and McCombs at the front of the residence."

"Correct. But what I want to know, lieutenant, is, how does a model citizen go from zero to ape-shit crazy in one weekend. He wasn't on anybody's radar as a stalker, pedophile, anything, and yet, he ups and kidnaps three children and murders six or seven people, before blowing up a house and killing three more?"

"Bobby, we'll get to your questions later."

"Please…don't call me Bobby."

"Sorry, Robert. Didn't know that was a thing. Mind if I ask why?"

"Because my mother named me Robert. And if Ethel Raines was alive to hear you call her son 'Bobby,' she would, in her words, conk you upside the head."

Deckard laughed. "I get it. Believe me." After a moment, he got back to business. "As I was saying, you and McCombs are out front, what happened next?"

"He called me."

"He being?"

"Keyes. Not only did he call me, he tried to goad me into going into that house."

"Which you resisted?"

"I did, and I told McCombs to stand down. We didn't know what we were dealing with, and we had backup in route."

"You're saying he disobeyed a direct order?"

"I'm not saying anything other than what I said. I asked you yesterday, were you looking for someone to blame?"

"I'm not, but the media's already found a place for it."

"And now it's your job to make sure it stays me, and not CPD? Listen, lieutenant, with all due respect, I've already told you everything that happened. If you're trying to cover the city's ass, that's fine. I don't care what anybody thinks about me, and I can tell you, that young man, McCombs, is already set to buried. I'm not going to help anyone toss any more dirt on him." I stood up. "This is over. If you want to hear anything else from me, make an appointment, but it's going to count as billable hours. No discount."

I left my debrief at the Chicago Police headquarters on Michigan Avenue, feeling the same as I had since this entire nightmare had begun. Confused. Speaking with Lieutenant Deckard the past couple of hours hadn't shined any light on why this happened. Call me crazy, but I needed to at least be able to formulate a theory. Given that his task was simply to make sure the narrative crafted by the media stuck to me, I knew there wasn't anything else he could help me with. I'm too old to care what people think of me. I just want to get to the truth.

Chapter

76

It HAD BEEN AS clean of an operation as he could've hoped for, all things considered. But the man that had recently been calling himself Ishmael Keyes, and also had been known as Orjan Brevik, wasn't satisfied. Even after he'd finished his breakfast of oatmeal with dried cranberries, three hard-boiled eggs, Greek yogurt, and matcha tea, and engaged in a twenty-minute shadow boxing session, he was still restless. On edge.

Yet he had to only watch the news to know that he was out clean.

On every channel, local and cable news, the reports were the same: *Ishmael Keyes,* the suspected murderer and kidnapper of three young black girls from Englewood, was dead. Taking his victims with him in a fiery hell in the conclusion of a case that had gripped the city for the past five days. Law enforcement would be weeks sorting through the carnage left behind. By the time they figured out that the thirty-two-year-old computer programmer, born and raised in America, had nothing to do with the crime, he'd be off on whatever island. It would be an open question: *who framed Ishmael Keyes?* The *real* Keyes had been a perfect patsy, specifically chosen.

On all levels, Keyes/Brevik told himself, he'd won. Ashe had been killed, Raines humiliated—for pity's sake, it appears the kidnapper lived just a few doors down from him—and his contracted task had been completed. Win, win, win. But there was one problem with that ending. Raines wasn't supposed to be humiliated. He was supposed to be dead. That's how this game works. Although he liked Raines. And being honest, he respected the old geezer. But the only one getting a pass this time around was Dale Gamble. No point in a kicking a man when he's down, or picking a fight with someone that can't fight back. But for Robert Raines, no, there was to be no pass. And this situation, as is, was just unacceptable.

After leaving his downtown suite at the Peninsula Hotel, Keyes/Brevik drove his BMW back to the south side. A light snow begun to fall. One thing he was certain of, he was sick and tired of snow. It was time to hit a warm, sandy beach, have drinks with plenty of rum in them, great cigars, and the company of morally flexible women.

But even as he pulled his vehicle alongside the shipping container that housed, not only the package he'd acquired from Wynn Pharmaceuticals, but those missing girls from Englewood, his mind again shifted back to Robert Raines. The explosion at eighty-seven-ten was meant for him. Not the mook that lost his life. Granted, had the cop simply been another victim, it wouldn't have been an issue. He got in the way. He took the hit meant for Raines. That would've been the ultimate victory. Walking Raines right into his own death. Everything Keyes/Brevik had said and done, was leading Raines to that door. It was a solid plan. Who knew the security camera system he'd hijacked at the real Keyes's house had an eight second delay and that Raines would get a phone a call?

Keyes/Brevik opened the container and stepped inside. Just where he had left them, the three young girls, bound and blindfolded, lay motionless on the mattress. They almost ended up in the inferno with the real Ishmael Keyes. If not for a sudden influx of traffic in the area that made moving them too risky at the time, they would have. So here they remained. They lucked out.

It was colder inside than Keyes/Brevik had expected. The space heater wasn't putting out much heat. Too bad, he thought. They could've at least died comfortably. But that wasn't his worry. He retrieved the package and took one last look at the girls on the mattress. They hadn't moved the entire time he'd been there. Maybe they were already dead.

This wasn't personal, ladies.

He exited and locked the container. Keyes pulled out his cellphone and dialed. "Sophie, it's me. The ruse is over. Keyes is officially retired," he said.

"And the man you impersonated? What happened to him?"

"What do you think happened to him?"

"So Orjan Brevik is alive and well again?" she said.

"Brevik may be burned by now as well. Prepare my exit under Alek Kralyck. Your package will be on its way to Paris within the hour."

"Thank you. Last chance. You're sure you won't reconsider my offer," Sophie said.

"No. I won't. But I'm sure I will see you soon, my dear. Take care."

Brevik ended the call. He'd have a new identity in a couple of hours. Everything was in place for him to walk away, back into the murky shadows he'd come from.

If only things were that simple, he thought.

Chapter

77

THROUGHOUT THEIR ORDEAL, LAYLA Montgomery had tried her best to keep her sister and their neighbor calm. That task became much harder after their kidnapper continually bounced them around, and moved them to...wherever they were now. Any time the two younger girls had been awake, they cried. They cried because they were tied up. They also cried because they were hungry. But after a while, their muffled grunts went quiet altogether.

It was much colder, too. Layla could hear the humming of the generator, and feel a faint source of heat, but neither of them couldn't move any closer to it. She had cried herself several times, wondering what was going to happen to them. The man hadn't been back to check on them for hours. *Or has it been days?* At least earlier in their ordeal, he would show up from time to time to make sure they could use the bathroom. Since he hadn't, they'd all been forced to let their bladder's go on the mattress they were laying on. That predicament only added to the cold and their discomfort.

Though she couldn't call out, and they couldn't respond, she could hear the girl's stomach growl as the time passed. It let her know they were still there, and they were still alive. If only she had seen that man sooner, Layla thought. Maybe they could've crossed the street, maybe they could've run and gotten away. Maybe—

She heard a loud creak and felt a rush of wind. A door being opened? She heard someone enter. It had to be *him*. Who else would it be? Layla heard him shuffling around. At no point did he speak to them, or lean in close and check on them. As nice as he'd been when they were in the house, he was just the opposite now. Layla no longer believed the man's promise that they would get to go home as long as they did what he said. There was no way they were going home at all. She knew that now. Layla did her best to keep from crying. She didn't sniffle, but she could feel tears running down her face. After a few moments, she heard the door creak closed again.

The man's voice was muffled, but Layla was certain that she heard him talking. Then she heard him get into a vehicle, crank it up and leave. Her tears flowed. She'd let everybody down. Her mom, Kayla, Shameka. She'd let them all down. Layla regretted every time she'd ever raised her voice at her little sister. Or anytime she didn't want to share a piece of candy. All the times she picked at Kayla when helping with her math homework (as long as their mother wasn't home, of course). Layla regretted all those things. She'd love nothing more than to share another of those moments with her sister again.

But now it seemed there was nothing left to do but die.

Chapter

78

Paris, France

WITH THE MERCENARY KNOWN as Orjan Brevik committed to seeing out what she felt was utter foolishness in Chicago, Sophie's choice was clear. He wasn't an option, so she'd have to go with her *plan B*. Even so, she couldn't help but wonder when he concluded his affairs where would he "lie low?" Maybe Bora Bora, or the Maldives?

While Sophie didn't agree with his side hobbies, she respected him for it. He was doing what he wanted to do. What he felt he needed to do. That was a turn on. It confirmed for her she would do the same. Without him. She knew she would see him later, as he'd said. They had always found each other.

Sophie dialed a number in her phone, and within moments was connected to French financier Aubrey DuChamps. The man she'd facilitated this last deal for. The man that would take her to the next level. Whether he knew it or not.

"Beautiful Sophie, so what did he say?"

"I've delivered, Mr. DuChamps, *Keyes* is willing to work with us again."

"Splendid! I couldn't not be happier mon Cherie. Now, what about the package?"

"The courier is already on the way to France."

"This is truly magnificent," DuChamps said.

"Indeed, it is. Perhaps we should celebrate. After all, we're partners now, right?"

"Yes, Miss Sophie, we are."

"Do you like champagne, Mr. DuChamps?"

"Of course, I do, and please, call me Aubrey. Did you not know I have one of the largest private collections of the finest champagne in all of France?"

"I did not."

"Of course, you did, my dear."

"Yes, I did," Sophie replied. "I just didn't want to impose."

"It's no imposition. A new partnership should be celebrated with the finest life has to offer."

"Are you inviting me over for a drink, Mr. DuChamps?"

"What could be better than celebrating with a beautiful woman?"

"Well, I do like a good celebration. Make sure mine is chilled, will you? If it's warm, it goes right to my head," Sophie said. "I can be there in the hour, if that's all right."

"Splendid."

Sophie ended the call. She laughed, figuring that somehow there would suddenly be an ice shortage in France, or the refrigerator in a billionaire's home would magically go on the fritz, but just the same, step one had been completed.

She walked over to her closet and pulled out a low-slung pullover. It would be perfect. Revealing just enough, but hiding the goods at the same time. One thing Sophie had been good at all her life was reading people. And Aubrey DuChamps was an open book. Most men were. That was what made the man known as Keyes so exciting. He was the proverbial curve ball every time. She stepped inside her walk-in closet and began perusing her shoe collection. There were rows and rows of shoes, and she found the perfect stiletto heels to go with the pullover.

Sophie stepped out of the walk-in and paused in front of the mirror. She teased her hair a bit and took a deep breath. This was it. There was no turning back. All that she had been advised to think about, the variables she needed to weigh, had been considered, and she couldn't come up with a single reason to back out of what she'd planned. None that carried weight, anyway. How many opportunities like this would come along? How many chances would there be to become independently wealthy?

Being honest with herself, Sophie reflected, she made more than a pretty penny being a facilitator. Hooking up parties with mutual interests or needs, ensuring whatever the business deal was, got done. It had been profitable, and yet, she needed to continue to do it. She became rich, but not wealthy. And wealthy, she reasoned, just had a better ring to it. And with wealth, comes power.

All things considered, there was only one question: continue to work in this life, or find a better one? She knew what her father would say. After all, most of who she was, and what she'd learned in life, came from him. He doted on her that way. And his being one of the most crooked politicians in France's history allowed her to make the connections she did, and become that facilitator she's known for being. But now she was playing high stakes poker and chess at the same time. To use the vernacular of the former, she was all in. It was time to put any remaining nervousness aside. As her daddy would say, *fear paralyzes, but ambition realizes*. And Sophie Bisset was ambitious.

Sophie dialed a number, and after a moment said, "Sheik, it's Sophie. We're in play. I need your answer."

Part Five

THE LAW OF UNINTENDED

CONSEQUENCES

Chapter
79

COMING HOME FROM MY debrief with Lt. Deckard, I had to park my Tahoe in the alley as the fire department had my street blocked off. They were back at work going through the wreckage of Ishmael Keyes's home. They were looking for the girls.

I got out of my truck. Right away I could smell burned wood and plastic in the air. I taste ash in my throat. I contemplated standing out in the cold and watching them. Waiting for the moment when they brought out three little victims in body bags. It didn't take much for me to change my mind. I have nightmares enough as it is, and this was already going to haunt me for the rest of my life. I may as well stay inside where it's warm and watch it on the news with everyone else. After shedding my winter gear, I put on a pot of coffee. A moment later, my cellphone rang. I looked at the caller ID. I couldn't believe my eyes. I blinked a few times to make sure of what I was seeing.

Staring back at me was *unknown number*. I felt the veins in my neck bulge and a pressure in my head that increased with my heart rate. I took a deep breath. *Calm down, it could simply be a telemarketer or some asshole running a scam*. I answered. "Raines."

"You are one lucky bastard. Do you know that?"

I recognized the voice. It was the voice of the man I'd been speaking with the past couple of days. The man that I had figured to be Ishmael Keyes. A man that was supposed to be sitting in the morgue, extra crispy.

"So, you are still alive," I said. The pressure in my neck and head had subsided, but my heart was pounding like a jackhammer in my chest.

"As are you. Though you shouldn't be." He said coolly. His voice wasn't as playful as it had been in the beginning of our previous conversations. It was sterile.

I said, "Is that right?"

"That bomb was meant for you."

"And the real Ishmael Keyes? And those innocent children?"

"Your neighbor was collateral damage. That's all. Those three little angels are fine though." *Keyes* laughed. "Fine may be overstating their current condition, but they didn't die in that house Raines. They were supposed to, along with you. They lucked out. You all did."

I felt a rush of blood to my head. Could he be telling me the truth? Are those girls still alive?

"That house bombing was supposed to put the final punctuation on your career, and your life. But the other guy went and ruined it."

"His name was Officer Sean McCombs, you sonofabitch. He had a family. The real Ishmael Keyes did too. His mother, father, and sister are going to miss him."

"Oh, boo-hoo. I don't give a shit about either of them! Your officer ruined a well-laid plan. All he had to do was let you be first through the door. But he had too much of a hard-on for that. Or was it that you were too much of a coward, and you let him go first?"

"This from the guy that kidnaps children, and I'm the coward?"

"Screw you, Raines! I could've killed you months ago. You and your entire team. I tried to engage you on my level, I showed you that much respect. Do me the courtesy of the same now!" His voice had gone cold, but I didn't care.

"Courtesy? You ambushed my friend. Kidnapped three little girls and killed innocent people. You want to tell me again why I'm supposed to respect you? I'd rather do you the courtesy of pissing on your grave!"

I heard laughter from the other end of the line.

"Glad to see you still have some spirit left in you, Raines," he said. "The way the media dumped on you, I thought your fighting spirit would've been diminished."

"There's plenty of fight left. Now why don't you tell me who you really are."

"Does it matter? You can still call me Keyes if you like. Or, if it makes you feel better, try Orjan Brevik. But what's in a name?"

He was right. What difference did it make what I called him? There was only one thing that was important. Only one thing that I wanted to know. "Where are those girls?"

"I'm glad you asked that. Good to see you get back on point. I'm willing to propose a trade."

"A trade?"

"Their lives for yours."

"And just how is that supposed to work?"

"I will give you a location. You meet me there alone. I'll tell you where the girls are, and you can text or call whoever you like. Your partner Gamble, CPD, the Marines, whoever. They can save the girls, but I get to kill you."

No surprise there. It was clear all along that was part of his plan. "How do I know I can trust you?"

"You don't. But it's those poor girls' only shot. What's it going to be Raines?"

What else could it be? I agreed to meet.

Chapter

80

Fontainebleau, France

ARMED WITH HER BEAUTY, Sophie Bisset made the hour-long drive to Aubrey DuChamps's estate in Fontainebleau. As she drove her midnight black 2019 Aston Martin V-12 Vantage up to the large, ornate gates that secured the 19th Century era mansion that sat on six acres of land, she marveled at the beauty of the structure. It was a castle.

Sophie's mind wandered, thinking of the possibilities that lay down the road in her own future. This was the type of security and opulence she sought for herself. This was why her plan had to work.

The structure was surrounded by giant oak and chestnut trees, and the lawn was perfectly manicured, of course. Stone sculptures mimicking Le Depart from the Arc de Triomphe adorned the front yard. There were also intricate carvings in the pillars that adorned the entryway. An older gentleman, dressed in a tuxedo and holding an umbrella to shield against the light rain fall, made his way down the front stairs as she brought her vehicle to a stop.

"Good evening, madame. I am Marcel," he said in French as Sophie rolled her window down. "You may leave your vehicle here and follow me inside."

Sophie shut off the ignition and exited the vehicle after Marcel opened the driver's side door. The starchy scent of freshly cut grass rode the cool breeze that accompanied the rain. Marcel covered her with the umbrella and led her inside the home. Sophie stared in awe of the beautiful entry hall, littered with artwork—paintings and sculptures. They came to a wide stone staircase which led them down to the dining room. The dining table was set with a bottle of chilled champagne, glasses, and a variety of h'ordourves.

"My dearest Sophie," DuChamps said as he rose from his seat. He was dressed in slacks and matching blazer with a turtle neck completing his ensemble. His wardrobe was plain but screamed money. He couldn't take his eyes off her as she removed her coat and handed it to Marcel. DuChamps eyes ran up and down her body, admiring the way the pullover dress gently hung on her frame. "So glad you could make it," he added.

Sophie extended her hand, which DuChamps gently caressed and then kissed. "Please, join me," he said, directing her toward the seat closest to his. "Perhaps we enjoy an apéritif, then I can have the staff cook up anything you like."

"You're very kind, Mr. DuChamps," Sophie said.

"Please. Call me Aubrey," DuChamps said, and poured her a glass of champagne. "Chilled. As requested."

Sophie smiled and took a sip. She had to give it to him. The man had good taste. Sophie took another sip, then said, "This is incredible. It's what luxury should taste like."

"You have a very sophisticated palette. It's Gout de Diamants."

"That goes for—"

"Around two million per bottle, yes, my dear. My wine, champagne, and cognac collections rival any in the world, I assure you, and you're welcome to whatever you'd like."

Sophie smiled her best smile and took another sip as DuChamps sat beside her.

"So," he said. "How did you convince our mutual friend to come to his senses?"

"I did what you suggested. I offered him a little something extra, to sweeten the deal. He has already gotten our package to the courier, and the courier is en route to Paris. He should arrive tomorrow."

"And how long before Mr. Keyes is back in Paris?"

"He's following behind the package. He'll be here within the next two days."

DuChamps poured both of them another glass of the Gout de Diamants. "Two days? My dear Sophie, what will you do with that time?"

Sophie picked up her glass and took a deep sip. "What indeed?" she smiled. "First though, I thought we might finalize our agreement as partners?"

"Ah. Business first, yes? Well, I'm prepared to cut you in on this next deal at thirty percent."

"Thirty? As opposed to fifty?"

"Equal partners? My dear, I do not think that possible. Appreciating all you've done for me, and what you are bringing to the table with you, I think thirty percent is more than fair."

Sophie sat up straight, the neckline of her dress dropped a little. "May I have more champagne," she said.

"But of course," DuChamps said and topped off her glass. "So, what do you think?"

Sophie took another long sip, nearly emptying the glass. "I think I'm hungry. What did you say was for dinner?"

"What do you desire, my dear?"

"How about steak," Sophie said, her voice low and seductive. "I love meat."

Chapter

81

TWO BOTTLES OF GOUT de Diamantis, one of Moet et Chandon Dom Perignon, and several drams of Hennessey Beaute du Siecle later, and Sophie could tell Aubrey DuChamps had reached his tipping point. She, however, was just fine. Something else she had learned during the years hanging with her father, before the French authorities carted him off to prison, was how to drink.

After their meal of perfectly cooked steak chateaubriand in a red wine sauce and French onion soup, they moved their party from the dining room to the main living room. Sophie noticed it was as opulent, if not more, as the other rooms she'd seen. DuChamps told her there were thirty-two rooms in the house. No doubt all adorned the same way.

As they sat on the sofa in the grand foyer, continuing to drink, Sophie made it a point to over-exaggerate her movements. She laughed at his jokes, even when they weren't funny. Which was most of the time. Sophie also made sure to lean into and brush against DuChamps occasionally, making sure he got the scent of her perfume and could feel her warm body against his. She could feel that he desired her and found her overwhelmingly attractive. She had no further to look than his trousers and the tent that had formed to know that she was right. It had to take all he could muster not to jump her, Sophie mused. *Let him feel you. Let him breathe you in. Above all Sophie, make him feel that he can have you. And that you want him to. No matter how repulsive you find him. Feed his fantasy. Sell him the sweetest dream.*

The more DuChamps drank, the friendlier he became. And the closer he came to toppling over. He may have expensive taste in spirits, but he's no drinker, Sophie thought.

"Sophie," DuChamps slurred. "Tell me, darling, can't we enjoy each other's company for two days? Before Keyes's returns? I don't mean to imply anything untoward, my dear, but I find myself taken with you. If there's anything I can do to spend one night with you, you have but to name it."

And there it was. *Gotcha.* DuChamps had an itch. And he wanted to scratch it. There was no doubt. Sophie had him, now. This was the distinction between men like DuChamps and men like Keyes. Sophie leaned in close to DuChamps until they were nose to nose. "You know, there is one thing, one favor you could do for me, and then, perhaps."

"Name it," DuChamps said, and almost fell into her lap. He smiled at her. "Forgive me, my dear. You were saying."

"When the courier arrives tomorrow, I'd like to be there, for the exchange. Then I can bring the package to you. And we could celebrate our new partnership, properly. We'd have all day, just me and you."

"You? You want to pick up from the courier? Nonsense, Sophie. We are too important for such menial tasks. I will send my head of security for that."

"It's what I'd like. I'd like to go and pick it up. I want to see the look in your eyes and see which you desire more. Me or the package?" Sophie smiled and her eyes took a seductive slant. DuChamps moved in for a kiss, but Sophie's index finger came between their lips.

"Do I get my wish?" she said.

DuChamps licked her finger, then sighed. "Yes, Sophie. If you must. You can go to the pickup. You may accompany Jean Luc and bring the package to me."

Sophie pulled DuChamps in close and engaged in a warm, passionate kiss, forcing her tongue into his mouth. She bit down on his tongue sharply. He winced and moaned with pleasure. She let a hand drop into his lap and massaged his thigh. DuChamps began to pant as her hand roamed higher, until, Sophie abruptly pushed him back. "That's just a brief preview. Tomorrow, you get the whole show. But now, I must be going." she said.

DuChamps couldn't hide his excitement from the kiss, nor his disappointment from her breaking it off. "But…"

"No, no, no," Sophie said. "We will celebrate when we have our prize in hand. Don't worry. It will be worth the wait."

"Of this I have no doubt," DuChamps said and tried to recompose himself. "Jean-Luc will be by to pick you up when it's time. And then—"

"And then I'll be back with a big surprise for you," Sophie said. She blew DuChamps a kiss and then made her way out.

Mission accomplished.

Chapter

82

Chicago, Illinois

THE MAN I'D KNOWN as Ishmael Keyes, who was just as comfortable being called Orjan Brevik, had set our meet. He was holding all the cards. Whether I believed those girls were still alive, or that he'd even keep his word—which I didn't—I had no choice but to go along, and pray that the hunch I had was right.

The location he picked was the abandoned Brach's candy factory on Cicero Avenue on the west side. The company closed down in 2003 over, believe it or not, the cost of domestic sugar. A lot of jobs walked out of the city with that closure. Its last claim to fame was making a cameo appearance in the movie *The Dark Knight*. The place has been silent since. Crumbling and graffitied, it looked like it was part of some ghost town, or post-apocalyptic movie, as I pulled my Tahoe into the parking lot.

The sky had been cloudy and grey all day long, and the sun was on its way down. That didn't help the ambiance. I trudged my way through packed snow and ice over to the building. I could feel snow sliding into my boots with each step in the near knee-high white powder. Brevik had instructed that I enter on the south side of the facility. I scoped out the parking lot, but there were no other vehicles. I wasn't sure how he arrived, but the man had said that he wanted to kill me. So, I didn't doubt that he would be here.

The chain that secured the doors on the south entrance had been cut. I was right. He was here already. I reached for the door and found myself hesitant. It was quite possible that if I walked through this door, I'd get a bullet in my brain. End of story. He wins. But I remembered that thing I'd said earlier about these "master plan" type guys. I figured he'd at least run it all down for me. Tell me how brilliant he was, otherwise, what was the point. He had to know that I knew just how smart he was. I grabbed the door handle, pulled the heavy metal door back, and walked inside. I pulled my flashlight from my left pocket and shone it into the darkness. Next, I drew my trusty Sig Sauer P250.

I cautiously made my way further inside the factory. The beam from my flashlight, and what ambient light from outside that could make its way in, played against some old machinery, making shapes and shadows appear and disappear. Broken glass and other debris crunched beneath my feet with each step. Even though it was cold, there was still a stale funk that permeated the air. Years of abandonment, human, and animal, piss and feces, hung thick in the place. I didn't even want to imagine how bad this place reeks in the throes of summer. The structure itself kept most of the winter wind out, but there was a steady breeze that flowed through due the windows having been "ventilated" by rocks or bottles or whatever kids and vagrants may have thrown through them over the years. I was a good hundred feet or so inside when a voice from behind said, "That's far enough, Raines."

It was him.

I turned around, and there he was. Stepping out of the shadows, the man responsible for the carnage and violence. He looked to be in his early thirties, Eastern European descent, based on his features. He was clean shaven and looked like he took pretty good care of himself.

"Don't raise that weapon," he said.

As my eyes adjusted, I could see he had a pistol pointed at me. At this range, any shot would be a kill shot. It made no sense to argue and trying to raise my weapon and get on target right now would be little more than suicide. "Okay," I said, and kept my pistol at my side. "How about our deal?"

Brevik laughed. "Robert Raines in the flesh. I didn't think you'd show," he said.

"And yet, I'm here," I said. I kept my voice calm. I needed to keep him talking.

"I didn't think you had the stones, old man. This means you truly were worthy. This made everything worthwhile."

"Well then, how about we get to it? Where are the girls? You wanted a trade, and I'm here."

"Where are they indeed," Brevik said.

"Are they even still alive?"

Brevik looked at his watch. "I told you they had seventy-two hours. Now, they've got in the neighborhood of twenty left, but you know what? That doesn't matter."

"Why is that? Aren't you a man of your word?"

Brevik sneered and said, "Partially. Because I *am* going to kill you. But I'm not telling you anything. I can't believe you trusted that I would."

"To be frank with you, I sniffed this out as a trap long before I got here."

"But you came anyway. You wanted to die? Is that it? Old age wasn't working fast enough for you?"

"I came here, hoping to understand why you did what you did, also because I had a hunch I felt was worth playing."

"You want to understand?" Brevik laughed again. "It's simple. I believe I'm the apex predator in the world. I find a target I think is worthy, and I test myself against them. Needless to say, I always win."

"Wow, you must have calluses on both hands from patting yourself on the back so much."

"You think you're funny?"

"A little."

Keyes ignored my dig and continued, "When I came to town, you and your team were all over the news. You saved a senator. Good for you," Brevik applauded. "Then I hear you found some missing women a while back, two more points for you. But I wondered how would you stack up under real pressure."

"And?"

"I guess you did okay. You got this far. But the ending doesn't change. It's the law of unintended consequences, Raines. An effect of random acts."

"Unintended consequences," I said. "I get that. The rest just sounds like a crock of shit."

"Fuck you, Raines. I got to you. I'm that pain in your chest. That needle in your eye. And now, we've come to the part where it's time for you to die."

"That's cute. It rhymes."

Brevik smirked. "It does, doesn't it? Anyway, now you know the why."

"I guess I do."

"And just so you know, Robert Raines, I meant what I said. I do like you." Brevik raised his gun. He was looking for a headshot. "You were fun to play against. In another life, maybe we'd even be friends."

"I seriously doubt that."

Brevik choked back a laugh. "Fair enough." He tilted his head to side, and after a moment, said, "Your turn. What was this hunch that you just had to play?"

"I had a hunch that if you showed up here, and we got a chance to talk face to face, you'd end up with that red dot on your chest."

Brevik looked down. Just as I'd said. A red laser beam was centered directly over his heart.

Chapter

83

"PUT YOUR WEAPON DOWN, Brevik. Or, I'll cut you in half."

The voice I heard was unmistakable. My hunch was right. After speaking with Detective Mark Royce, I concluded that Ashe was alive. I believed. And not only was he alive, I had figured that he was tracking me, or Brevik, or both of us. I knew he'd be here, and sure enough, the big man stepped out of the shadows behind me, holding a hand cannon with a laser sight. He angled off, so he had a clean shot at Orjan Brevik.

I smiled my widest smile. It was my turn to grin like the cat that ate the canary. "Guess my hunch paid off," I said.

The area we were in was dimly lit, but my eyes registered the look of shock that rolled across Brevik's face. He did his best to recompose himself. "Fifty cal, huh? Oh, yeah. That'll do it." He smirked, then continued, "You're still alive. Soldier to soldier, I might have underestimated you. That's what I get for not making certain."

"Sucks when you think you're really good at something and find out you're not, doesn't it? Now, last time I'm going to tell you, put that weapon down."

Brevik dropped his weapon to the ground. "You look like you recovered well."

Ashe took a step forward. "Had a great doctor."

"Good to know. Maybe I'll make use of that doctor's services after this is all over," Brevik said.

"I haven't met a doctor yet that can cure what you're about to come down with."

"You're going to shoot me now? Get your revenge that way?" Brevik raised his hands. "Fitting, sure. But a man like you—"

"Motherfucker, you don't know anything about me," Ashe said.

Brevik nodded. "You just struck me as a man that, in a situation like this, would prefer to get his hands dirty."

"I owe you two bullets," Ashe said, then handed me the Desert Eagle he was holding, and removed his coat. "But honestly, I was hoping you'd say that."

That Cheshire grin I'd envisioned Brevik as having sprouted on his face. He removed his coat as well. I took a step back. These two were determined to go hands on, and I was determined not to catch a stray punch. The two men squared off. Alternating between the shadows and vestiges of remaining daylight that filtered into the building. Ashe was easily the more physically imposing of the two. He had the height advantage by a little over two inches and had to outweigh Brevik by forty pounds easy. His massive frame dwarfed Brevik.

337

But to Brevik's credit, he wasn't fazed by that. In fact, the look on his face said that he was going to enjoy this.

Ashe lunged, but Brevik quickly side stepped, throwing a hard, crunching punch into Ashe's ribs. I heard him moan. Brevik followed up with a deft right-left combination, ending the flurry with an elbow strike that caught Ashe flush and made him stagger backward.

Brevik tried to press his advantage but walked into a straight right hand from Ashe that buckled his knees. I had to stop myself from cheering out loud. There was no denying, though, I wanted him to take this guy's head clean off.

Ashe unleashed a straight left, right elbow combination of his own that dropped Brevik to his knees. Brevik lunged upward, using his head as a ram, striking Ashe's chin. Ashe fell in a heap, and Brevik pounced on top of him.

"Let me shoot this prick! I'll just wing him!" I yelled.

"No!" Ashe called out.

He fended off a flurry of punches from Brevik, who was trying to get into a mounted position. Ashe whipped one of his legs up and caught Brevik's left arm as he reared back for a punch. Throwing him off balance, Ashe twisted his hips and tossed Brevik away from him. Both men quickly bounded back to their feet.

They circled each other warily. It was like watching two heavyweight boxers that had gone a few rounds, each having had their moment of owning the advantage. And now there was a mutual respect. If I was judging, I'd say that things were even.

Again, I raised Ashe's Desert Eagle .50 caliber, all I needed was permission. The gun was heavy; far heavier than my Sig.

But I could manage it. I just wanted to shoot the man in the leg since we needed him alive. Ashe had seen me out of the corner of his eye and waved me off. There'd be no bullets in this battle. He was clear about that, and I accepted it. This man had shot him with the full intent of killing him. I could only imagine he felt the need to mete out a little pain as payback.

Brevik threw a quick, snapping right hook that was blocked by Ashe. Ashe stepped inside with an elbow strike that nearly separated Brevik from his senses, then scooped the man up off his feet and slammed him hard against the debris ridden concrete floor. I heard a rush of air leave Brevik's body.

Ashe lifted the man's head from the floor and wrapped one of his massive arms around his neck. Dropping to the floor with Brevik, Ashe's legs wrapped around his opponent's torso in a vice. He squeezed. Brevik's eyes went wide. Even in the failing light, I could see them bulge as red filtered in. Brevik's arms flailed in a desperate attempt to reach behind him and maybe land an eye gouge. Something, anything that could win his release. It was in vain.

I noticed Ashe's grip tightening.

I felt panic well up inside of me. "No!" I shouted. "Don't kill him! We still need him!"

Chapter

84

BREVIK FELT THE GRIP around his neck tighten. He continued trying to reach behind his head, pawing at his opponent's face. He wasn't able to make firm contact. This was a powerful man that had him in a compromising position. He needed to get out of it. Fast.

Brevik tried to twist and shift his hips, hoping to gain leverage that way. But Ashe's legs were wrapped tight. Brevik tried striking Ashe along the elbows and digging his thumbs into Ashe's ulnar nerve. But the big man's muscular arms were hard as granite.

None of it worked.

"Wait," Brevik managed in a hoarse whisper. "I never told anyone where the girls are."

Ashe said nothing.

How did I get here? Keyes thought.

Overconfidence, he reasoned. Plain and simple. His willingness to accept that his target had expired, without hard proof, well, that was just unprofessional. What's that old expression about when you assume? That was the kind of mistake that he couldn't afford. Might come back to haunt him.

Brevik felt Ashe's boa constrictor like grip tighten another notch. And for the first time he could remember, he felt fear. His was a high stakes game. Coming in second best meant you weren't going home. He'd never considered that outcome a possibility before. For as long as he'd played this game, he sought out the most difficult challenges he could find. And he'd won. Each and every time. That wasn't a fluke. It meant he was just that good. Yet, he was now staring in the face of the possibility that this time around he had bitten off more than he could chew. And that was scarier than losing. But that's what happens when your eyes are too big for your stomach.

"You...still...need...me," Brevik hissed, fully coming to grips with his mistake.

A couple of stones left unturned.

Damned shame when that happens.

Brevik's mind flashed over Sophie Bisset and her invitation to work abroad. *If she could see me now*, he thought. But this was too important. So, there can be no regrets. Regardless of the outcome. The chance to challenge oneself was way too important. Memories of a time he and Sophie had spent together—two full weeks in Bora Bora two years ago—played out in his mind even as the pain he was feeling intensified. Regardless of the great food, drinks, sex, and time spent on the beach, what he treasured most, was her smile. Seeing her smile those entire two weeks was what he enjoyed the most about their time together.

Though he felt the life being squeezed from him just now, the thought almost brought a smile to his face.

"No," Ashe said. "I don't need you."

"But…those girls…" Brevik eked out. "I never…told you… where they…are."

"And I don't need you to."

Second best, Brevik thought. *This time around, I come in second best. Can't win them all.* Brevik found it easy to make peace with his fate. Besides, he lost to a warrior. A man that he'd put a couple of bullets in just two days ago. He was more than impressed with that. *Ha! Should've been three.* He'd finally found that one opponent that was, in a life and death struggle, better than him. *It's okay.* This result was better than prison, anyway. Who'd want to rot in a cell for the next fifty to sixty years? It's been a great life. Lived with no regrets. Well, maybe one.

Goodbye, Sophie.

Those were the last thoughts to roll through Brevik's mind before the sound of his neck breaking filled his ears and his eyes went dark.

Chapter

85

"No!" I YELLED.

My heart sank as the ugly, crunching sound of Ishmael Keyes, Orjan Brevik, or whatever the hell his name was, neck breaking, had filled the abandoned candy factory for a moment. And just like that, the place was silent. Same as it had been when I'd first walked in.

I slowly walked over to Ashe as he got himself up off the ground. I could see that he was bleeding from his lip, and blood had seeped through his sweater in the left shoulder and abdomen area. He nearly collapsed in my arms as I got closer. Luckily, he held his weight, otherwise we both would've gone crashing to the concrete.

His breathing was a little heavy, and beads of sweat poured down his face after his vicious battle with our madman. The fight might have been brief, but they both had packed a lot into it. They had traded some hellacious blows. Shots that I figured would've felled most men, and would've made many more think twice about getting up for another helping. Yet, they had both seemed to say, "*Thank you, sir. May I have another?*"

I looked him over and said, "Are you okay?"

Ashe managed a half smile. "Not really, no."

I couldn't find a smile at all. I was thrilled that my friend was alive, there was no question about that, but I had to wonder if he had let his rage, maybe even some thirst for revenge, get the best of him in the heat of the moment. It wasn't impossible. It reminded me of the time when he confronted Orrin Robicheaux in Louisiana. The circumstances surrounding both instances were different. Except for the ending. But there was still the reason that I had put my life on the line to come here.

"The girls," I said. "He never told me where they were."

"I think I know where they are."

"You think?"

"I know," Ashe said in between sucking in huge gulps of air.

My body became less tense. My knees almost gave way. I gasped. "But…how?"

"He thought I was dead, remember. I picked up his trail after the explosion on your block, Brevik showed his face in the aftermath."

A thought occurred to me. "He was probably trying to confirm whether or not I was dead. Couldn't resist showing up at his own crime scene."

"I had been on him ever since. It occurred to me as we were fighting. There was one location he visited repeatedly. He had to be holding something important there. It's the only thing that makes sense. But we'd better hurry."

I did my best to support Ashe's weight as we made our way back out into the Chicago cold. The sun had all but gone down now, and dark skies were taking over the city.

"You know you could've saved me a lot of worrying if you had told me you were alive," I said.

"Well, don't send me flowers until you're sure I'm dead," Ashe deadpanned. He took a deep breath, then continued, "I thought about that. But I wasn't sure what we were dealing with. I didn't want to put you, or Dale, in any danger by reaching out. It was best that the man who tried to kill me thought I was dead. Unfortunately, that meant you had to be kept in the dark, too. After I got a line on him, I figured my best bet was to follow you next."

"I'm glad you did. A minute or two later, and this might've been my final resting place." I felt his weight leaning against me increase. "You need to get to the hospital," I said.

"You're right. I do," Ashe said through gritted teeth. "After we get the girls."

Are those girls okay? I wondered. I had no idea what that madman might have done to them. Regardless of what I may have thought of Brevik in the beginning, I knew now he was an evil, sadistic man. How much of that transferred into his plans with the girls, I didn't know.

I helped Ashe into the back seat of my Tahoe. For a moment, he put up a fuss, determined to drive himself. Stubborn mule. But, given the shape he was in, it didn't take much for me to convince him to let me drive him. There was enough space for him to lie out in the back seat. I did have to promise that I'd come back for his car sooner than later.

I got the Tahoe in gear and floored it. Time was of the essence.

Chapter

86

We arrived on the south side in no time. I drove in full bat-out-of-hell mode, with Ashe directing me from the back seat.

The three snow covered shipping containers caught my eye immediately. There they sat, in full view, just as Ashe said they would be. Brilliant when you think about it. Hiding the girls in plain sight like that. Whatever I thought of Brevik as a human being, I had to give it to him. He had some moves. He was well prepared. I brought the Tahoe to a stop beside the third container. The opening was shielded away from the street. It offered privacy. Just what Brevik needed while he carried out his evil deeds.

Ashe struggled to sit up in the back seat. "I got this," I said.

"Can you pick a lock?"

"I was picking locks before you were a twinkle in your daddy's eye."

He didn't offer any resistance or a snarky comeback, which let me know he was hurting for sure. And rightfully so. No way he should've been out in these streets. But he did it to save a friend, and as Ashe would say, because there were things that needed doing. Him going hand to hand with Brevik, proving who really was the apex predator, well, that's just who the man is. I wasn't present for Ashe's showdown with Orrin Robicheaux, but I imagined it had to be something like that. We never got too deep into "why" Ashe handled things the way he did. Being honest, I don't think I wanted to. But, be it the fog of war, or something that was bred in him by his father, he had a code. A way he did things. He always pushed the enveloped and even moved the line of where justice ended and vengeance began to suit his needs. This was something I knew when I brought him on as an investigator. Something I lived with. And truth be told, it was great to have a friend that could do things you could not.

I made my way over to the container and the fancy lock that was securing it. I reached inside my coat, pulled out my picking tools, and set to work. The wind was brutal against the bare skin of my hands. They started going numb quickly. That wasn't enough to stop me. If Ashe was right, those girls were inside, and it was well past time we'd gotten them back home to their mothers. Past time we ended this nightmare.

After a few minutes, I heard the satisfactory clicks of the lock coming undone and ending its shift as a security guard. In the faint light that filtered in from outside, I saw one of the girls flinch. Hard. I suspected she thought it was their kidnapper, their tormentor, back again.

A NEEDLE IN THE EYE

An icy breeze blew in at my back through the open doors. It seemed to last forever. I turned on my flash light. My eyes moistened when I noticed the gags and blindfolds and thought of the ordeal they'd been through. I also noticed that the other two girls weren't moving. They didn't stir at all when I came in. The snow trapped in my boots crunching on the container floor caused the one girl to shift. *Were the other two okay? Were we too late?* My chest tightened, and a knot formed in my stomach as thoughts of having lost either of these children crept into my mind and began to take root.

The kid in the middle, the one that shifted when I came in, began breathing in shallow, raspy gasps. I kneeled down on the mattress and could feel her entire body tense up. I put a hand on her shoulder. Her body seized.

"Relax. My name is Robert Raines. Your mothers sent me."

From her reaction, I could tell she noticed my voice was different. I could still feel a little tension in her body as I undid her blindfold and removed the gag from her mouth. Her eyes struggled against my flashlight. She blinked rapidly. But after a moment, those eyes sent me a message that said she knew for sure I wasn't their tormentor. There was relief in her gaze.

"Can you take us home, please?" Layla said and cried.

The other two girls stirred. *They're alive. Hallelujah! They're alive!*

A wave of relief rushed over me like a tide breaking on a beach head. "That's exactly what I'm going to do," I said with a smile. "Get you all back home."

Chapter

87

THE MOMENT OF TRUTH had arrived for Sophie Bisset when she received the much-anticipated phone call from Jean-Luc. The meet had been set with the courier. They were to pick up the package from The Pont Nuef, before heading to Aubrey DuChamps's Avignon estate. *Two mansions*, Sophie thought. *He has two mansions!*

Jean-Luc was punctual. 10:00 a.m. on the dot. As he drove them across the city, Sophie noticed how his eyes continually wandered down, staring at her bare legs, visible because of the waist length fur coat she wore and dress that rose nearly as high. She crossed them playfully back and forth, noticing each time the movement caught his eye.

Men.

They drove along the Seine River, until they reached The Pont Nuef, the oldest bridge in Paris that crosses the river. There was an alcove just under the bridge. Jean-Luc pulled the car over about thirty meters from it and brought the car to a stop.

"Wait here," he said.

"I wanted to come with," Sophie objected.

"You'll wait here. I will be right back with the package, then I take you for your date with DuChamps." Jean-Luc snickered, then exited the vehicle.

Within moments, he was out of sight. Sophie felt her pulse racing again, and though it was chilly out, she felt beads of sweat form on her brow. Her hands felt clammy. She took three deep breaths. Words her father had shared with her years ago rattled in her head. *Once you make up your mind to do a thing, you don't think about it. You just do it.*

But what Sophie planned to do, if she could go through with it, would even make her dad blush. Sophie rubbed the back of her neck and bit down on her lower lip. A light mist of rain fell just as Jean-Luc ducked into the alcove and out of her field of vision. The trees that lined the river didn't have leaves, but their branches swayed in the breeze that accompanied the rain. She thought of the man that had taken to calling himself Keyes of late, and the time they'd spent in Bora Bora. She would've given anything to be there now, with him. How much simpler that would've been. Sophie didn't recall the name he was going by at that time, but she recalled every moment they spent on that beach. But he made his choice, which meant she had to make

SHAWN SCUEFIELD

hers. Move forward, or stand pat. *And*, she reminded herself, *I've got too much ambition for that.*

Sophie opened her purse and removed a flask. She unscrewed the cap and helped herself to several gulps of cognac. After screwing the cap back on and placing it back into her purse, she checked her watch. *Last chance, Sophie. You can get out of the car now and walk away clean.* Her mind had flipped again. Doubts crept in. Again. But then she flashed back to yesterday, and her arrival at the estate of Aubrey DuChamps. *Two mansions! He's got two mansions!* Higher ambitions once again pulled ahead of any fears and doubts.

If she moved forward, every aspect of her life would change. As she began putting things in motion, she constantly wondered if she was fine with that. If she could not only face, but embrace, that new reality. Just as important, what would it mean if she couldn't?

Jean-Luc reappeared from the alcove on his way back to the car.

It was now or never.

Sophie's hands shook. She clutched her purse just to keep them still.

"See, no problem," Jean-Luc said as he entered the car and closed the door.

It's now or never.

"Can I see?" Sophie said, doing her best to keep her voice level.

"You can see when we get to Mr. DuChamps," Jean-Luc replied.

352

"Please?" Sophie said. She did that thing again, moving her legs back and forth.

On cue, Jean-Luc's eyes drifted south. He looked at Sophie, and she smiled. Jean-Luc smiled back. "Okay. Look," he said and pulled a small package wrapped in plain brown paper from his jacket pocket. It was about the size of a deck of playing cards. "Now, if you want to see more, perhaps, you show me more?" Jean-Luc said and put the package back into his pocket.

Sophie raised an eyebrow. She took her right hand and unzipped her fur coat. Jean-Luc licked his lips.

Sophie wasn't sure it worked. Sure, she heard the loud pop and saw blood, but it was the shocked look on Jean-Luc's face as he clutched at the hole in his throat, that confirmed success. Sophie pulled the Luger .22 caliber she had hidden from inside her coat and fired again. Jean-Luc slumped over in the driver seat, his head thudding against the driver's side window.

She had done it. Sophie felt her heart pounding hard in her chest. A lump developed in her stomach and rushed up to her throat. She was a volcano ready to blow. And blow she did. Sophie opened the passenger side door, leaned out and vomited. She stepped out of the vehicle. The cool air and rain hitting her face helped tremendously. Her stomach settled and her head cleared.

Pull it together, Sophie. You did it. Believe it or not, you really did it. But we don't have time for this. It's done. It's time for the next move.

Sophie pulled a soft cloth from her purse and wiped down any surfaces in the vehicle she'd touched. When she'd finished, she raced around to the driver's side of the car, her heels clicking loudly against the wet cobblestone. Sophie opened the door, being careful not to let Jean-Luc fall out of the vehicle. She reached into his pocket and grabbed the package and his cellphone. She closed the car door and tucked the package into her purse.

Sophie Bisset checked around, her head whipping back and forth. There were no on-lookers, a crowd hadn't formed. She was alone with the deceased Jean-Luc. Sophie pulled out her cellphone and made a call as she walked away, disappearing under the bridge. She took another deep breath. There was no turning back now. This was real.

"It's Sophie."

"Miss Bisset. I take it things have gone as planned?" Sheik Al-Assan said.

"Yes. I have the package and I'm ready to leave Paris."

"My plane is at de Gaulle, waiting for you."

"I'll make contact when I arrive in your country. Once I'm settled, we can start the bidding process."

"We look forward to your arrival. I extend my every courtesy to you."

"Thank you, Sheik."

After ending that call, Sophie used Jean-Luc's phone and dialed another number. "Yes, Interpol? I have information for the Americans concerning a theft."

Chapter

88

Chicago, Illinois

SEEING THE LOOKS ON the faces of Latesha Barnett and Tracey Montgomery as they hugged and kissed their daughters in their shared room at Stroger Hospital was beyond satisfying. While I had some angst that I wasn't able to do this for those parents some twenty years ago, it wasn't enough to dampen my mood.

Their reaction to seeing me was a complete one eighty from the last time we were face to face. "Mr. Raines, we can't possibly thank you enough," Tracey Montgomery said.

"You don't need to," I said.

"Well, we're saying thank you, anyway."

"And I want to say I'm sorry," Latesha Barnett said. "When I blew up at you—"

"You definitely don't need to apologize. You were living a parent's worst nightmare in that moment."

355

Latesha and Tracey both took turns hugging me again. Afterward, Latesha asked, "How's your friend? Is he going to be okay?"

"Ashe will be fine, thanks for asking. We're both just glad we were able to get your daughter's home and that they're going to be fine."

Latesha smiled and said, "Best dollar I ever spent."

"Hardest buck I ever earned," I said, then excused myself and headed out.

Layla, Kayla, and Shameka had been in the hospital the past two days, and would spend at least another couple before checking out. All of their physical wounds would heal without a trace, the doctors said. Of course, they'd probably all need therapy—including their mothers—given their ordeal.

The media had changed their tune as well. I went from goat to hero, along with Ashe of course. I wanted him front and center on this one. He found those girls after all. But once he'd gotten wind of all the grief, the media had given me when we thought we had lost them in the house explosion, he lost his appetite for interviews. I personally didn't care. If I spent my entire life worrying about what people thought of me, I doubt I'd have made it to this age. Just the same, it's good when you're not being dragged through the mud on a twenty-four-seven media cycle.

Speaking of Ashe, he spent a couple of nights in the hospital himself. Against his will, but I had convinced him to put aside his objections. There was no way he should've been out on those streets so soon after being shot. But he felt he had work to do, so he got up and did it. And boy, was I thankful for that. Especially since part of that "work" was saving my hide.

I made one more stop later in the week to see the girls and their mothers before they were released. It was good to see those young ladies in much better spirits than they had been. They were eating again, joking around a little. It did my heart good.

It was just passed two in the afternoon when I made my way home. I had stopped off at one of my favorite cigar shops and brought a fresh cigar, a Dominican called the San Cristobal Revelation. This was a victory, and victories deserve a fresh cigar. I blame Dakota Quinn for me revisiting this old habit. I smoked with her when we were in New Orleans two years ago and have had them occasionally ever since. And no, I don't have any problem laying the blame for that at her feet.

I was out of Blanton's but had a bottle of Maker's Mark on my kitchen shelf that had celebration written all over it. I parked my Tahoe in front of my house. Again, I had to pass the burned-out remains of the home of the *real* Ishmael Keyes. That would be a constant reminder for a long time of the events that had taken place over the past week. I walked up my porch steps. Hearing the snow crunch underneath my feet reminded me I hadn't been around to shovel the past couple of days. Hearing snow crunch as I stuck my key in the door, however, let me know that there was someone walking behind me. I went for my Sig.

What now? Did Brevik have an accomplice? When will I get a chance to rest? Then again, I invited all of this, hadn't I? I could've stayed retired, and maybe, well…maybe none of what has happened over the past two years would've happened.

I turned around. My hand was firmly on the butt of my gun, ready to draw if need be. Standing before me was a fresh-faced young man, dressed for the weather in a heavy coat, skull cap and scarf. I didn't know him. Never seen him before, in fact. And I was sure of that. Yet he somehow looked familiar, though in the moment, I didn't know why.

"Sir?" he said.

The kid's voice squeaked. I put him at no older than eighteen, nineteen years old. "Yes," I said.

"I seen you on the TV the past few days."

"You probably have."

"Robert Raines, right?"

"I am," I said. Given all that had happened, I had yet to take my hand off my weapon. "How can I help you?"

"My name is Jacob. Jacob Latham. This is going to sound crazy, but…I would've preferred to do this another way. It's…"

"Come on. Out with it, young man."

"I'm your grandson."

I heard the words, but they made little sense. And as my brain processed them over and over, they took my breath away. "W-what? How?"

The young man stepped closer. He pulled his skullcap from his head. His features were in full view now. He looked just like a young Robert Jr. My son.

"My mom, for a long time, wouldn't talk about my father. It wasn't until I turned sixteen that she told me my father was a cop and that he died in the line of duty. She'd said that, given he had never introduced her to the family, she was hesitant to say she was pregnant with his kid at the time. Like you guys wouldn't believe her or something. We were watching WGN the other day, the story about that house blowing up, and those girls missing. When they put your picture up, she said, 'hey, that's your grandfather.' Just like that. Out of nowhere. I go from not knowing much of anything about my dad, to seeing my grandfather on TV."

My hand slid away from my gun. My eyes watered and I instinctively wiped them. I studied the kid a little more. I had no idea if he was telling me the truth or not, but no way he could look so much like junior as just some coincidence. I walked down the stairs. We stood face to face. He had some height on him, broad shouldered. The look in his eyes, his demeanor, led me to believe he wasn't being deceptive. It's what he was told. It's what he believes. It was what I believed. He's my grandson.

Oh, my God!

I hugged him. He immediately returned the embrace. Years of emotions poured out of him as he hugged me. And that's when I lost it. I cried probably as hard as I cried the day I lost my son. What were the odds, all these years, feeling that I'd lost the connection I had with my son, other than my memories, and all along, out there in the world was a piece of him? A piece of me.

I invited the young man, Jacob, into my home. The pictures on the wall of Robert Jr. were like a reflection in the mirror to him. One in particular was taken at a CPD picnic back in 2000. Junior was in the foreground with his mother, I was in the background talking with a few officers.

"Is that my grandmother?"

"It is. That's your grandmother, and kid, she's going to be so thrilled to meet you."

Chapter

89

ASHE'S CELLPHONE RANG, INTERRUPTING Miles Davis's *All Blues* as it pulsed from his sound system. He had no intention of taking any calls. He preferred to rest, enjoy some jazz, and a few glasses of Bulleit bourbon. But glancing at the number on his caller ID, he figured it best he did. He paused the music.

"Sir," he answered.

"How're you feeling, chief," Colonel Harrison said.

"I'm better, thanks."

"Saw you on TV the past few days. Surprisingly short lived."

"Well, if I was living for applause, I would've joined the circus, or the Harlem Globetrotters. To what do I owe the pleasure, Colonel?"

"First off, I wanted to say good work with Brevik, even if it was ten years late."

"Gee, thanks."

"Found out something interesting concerning Brevik, by the way. He had another agenda here in the states, aside from stealing identities, committing murders, kidnappings, and such."

Ashe slumped back on his sofa. "No shit," he said and emptied his glass.

Colonel Harrison continued, "None. Appears he had been hired by a French billionaire."

"Hired to do what?"

"He robbed a place called Wynn Pharmaceuticals, just outside of Lake County, Illinois. Made a bit of a mess on his way out."

"Let me guess, they make more than Viagra and Lipitor."

"In fact, they do, master chief. Brevik stole an experimental augmented neurotoxin."

"A what?"

"Based on what we've learned from DOD, it's a combination of ricin, strychnine, and tetradotoxin."

"So, Wynn is owned by the Department of Defense, I take it?"

"You'd be right, old friend, though they contracted out for security. Some heads are going to roll on that one, let me tell you. Anyway, the sample that was stolen was the only one in existence. And here's more sunny news. There's no known cure."

"There was nothing found in the container where Brevik hid the kids, or his vehicle?"

"No. And I wouldn't have expected there to be. CIA got a call from Interpol, an anonymous tip regarding the theft, put us on to French billionaire, Aubrey DuChamps."

"You pick him up?"

361

"No, we kicked it to the feds. They have him. Say he gave them some story about a woman that double-crossed him, and that she must have the toxin now. He gave them a name, Sophie Bisset. But right now, she's in the wind. No one has anything on her, other than in certain circles she's known as a fixer. Right now, her trail is cold."

"Son of a gun."

"Or daughter. Her father, Francois Bisset, was one of the few politicians to go down for Angolagate. Big scandal in France, but he ended up carrying most of the weight. He's the only one that's received a prison sentence so far. Anyway, appears he's passed on the criminal gene to daughter dearest. If what DuChamps says is true, she sure did a number on him."

"And you called to tell me this, why?" Ashe poured himself another shot of bourbon.

"This? This was small talk. We've got bigger problems, old buddy."

"Being?"

"When we did that run up on Brevik, we found something even more interesting. There was someone else that made it into the states that shouldn't have."

Ashe downed his shot, then sat forward on the sofa. "I'm listening."

"Yusef al-Raza."

"I thought he was dead."

"We all did. The entire intelligence community. CIA, NSA, FBI, Homeland, you name it. Whole alphabet. Frankly, I believe that's why he was able to slip into the country. No one was looking for him."

"Well, where is he now?"

"Gone. He left the states two weeks ago. Last intel put him in Afghanistan. Kandahar province. We need to find him. We need to know what he was doing in the United States. A man like that doesn't show his face for no good reason. He certainly wasn't here to see the sights. And he's more than just a bag man, so, something's up. And we need to know what. Remember that thing I said earlier about needing a favor to come back my way?"

"I do."

"I called to see if you were willing to join our hunting party. Get your nose back in the dirt. I'd be coming with."

"You?"

"You think I'd have you working with just a bunch of no rank fuzz butts that would be falling all over themselves to get a war hero's autograph? Not on this one, pal. This one is enough to get me out of bed before sunrise."

After an extended pause, Ashe cleared his throat. "Let me think about it."

"That's all I ask. But we're wheels up in twenty-four, so think fast."

Chapter

90

IT WAS JUST AFTER four in the afternoon when Elena arrived at my house. *Our* house. She wore a concerned look on her face as she came inside and began removing her coat. That was my fault, calling her as I did and vomiting words at her that I'm sure made very little, if any sense. One thing I got out, which she could understand, was that she needed to come over right away. I had news and couldn't give it over the phone.

"Talk to me, Robert. What's going on? Are you okay?" she said, worry dripping from her words. She sounded like someone expecting to receive some terrible news. There was a sadness in her eyes that said so as well.

I hugged her and felt her body almost go limp. "Are you okay, Robert?" she asked again. "I've got something to tell you," I said finally. I found my emotions roiling up from my stomach and into my chest. Each breath felt heavy. "But first, I need to apologize. Again."

"Apologize?" Elena pushed back from my hug, her head turning sideways. "For what?"

I took her by the hands and led her to the sofa. We sat down and her hands tightened around mine. "I'm sorry," I began, and had to choke back tears. "For everything that happened after junior died. As I've said before, I pulled away from you. I couldn't deal with losing him. Being selfish, I acted as if I was the only one hurting. I wasn't there for you like I should've been. Like you needed me to. Even after I retired."

Elena's shoulders slumped and her mouth fell open. "Robert…I…I don't know—"

"Wait," I interrupted. "There's more." I took a deep breath and cleared my throat. My words had become sticky and were getting lodged there. This had gone a lot smoother in my head. But hearing me speak these things aloud coupled with the look on Elena's face as she heard them was like having salt poured into a gaping wound. "Every time I looked at you, I saw him. I saw the promise of his life denied. I convinced myself that you resented me for it. I know you didn't want him to become a cop, and I you had wanted me to talk him out of it. But he wanted to be like his dad, and that made me proud."

I noticed Elena's eyes watering. At that point, I felt tears streaming down my cheeks. I wanted to wipe my eyes, but she hadn't let go of my hands yet. And I didn't want her to. "It was that pride," I continued, "that prevented me from ever having that conversation with him. For that, I want to say I'm sorry."

365

Elena released her grip on my hands, and in the same motion, her right hand came up and rested on my face. Her touch was gentle, and like in my dream, it felt good. Tears were also flowing down her face now, and her voice cracked when she spoke. "Robert, I never resented you. I never even blamed you. Our son was his own man. He was going to follow in the footsteps of his hero no matter what. Despite my fears, I was always proud of that too." Elena took her thumb and dabbed at the tears on my face. "But thank you."

"For what?"

"Your apology. You explained yourself a lot more than you had in the past, and I appreciate that." She paused. "I'm glad we had this conversation. But I made up my mind when I left—"

"This isn't about that."

"It's not?"

"There's no need to go picking over those old bones. Not right now, at least. There's something more I have to tell you about junior."

Elena's face went flush, and she slumped back on the couch.

"This…this is a good thing. A wonderful thing. That connection we'd lost with our son, well, I found it."

"You're not making any sense, Robert. What are you talking about?"

I stood up. I felt light headed for a moment, as if I couldn't believe what I was about to say. Being honest, I couldn't. Quickly regaining my composure, I said, "You're a grandmother. Junior had a son."

Elena's eyes widened. "What?"

"I met him. Today."

"You met him today?" she said. "This isn't possible."

"It is. It's true." I turned toward the kitchen. "Jacob? Can you come in here, please?"

All the color went out of Elena's face as Jacob entered the living room. Her eyes darted back and forth between the two of us.

"Hi, grandma," Jacob said.

Elena let out a shriek before leaping to her feet and wrapping him in the biggest bear hug. She'd recognized the resemblance immediately. *How could she not?* The tears flowed fast and free again. From all of us.

Chapter

91

JACOB AND HIS MOTHER, Kelly Lathom, returned to visit me the next day. She brought with her a photo album containing many pictures that she'd taken with my son during the year and a half they dated.

Kelly explained, same as Jacob had said, that she didn't feel comfortable introducing herself with child, after my son had passed. They hadn't discussed marriage, or the baby. She was waiting for the right time to tell him. Unfortunately, that time never came. She held onto this secret for near twenty years. I was disappointed to hear that, but not at all mad. I would've loved to have been in this kid's life, from the time he could crawl and take his first steps until now. Yet, the excitement, the thrill I've gotten each time he's walked through my door, has been incredible. It's come at a time that I needed it the most.

Thoughts that I had about visiting disgraced former Chicago Police Officer Elliot James, my son's former partner, in the hospital had gone. Prior to our involvement with Brevik and his kidnap/murder spree, I had been visiting Elliot at least once a week. Faithfully. Each week, and each visit, went exactly the same. He lay motionless, connected to life support systems that did his breathing and kept his heart pumping, unaware that I was even in the room. I'd talk for ten, maybe fifteen minutes. Sometimes it was about the old days. Times we'd all spent at my home, brats on the grill and brews in hand. Sometimes I talked to him about the job. Or the events that led him to being in the hospital in that vegetative state. But most times, more often than not, I talked about what happened to my son, Robert Jr. And what Elliot said to me before he shot himself. That there was more to the story with my son. That there was a truth that I deserved to know. I'd always ask what was it. For his part, Elliot would always not answer.

Since meeting Jacob, however, I've had to ask myself: do I need to know? Do I have to know? It's quite possible that Elliot was speaking from a drug induced haze. He may not have had any idea what reality was at the time he'd said those things. I've let it consume me the past few months. No matter what he'd say, if he were to come out of that coma, and actually have any of his faculties, I'm not getting my son back. But now I have Jacob. My grandson. A piece of my son. And that, I believe, will allow me to make peace with that loss. I won't forget, that's for damned sure. But I don't have to torment myself by wondering what Elliot wanted to tell me. That alone was freeing.

Elena joined us as well. We wanted to make up for all the lost years in one day. Everything that we had missed: birthdays, graduations, you name it. It was interesting to learn that just like his dad, Jacob was quite the high school athlete. Jacob starred in both football and basketball. There are a couple of local D-II schools, Quincy and McKendree University, looking at him. The coaches have even mentioned the possibility of a full scholarship. Funny how that happens. His dad was quite the baseball player himself.

It didn't take long before Elena was in the kitchen cooking. This old house hasn't smelled this good in some time. I have a bit of skill in the kitchen, but most nights I'm eating takeout. So many memories fill my mind as the smell of Elena's fried chicken wafted into the dining room. She also made one of my personal favorites, her potato salad, to go along with her buttermilk biscuits.

After a wonderful, filling meal, I broke out all of my photo albums, had jazz tunes playing, and Elena and I told Jacob all about his dad. There wasn't a dull moment. Suddenly my living room wasn't an office anymore. It was actually for living. Of all the things I didn't see coming, this registered as the biggest surprise. A good one, for a change. I found myself hanging just off the kitchen, while Elena sat with Jacob and Kelly, just staring. This wasn't what I'd call a second chance, but it was as close as I was going to get. I decided that I couldn't let anything get in the way of that. Not anything at all. It was a decision that had to be made, but one I didn't take lightly. How could I? It didn't only affect me.

I excused myself and made a call.

Chapter

92

"Ashe, it's Raines. How's it going?"

"It's going good, how about with you?"

"That's why I'm calling, actually."

"Is everything okay?"

"Things are better than okay," I said. "You won't believe who I met."

"Don't tell me, you've met the girl of my dreams and want to hook me up," Ashe said, and laughed.

"My grandson," I said. I felt the excitement in my voice as the words came out.

"Say again?"

"Before junior died, he was on his way to being a father. I just found out. We've all been playing get to know you. It's been unbelievable."

"That's incredible news, Robert. I'm happy for you."

"Thanks. Now, comes the hard part of this call," I said.

"I get it, Robert. You need to take a step back. Just like Dale did. Be with your family."

"I do, but I don't want you to feel like I'm turning my back on you."

"You're not and don't you dare think that. I understand."

"I know you do, and that's why I feel bad about it…it's just that…"

"Robert, you don't need to explain anything to me. We're friends, and I get it. I do."

"You're wrong about one thing," I said.

"What's that?"

"We're not friends. We're brothers."

"You're right. We are."

"Why don't you stop by, I'd love for you to meet him. I've already told him stories about you."

There was a pause from Ashe's end. After a moment, he said, "As soon as I get a chance, I will. But I'm going to be taking off soon."

"Oh? Where to?"

"Can't say."

"Can't say? Because you don't know?"

"National security can't say," Ashe replied.

The news made my heart sink. I knew what that meant he'd be getting back into. He'd told me before that his former commanding officer had asked him back. Being happy working with Dale and me, he'd repeatedly turned the offer down. I couldn't help but feel that my stepping away from the business solidified his decision just now. I also knew that if I asked, he'd say that wasn't the case. Once again, unintended consequences. There's been plenty of that going around.

"I'll leave a number," Ashe said. "If you or Dale ever need me, you call it. They'll be able to find me, and I will come. You have my word on that. Thanks for everything, Robert. I mean that."

"Thank you, Ashe, for always being there. It was my privilege to work with you."

"I'll see you again," he said.

"I look forward to it. RDC Investigations isn't over. We're just on pause. But you make sure that you make it back. RD Investigations sounds terrible."

***

Ashe hung up from his call with Robert. He sat down on his sofa in his living room. The events with Brevik now seemed like a long time ago. There were other matters to be attended to.

Important matters.

Ashe dialed a number on his phone, and after going through the security protocol, he said, "Colonel Harrison. I'm in."

Chapter

93

IT ALL HAD COME as a shock to Dale Gamble. First, the news that Robert Raines had a grandson whom he'd just met, and then the news of Ashe heading back to covert ops with the CIA's Special Operations Group (SOG).

Within a three-month time-frame, RDC Investigations had been put on hold. There was a lot of good that had come from their endeavor. But a lot of personal pain as well. Dale had no further to look than at his wife, who'd fallen asleep on the sofa in front of the TV again. There had been a lot they had lost over the course of two years, but things at least ended on a high note. Those three young black girls were rescued, a madman taken off the streets, and Bobby's good family news. It was definitely a win.

Dale made his way into the kitchen to prepare dinner as Millie would wake up from her nap soon. He peered out of the window, over the kitchen sink, and into the backyard. Dale's skin went white as a ghost. What he saw shouldn't be there. Not now. This was all over. It had been for a few days now.

He reached on the top of the refrigerator and grabbed his Kimber 1911. Dale fumbled getting his boots on and didn't even bother for a coat. He ran outside and over to the garbage cans. There, flapping in the wind, was an envelope taped to the top of one of the cans.

Dale raced to the alley, but it was empty. He looked in both directions, staring intently, but he was alone with the February winds. Dale returned to his yard and ripped the envelope from the trash can. He opened it, and inside he found a note, written in red crayon:

I know what you did. You never said sorry. You're going to pay.

Ashe will Return
In
SLOW BURN

Coming Soon!

Made in the USA
Columbia, SC
22 July 2021

42225181R00233